Seb's
SUMMER
Maine Men Book Three
K.C. WELLS

Seb's Summer
Cover Art by Meredith Russell
Edited by Sue Laybourn

Warning
This book contains material that is intended for a mature, adult audience. It contains graphic language, explicit sexual content, and adult situations.

Maine Men

Levi, Noah, Aaron, Ben, Dylan, Finn, Seb, and Shaun.

Eight friends who met in high school in Wells, Maine.

Different backgrounds, different paths, but one thing remains solid, even eight years after they graduated – their friendship. Holidays, weddings, funerals, birthdays, parties – any chance they get to meet up, they take it. It's an opportunity to share what's going on in their lives, especially their love lives.

Back in high school, they knew four of them were gay or bi, so maybe it was more than coincidence that they gravitated to one another. Along the way, there were revelations and realizations, some more of a surprise than others. And what none of the others knew was that Levi was in love with one of them…

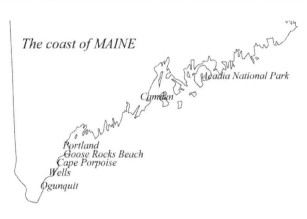

The coast of MAINE

Acadia National Park

Camden

Portland
Goose Rocks Beach
Cape Porpoise
Wells
Ogunquit

For Jack Parton

One Skype call when I was thrashing out my ideas for Seb's Summer, and suddenly I knew where I wanted to go with this book.

Thank you for two wonderful road trips through Maine – and for your inspiration.

Prologue

From Ben's Boss:

"Christ on a cracker, I do not fucking believe this!"

"Seb. You'll wake Grammy," Ben said. "Get over here. What's wrong?"

Seb strode over to where they were sitting, his hands clenched, his hair unruly. "That was my mom on the phone." His chest rose and fell rapidly.

"Breathe, dude." Ben had never seen Seb in such a state. "Now calmly… what happened?"

Seb made an obvious effort to comply. "My uncle Gary went and broke his goddamn pelvis, that's what happened." He scraped his fingers through his hair, not for the first time, Ben suspected.

Ben frowned. "Are you and he close? Is that why you're so upset?" Except Seb wasn't upset—he looked pissed, to the point where he was visibly vibrating with rage.

"No, we're not close. Wait—we were, when I was a kid, but I haven't seen much of him. We kinda drifted apart. And what's happened is that my mom told my uncle I'd help him out. Because I'm the only one who can, apparently."

"You're not making any sense," Ben told him.

Seb sat on the nearest chair and leaned forward, his head in his hands. "I had plans, goddamn it. I was gonna chill out, get laid, get laid some more…" He took a deep breath. "Uncle Gary has his own fishing business, down in this tiny little place along the coast. Cape Porpoise. Cute name, huh? It's exactly how it sounds. Cute, quaint, idyllic—and quiet. Like, deathly quiet, because there's nothing going on. And Mom told Uncle Gary I'd go stay with him for the rest of my summer vacation, and take over for him."

Ben bit his lip. "You're gonna fish?" He shouldn't laugh. He really shouldn't.

Fuck, it was hilarious.

Seb jerked his head up, his eyes wild. "It's not funny, dude."

"It is from where I'm sitting. I remember when you were younger, that summer you went and helped out. That's what all the family did, wasn't it? You took turns being a deckhand for the summer." Ben grinned. "And you bitched and complained, then said that was the last time anyone would ever get you on a fishing boat."

Seb gaped. "What makes it worse? I'm gonna be doing it for free. You should've heard my mom. 'You're a teacher, you're already getting paid. You don't need the money.' Like fuck I don't. 'Take over for him,' she says. Yeah, right. Can you really see me getting up at the crack of whenever, to go out in some boat and be a glorified deckhand? Because that's all I'd be." He straightened in his chair. "You know what? I'm not even gonna think about it. Because that would be like talking it into existence, and it ain't happening. Gary can find some other schmuck." He got up. "Sorry, guys. I'm outta here. That call has given me a sour taste in my mouth. I'll call ya, soon." And with that, he strode back into the house.

Chapter One

June 13

Whatever Seb Williams was feeling right that second went *way* beyond pissed. And all it had taken to get him there was one phone call from his mom.

He strode back into the house, stopping short of slamming the door at the last second, because the logical part of his brain kicked in and reminded him he'd wake Grammy if he did that.

The nerve of my mom. He still couldn't believe she'd come out with all that crap. *Uncle Gary must've put her up to it. It's revenge, that's what it is. Revenge for that time he took me out on the boat when I was just a kid, and I barfed all over the deck.* Well, no fucking way was *this* guy gonna spend his long-awaited, dreamed-of, *fantasized*-about summer vacation cleaning buoys, prepping bait, hauling traps, and securing lobster claws. It horrified him that he even *knew* about all that shit. Those tasks were burned into his memory.

Uncle Gary scarred me for life.

Levi came out of the kitchen as Seb was grabbing his jacket from the hooks by the door. "Hey, what's wrong?"

Seb forced himself to breathe deeply before he spoke. "Hey dude. Great party, but I'm outta here. I just finished a really bad call from my mom, and if I stay, I'm gonna ruin it for everyone. I'll call, okay?" Then he was out of the house and heading for his car, thankful he hadn't been on the booze all night. He'd had a beer about two hours ago, but that call had rendered him stone cold sober in a heartbeat.

He unlocked the door, got behind the wheel, and resisted the urge to let loose with a yell. *Fuck you, Uncle Gary. You are not gonna ruin my summer.* His phone rang, and he squirmed in the seat, trying to free it from his jeans pocket.

"Did you forget something?" Levi asked as the call connected.

"Apart from my manners? Don't think so." He shouldn't have left like that.

"How about your overnight guests? Aren't Ben, Dylan, and Aaron staying with you tonight?"

Aw fuck. "Shit, yeah." He'd forgotten about them completely. *Duh. That's why you weren't drinking tonight, you dickhead.*

Before he could get another word out, Levi got in first. "Look, don't worry about it. They can stay here tonight. I'll make up the guest bed."

That sweet guy. "You don't have to do that."

"Yeah, I do. I don't think you're in any mood to entertain guests. Text me when you get back to your place, okay? Just so I know you didn't wrap your car around a tree or something."

"Sure. Thanks, Levi." He disconnected. *Thank God for Levi.* Then Seb recalled the rest of his weekend plans. The guys were coming over for lunch.

We'll see. If he could shift this mood, then maybe.

He drove back to Ogunquit in almost total silence, except for the odd vehement "fuck!" yelled here and there. By the time he was home, his rage had subsided to a simmer.

Not gonna get mad about this. I'm just gonna tell Uncle Gary it ain't happening, no matter what my mom says. Seb had worked his ass off. He needed to recharge his batteries, and the way he was feeling, it would take until school started again at the end of August to accomplish that.

He opened the fridge and grabbed a bottle of beer. When his phone buzzed on the table, he peered at the screen with trepidation. *If that's Mom, I don't think I can pull my punches.* He breathed easier when he saw it wasn't her—it was an unknown caller. Seb picked it up and hit *Answer*, waiting for whoever was on the other end to speak first. If it was a spam caller, he was in the perfect mood to blast them.

"Seb? You there?"

He recognized his uncle's voice immediately. "Hey, Uncle Gary." *Aw fuck.* It looked like shit was about to get real.

A wry chuckle filled his ears. "Jesus, kid, you're a bit old for that uncle crap. Call me Gary." His voice sounded strained.

Seb had to agree. It felt as though he was eight years old again. "Mom called. Said you've had some bad luck." He pulled out a chair at the small kitchen table and sat.

Gary snorted. "Fuck, you can say that again. Pardon my French if my fuckin' language offends your delicate ears."

Despite his mood, Seb laughed. Gary hadn't changed. "So how did you break your pelvis? Don't tell me. You slipped on a fish. Oh, *I* know—a lobster tripped you up with its claw."

"Har har. Funny man. I wiped out on my

friggin' motorcycle. And it's not a break, it's a fracture. Trust your mom to exaggerate the fuck outta this." Seb caught a muffled voice in the background, followed by Gary's growl. "No, I will *not* stop cussin' in my own friggin' home. Christ on a cracker, woman, I'm gonna be in your clutches for eight weeks or more. You'd better get used to my cussin', 'cause I don't aim on lettin' up anytime soon."

"Who's there with you?"

Gary groaned. "Your Aunt Annie—and she's bein' a royal pain in the ass!" Seb caught Aunt Annie's raised voice, then what sounded like a scuffle.

"Hi, Seb. Annie here."

"Did you just wrestle Gary for the phone?"

"Stupid ol' mule." He didn't miss the affection in her tone, however.

"How bad is it?"

"Bad enough that they had to use screws to pin him back together. And don't listen to a word he says. Fracture, my ass." She groaned. "Now he's got me cussing too. Five minutes around him, and I'm swearing like a sailor. Now, what he needs is complete bed rest. The doctors said it could take eight to twelve weeks for him to fully recover, so I'm taking him home with me. He can't very well stay here. Besides, you'll have enough on your plate, without being a nursemaid to a cantankerous old—"

"Hey!"

"Oh hush. You know I'm right. Besides, if you stay, all you'll do is pull-haul everything Seb does. Tim knows what he's doing, right?" Seb caught Gary's muttered, grudging agreement. "Well, that's fine. You leave Tim in charge, Seb will do what he's told, and *you* get to heal up." Another pause.

"Go make me some tea," Gary barked out. Annie's voice dimmed, and Gary sighed. "She means well. I know why she's doin' it. All your cousins have quit the nest, and she has to have *someone* to mother, right? And she *will* look after me."

If you don't kill each other first. "You in pain?"

"Are you kiddin'? They've got me on these painkillers that got me high as a fuckin' kite, till they wear off." There was a pause. "Look, I'm sorry 'bout this. You were the only one I could think of."

Seb pushed out a heavy sigh. "I get it. Mom already laid out the whole you're-free-for-the-summer argument. And Annie's right. At least she'll be able to take care of you."

"So what time can you get here in the morning?"

Wait—what? "Excuse me?"

"There's stuff I need to tell ya before she whisks me away on her broomstick." Annie's voice rumbled in the background. "Hush yourself. I'm talkin' to Seb, and it's important. So yeah, I've got stuff I need to go over with you, so you're ready to start Monday."

And just like that, Seb was back to being pissed. *Looks like lunch with the guys is canceled.*

"I'll send her out in the morning with a grocery list over't Bradbury's. That way, you don't have to think about food for a while. I'll make sure she stocks up on the basics."

Seb knew Gary was doing his best to lessen the blow, but it still sucked. And there wasn't a damn thing he could do about it, not if he didn't want to come across as a cold-hearted bastard.

"I'll be there before noon. That good enough?" Cape Porpoise was about a half-hour's drive from Ogunquit, if that.

"Yeah, that'd be great." Another sigh. "I'll try not to kill your Aunt Annie by then." A pause. "Thanks, Seb. I know we haven't spoken in a while, but—"

"You get some rest, and I'll see you tomorrow." Seb disconnected. He put the phone down, then took a long drink. *Well shit. So much for not talking it into existence. Looks like the cosmos is gonna steamroller me into it.* Seb raised his bottle. "Summer is officially canceled," he announced to the world.

He got up from the table, his phone in one hand, the bottle in the other, went through the arch that led to his living room, and flopped on the couch, careful to hold the bottle steady. He gazed at his surroundings. *Let's look on the bright side. I don't have plants to die on me while I'm away.* Seb did *not* possess a green thumb. And it was the only bright side he could see.

Sucks donkey balls.

His phone buzzed once. It was a text from Levi.

You okay?

He clicked *Call.* "Nope." He relayed the key points. "So that's it. What a shitshow."

"Hey, at least there's a positive side to all this."

Seb snorted. "There is? Not from where I'm sitting." Except for the whole plants thing, and he wasn't going into that with Levi.

"Sure there is. You're going to spend the

summer working that body. By the time you're through, you're gonna be so buff you'll have to fight off all the guys drooling over you."

He had to hand it to Levi. The guy was a regular Pollyanna.

"Thanks for that. I'll let you go back to the party."

Levi chuckled. "What party?"

Seb's stomach clenched. "Hey, I didn't kill it, did I?"

"Relax. Almost everyone had gone by then. Right now the guys are in the guest room, talking over hot chocolate and Grammy's oatmeal raisin cookies."

"Aw, fuck, I missed out." She made the best cookies.

"Don't worry. Next time you're here, I'll make sure we've got some for you. And you stayed at the party longer than Finn and Joel did."

Seb cackled. "Yeah, but they had an excuse to leave. They had a date with a hotel bed."

"Speaking of beds... get some sleep. And keep in touch? You ever need to talk to someone, you know where I am. Especially if you need a change of scenery."

"Thanks, man." Seb disconnected. He set both phone and bottle down on the carpet, folded his arms under his head, and closed his eyes.

What came instantly to mind was the light in Joel's eyes when he looked at Finn.

Someone wrote about that light in a song. Because *lovelight* nailed it.

The first time he'd seen Finn and Joel together at Maine Street, Seb had known they were a good fit, but the party had been a revelation. He'd never seen Finn so goddamn *happy*. Seb had kept sneaking glances across the patio all evening, watching him and Joel as they sat together, talking quietly, laughing, and so *many* smiles shared between them.

Fuck, the way Joel looked at him... There was such intimacy in that gaze. A weight settled over Seb's chest, and his limbs felt heavy as fuck.

I want that.

He wanted someone to *know* him, balls to bones. Someone to care when he was angry, or hurting, or just plain tired. Someone to come home to at the end of a long day, to give him a foot rub and listen to him rant about the little bastards he had to teach.

And the fact that I don't *have someone like that? Is that down to me?*

Seb knew how he came across—no-strings, no-commitment, two-dimensional kinda dude. It wasn't his fault the guys he went most for—older guys, with a bit of silver here and there—weren't into commitment. They were mostly out for all the fun they could get, so why not give 'em what they wanted?

Maybe that's why those guys never make it past one night with me. Maybe they saw more than Seb thought they did, saw the need in him, and perceived him as being too much work.

Except Joel was an older guy, and he clearly had no issues with commitment. *There have to be more like him out there, right?* Seb didn't doubt for a second that as soon as he'd gone to the bathroom that afternoon, one of his friends would've made a comment about how Joel checked all Seb's boxes. Sure he did—but he was Finn's guy.

Seb wanted a guy of his own.

Even my friends don't know the real me. They think I'm like a peach, with a stone where my heart should be, but I've got more layers than an onion.

That stopped him dead. *Whoa.* Seb wasn't one for philosophical musing. *What the fuck brought that on?* Maybe it was seeing Finn and Joel. And as for them not knowing the real him, that wasn't true, not anymore. Only a month or so ago, Seb had confessed something to Finn that not one of the others knew—he had one-night stands because that was all he could get.

Have I talked myself into this corner? Am I subconsciously putting up barriers, signs that read Alert—commitment-phobic?

All Seb knew was how he'd felt when he watched Finn and Joel.

He wanted what they had.

I'm not gonna find someone in Cape Porpoise. All I'm gonna find there is a lot of hard work.

Thank God for porn. He had a feeling it would be a lifesaver in the coming weeks.

His phone buzzed, and he reached down for it. When he opened Finn's WhatsApp message, his throat tightened. It was a selfie. Finn had taken it from above, and it showed him in bed, beneath white sheets, and Joel curled up around him, asleep.

The message contained one line: *So fucking happy.* As if Seb needed to be told. Happiness shone out of him. His face *glowed* with it.

And there was that goddamn weight on Seb's chest again. He didn't begrudge Finn his sparkly new relationship, not for one goddamn second, but it did throw Seb's own situation into sharp relief.

I want to be happy too.

More than that, he wanted what Finn had— someone to look at him with lovelight in their eyes.

Chapter Two

June 14

Driving along tree-lined Main Street confirmed Seb's worst fears. Cape Porpoise was picturesque and quiet—*way* too quiet. He recalled his childhood visits here, when he'd whined to his mom that there was 'nothing to do.'

Little appeared to have changed.

So far, he'd passed Bradbury's Market, which looked big enough to provide whatever he needed in the way of food and other necessaries. Apart from that, there were houses, set back from the road, with well-cared-for front yards and neat flower beds, and that was it. As Main Street became Pier Road, he spied boats in the harbor to his right through the trees, the sun glinting on the calm water.

I suppose if I were here just to chill out, it'd be perfect.

It wasn't as if Seb was going to get much time to himself to do any chilling.

He followed Pier Road as it snaked around a bend. He slowed at its closest point to the water's edge, took a left, and pulled onto the narrow dirt road that led to Gary's place. He smiled when he saw the dilapidated truck out front. It was the same one he remembered from his childhood.

Come to think of it, the house looks so much smaller, and it wasn't big to begin with. Seb parked beside Gary's truck, noting another car at the side of the house.

That had to belong to Annie. He got out of the car, and climbed the four steps up to the front door. Before he could knock, the door opened, and there was Annie, her gray hair cropped close to her head, her glasses perched on the end of her nose, just like he remembered.

"Hey stranger. How's the teaching going? Strangled any kids yet?"

Seb smirked. She and Gary were alike in one aspect—neither of them had a filter. "Good to see you too, Annie."

She peered at him with a frown. "Where's your stuff?"

"In the car. It can stay there a while." He grinned. "Gonna let me in?"

"Sure, but keep the noise down. He's dozing on the couch." She stood aside to let him enter, and Seb crossed the threshold into the compact interior. They were in the main room of the house, where the kitchen was separated from the living room by a low wall.

Good God, what a mess. There was clutter everywhere, except once he looked past that, he could see there was dirt too. *When did he clean last?* His uncle lay on the couch, supported by pillows, with a throw over him. The couch was big enough to serve as a bed and it was the only seating in the room. A long low coffee table sat in front of it, and there were more tables and bookcases against every wall.

Seb couldn't see one clear surface.

Annie beckoned him with her finger, and they crept past the couch and through the door into Gary's bedroom. She closed the door quietly.

"I thought we'd talk in here." She kept her voice low. "He didn't have a good night and I wanted him to get some rest before I made the trip home." Annie grimaced. "He's going to be in the car for four hours, and that'll be as uncomfortable as hell." She sat on the end of the bed and gestured for him to join her. "You still teaching at Wells Jr High?" He nodded, and she huffed. "Rather you than me. Kids are so different nowadays."

Seb chuckled. "I bet every generation says that. When I was in college, one of my professors read us this account, someone's comment about the youth of the day. It was the usual stuff: kids loving luxury, having bad manners, disrespecting their elders, not standing up when said elders came into the room, contradicting their parents…"

Annie nodded vehemently. "My point exactly."

"He asked us if it sounded familiar, and someone said, 'yeah, sounds like something my granddad says.' The professor nodded and told us it was written by Socrates, and not to let anyone tell us kids are different." He glanced around the room, doing his best to disguise his feelings.

Jesus. This place needs a clean. Then he noticed the beige fur-covered cat tree. "Gary's got a cat?"

Annie snorted. "He *had* a cat. Flea-bitten bastard died five years ago, and he *still* hasn't gotten around to throwing that thing out." She patted Seb's knee. "See if you can do something about the mess once we're gone," she said in a low voice. "I'd like him to come home and find it in a better state than he's leaving it."

Seb bit his lip. "That won't be difficult."

"You got some fella in there?" Gary's voice shattered the quiet. "Not that I mind, but keep the noise down. Don't want the neighbors complainin'."

Annie's eyes twinkled. "It's awake." She opened the door, and they went back into the living room. Gary didn't move, but his eyes followed Seb as he approached.

"You got here then." He winced, and Annie didn't hesitate. She picked up the bottle on the coffee table, tipped a couple of pills into her hand, and handed them to Gary, along with a glass of water. He didn't argue, so Seb guessed the pain was pretty bad. Gary squinted at Annie. "How about you make some coffee? Me an' Seb need to talk."

Annie arched her eyebrows. "Fine."

"I'd love some coffee," Seb told her. He waited till she'd walked into the kitchen, then he perched at the end of the couch where there was space, and shrugged off his jacket, laying it over the end of the coffee table. "Do you need anything?" he asked Gary.

He shook his head slightly, wincing again. "About tomorrow. If you follow Pier Road right to the end, that's where Tim will pick you up in the boat. Make sure you're there by four-thirty."

Seb blinked. "I guess I'm having an early night." It wasn't really a surprise. Nor was Gary coming straight to the point. *He never was one for small talk.*

"He'll take the boat out, and work out where to put the traps." Gary focused his eyes. "You remember how to prep bait?"

Seb snorted. "You had me sliding redfish and porgies onto bait needles when I was just a kid, remember? *And* you had me plunging buoys into a barrel of hot water to boil away all the gunk and algae."

Gary sighed. "I know you hated it, but you were the best of the bunch. You were also the best at bitchin' about it." There was a hint of a twinkle in his eyes. "Is that a gay thing?"

"Excuse me?" Annie said loudly from the kitchen. "You can't say things like that."

"Oh hush. My house, I can say what the hell I like. And in case you haven't noticed, I've toned down the cussin', seein' as you made such a song-and-dance about it." He glanced at Seb and rolled his eyes. Seb did his best not to laugh.

"I had noticed," Annie fired back. "I wasn't going to mention it, in case you decided you'd been civil long enough."

Gary's comment told Seb one thing for certain—his mom had been talking about him. "Back to your question. Not necessarily. I know a few gay guys who wouldn't know how to bitch to save their lives."

Gary made a noncommittal noise. "Tim'll take you through measurin' the catch and decidin' which ones to throw back." He cleared his throat. "I'm gonna say this now. You need to keep in mind you've gotta catch one hundred fifty pounds of lobster at least, just to cover gas and bait. So no slackin' off."

"One hundred fifty pounds doesn't sound like a lot." Seb cocked his head. "Is it getting tougher out there?"

Gary pushed out another sigh. "When you were here last, soft-shell lobster sold for three to four dollars per pound on the wharf. Now? Two dollars seventy-five."

"I guess fuel prices have gone up too."

Gary's face tightened. "S'not just the fuel. Bait prices too. That summer you were here, I reckon a drum of bait was thirty-five dollars. Today it'll cost you a hundred and eighty."

"Can you make up for the low price by catching more lobster?"

Gary gave a slight shake of his head. "Can't handle a higher number of traps. Maine law. Eight hundred is the limit, and we set and haul a portion of that figure every day."

Seb gazed at him with renewed admiration. "But you're still here."

Gary's eyes gleamed. "I'll be doin' this till I can't do it no more. I love it."

"That's because you're too stubborn to know any better," Annie said as she brought them coffee. She patted Seb on the shoulder. "I'll be in the bedroom, packing up the last of his clothes." Then she gave Gary a mock glare. "I don't want to hear you cussing, just because you think I can't hear you. Because I can."

Gary pointed to a drawer in the coffee table. "You'll find earplugs in there then." Annie rolled her eyes and walked out of the room, pushing the door to but not closing it.

Gary studied Seb for a moment. "They let you teach with hair like that?"

Seb could give as good as he got. "Fuck you," he said good-naturedly, knowing it would tickle Gary.

Sure enough, Gary chuckled. "Damn, it's good to see you." His brow furrowed. "You okay?"

"You mean, apart from being here?" No sooner had the words left his lips then Seb regretted them.

Gary waved his hand. "It's all my fault. I was going way too fast." A look of horror flickered across his face. "You weren't goin' on vacation, were ya? Your mom didn't mention that."

"Relax. The farthest I was gonna get was Ogunquit Beach." Except Seb didn't want to think about that.

Gary's lips twitched. "I guess I know how you were gonna spend your summer then."

Seb didn't hold back. "You knew that anyway. You've been talking to Mom."

Gary gestured to the pillow near Seb. "Pass me that, will ya?" Seb did so, and when Gary tried to shove it under his head, Seb helped. He sat back down, and Gary regarded him thoughtfully. "I have two brothers and three sisters, and you had to get saddled with the only one of us who don't like gays. Sucks to be you, I guess."

Seb's chest tightened. "We just don't talk about it." It was better that way.

"You wanna laugh?" Gary grinned. "When you told your mom you were gonna be a teacher, she called me and said you'd finally seen the light. She figured you couldn't be a teacher *and* be gay."

Seb stared at him in frank amazement. "Seriously? Where the fuck did she get that from?"

Gary cackled. "I gave up tryin' to figure out how your mom's mind works long ago. I asked her if you were seein' anybody."

Seb snorted again. "Bet that went down well."

"Like a lead balloon." Gary's gaze flickered toward the bedroom door. He lowered his voice. "Gonna tell you something now, but you gotta promise not to tell your mom I shared this with you, all right?"

What the fuck? "Okay."

There was a moment of silence before Gary spoke again. "When you were sixteen, your mom was tryin' to find a place to send you."

Ice crawled over Seb skin. "What kind of place?" As if he couldn't guess.

"Oh, somewhere with people who were gonna put you back onto the path of righteousness, and make you straight again. She'd found a couple of places too."

Holy fuck. "Tell me this is a joke."

Gary shook his head. "I was the one who told her to pull her head out of her ass, and leave you be. I told her this wasn't a choice, it was just how you were. She didn't much like that answer. So I told her, what she was suggestin' amounted to brainwashin', and it might damage you. *That* slowed her down a tad."

Seb sucked in a breath. "I guess I owe you." His head was reeling.

Gary waved his hand. "That's okay. The way I see it, you're payin' me back."

And then some. Seb pushed aside his frustration. He knew the heart of his anger was directed at his mom, not because of what she was asking of him, but because it was *her* doing the asking. And yeah, he hated the fishing part of it with a passion, but in the light of what he'd just learned?

He owed Gary, big time.

I guess it's time to put on my big boy pants, suck it up, and just get on with it. What's one summer, compared to what I could have lost if Mom had gotten her way?

The door opened and Annie came out, a suitcase in each hand. "That's all your clothes. And the first thing I'm going to do when I get you home is the laundry."

Gary rolled his eyes. "Judas Priest, woman. Don't you ever quit naggin'?" His gaze met Seb's. "I'm startin' to think this is *not* such a great idea."

"Well, that makes two of us," Annie retorted.

Seb held up his hands. "Do I have to be the grown-up here? You're gonna be sharing the same house for two months or more. It *might* be a good idea to try to get along." He gave Gary a pointed stare. "So you might need to cut back on the cussing for a little." He glanced at Annie. "And *you* need to cut him some slack."

Annie blinked, her mouth opening and closing. Finally she coughed. "I'll just take these cases out to the car." She walked out of the front door, shutting it behind her.

Gary's eyes twinkled. "Well look at you. All growed up." He sighed. "I know I said it last night, but it needs sayin' again. Thank you for this."

Seb bit back a smile. "I think I'm gonna be having an easier time of it than you are."

Annie came back into the house. She stood at the end of the couch, her hands on her hips. "I think between us, we can get him into the car."

Gary glared at her. "Jesus, I'm right here. And I still got legs, case you haven't noticed."

Annie glanced at Seb. "See what I mean? Stubborn ol' mule."

Seb didn't think there was all that much to choose between them.

Three hours after Annie and Gary had driven away, Seb was exhausted. He'd taken all the bed linen and put it in the washer. Then he'd started cleaning. Five large black garbage bags sat outside, ready to be collected, along with the forlorn-looking cat tree. He'd removed all the clutter, intending to clean every surface.

Then he ran into a problem. There wasn't a single cleaning product in the house. *What the fuck, Gary?*

Seb glanced at Gary's notice board. Among the receipts for bait, fuel, and catches that were pinned to it—which seemed to be Gary's only filing system—there was a leaflet for the Bradbury Brothers Market. They closed at seven on Sundays, and the store had to be less than five minutes away on foot.

I need some air anyway.

Besides, what were the chances of him running into a sexy hot guy, also doing a little shopping? Seb laughed.

Pretty fucking thin.

Chapter Three

Marcus Gilbert poured himself a cup of coffee and walked into the living room to gaze out at the yard. All was peaceful, apart from the squirrels who were darting here and there, and the birds singing their hearts out in the trees surrounding the house on three sides. Marcus's day always began the same way—sitting in the big armchair facing a wall of glass, a cup of coffee in one hand, taking the opportunity to breathe in the peace. And by late afternoon, he returned to the same spot to enjoy the sunlight.

His phone vibrated, and Marcus sighed. *So much for enjoying the quiet.* He pulled his phone from his jeans pocket and glanced at the screen. It was a text from Nick.

Well, what do you think? Do you like it?

Nick wasn't usually this cryptic. Marcus composed a reply. *Do I like what? And good afternoon to you too.*

Seconds later Nick pinged back a response. *My package.*

Marcus almost sprayed the window with coffee. He put down his cup, and clicked *Call.* "Does your husband know you're asking guys their opinion of your package?"

Nick guffawed. "Okay. I guess I didn't

phrase that very well. The package I sent. Did you like it?"

"What package?"

Nick made an impatient noise. "The one I got a text about yesterday? Saying it's been delivered?"

It was then Marcus realized he hadn't checked the mailbox for a couple of days. "Oops. Let me go see." He got up from his chair, went through the house and out of the front door. It may have been June, but the air still had a chill to it, despite the hour. The mailbox was open, and several items could be seen sticking out of it.

Thank God for law-abiding neighbors. Not that Marcus expected anything less in Cape Porpoise. He hurried over to retrieve the envelopes, and found one fat brown cardboard package stuffed into the black metal box. When he got back inside the house, he picked up his phone from the kitchen countertop where he'd left it.

"Oh. Looks like I have mail," he joked. At first glance, the rest was stuff for his parents, or leaflets that would be filed in the trash can. *Hey, dude. There's this thing called recycling, remember?*

Nick laughed. "Gee. I wonder who it's from?"

The package bore the word *Fragile*. "Oh God. What have you sent me?" He pulled the tab to open it. A bubble-wrapped shape came out, along with a smaller package also wrapped in plastic. Marcus put the phone on speaker, grabbed a knife from the block, and sliced through the wrapping. He stared at the items, perplexed. "Nick, why are you sending me aromatherapy oils and an oil burner?" It was a *very pretty* oil burner, made from what resembled soapstone, with a cut-out design that he guessed would produce a nice effect when a tea light burned inside it.

"Hey, I chose those five oils very carefully. Lavender is to relieve stress, sandalwood calms the nerves and helps you focus, rose reduces anxiety, chamomile improves mood and relaxation, and jasmine just… lifts you."

"I'm sensing a theme here." Marcus was touched. "Thank you."

"So… How are you?"

"I'm good." When silence met his response, he sighed. "No, really, I'm good. I've been meaning to call to thank you."

"What did I do?"

"You convinced me I needed to break the cycle. That I couldn't stay in New York and expect things to change." And when Marcus hadn't listened, Nick had persisted, because that was what good friends did. *I thought I had a lot of those.*

Marcus could count his good friends on one hand now.

"I'm glad." Nick's voice was warm. "Juan was worried sick. And I know I said call if you need anything, but when you didn't… I guess you didn't need anything."

"I'm sorry." He *had* meant to call, but it had slipped his mind. *I was too busy getting my shit together.* Which was a piss-poor excuse, seeing as it was thanks to Nick's intervention that he was in his present—vastly improved—state.

Marcus picked up his cup and wandered back to the living room. He had to smile at the sight of a squirrel gazing through the window. As Marcus drew closer to retake his seat, the squirrel shot back into the woods.

"So what are you doing with yourself up there in Maine?"

Marcus settled back against the seat cushion. "The first month, I didn't do anything apart from sleep. Oh, and walk. I walked my ass off." He figured he'd covered every inch of Cape Porpoise on foot during April and May. It was amazing what there was to see when not viewed from a car window.

"Hey, if you need to sleep… Sounds like my gift is useless. Just listening to you, you seem way more relaxed."

"Like I said, I'm in a good place." The house had provided exactly what Marcus had needed—a calm safe space to regroup his thoughts, recharge his batteries, renew…

"So what's it like? The house, I mean."

"I suppose you could describe it as quirky." That was always how it had struck Marcus. "It started out simple, but various bits got added on over the years. It's quiet here, though." He gazed out at the back yard. "All I can see right now are trees." Exchanging Manhattan's noise and… temptations for the tranquility of Cape Porpoise had been the right thing to do.

"Can I come visit?"

"Sure. Just pick your dates carefully. The family is going to descend on the Fourth. Everyone will be here—and I do mean everyone. My brother, his two kids who are home from college, my sister, her son, also home from college, my cousins Lisa and Rob, their kids, Lisa's grandkids—and of course, my parents."

"Holy fuck. How big is that place?"

"There are four bedrooms, the attic room, and the summerhouse. And a lot of sofa beds." Having the family there would be like stepping back into his childhood.

Marcus couldn't decide whether the prospect excited or terrified him.

"Are you ready for that big a gathering?"

He blinked at the coincidental question. "Why wouldn't I be?"

"Do any of them know what's been going on?"

Of course they don't. Why the fuck would Marcus share that? He forced himself to take a calming breath. "All my parents know is, I needed a change of scenery, and a break from New York. That was why they suggested the house." They had no idea what led up to that, and it was going to stay that way. "And I'll be fine." Thank God he got along with his family.

"So I'm okay before the Fourth... What about after?"

Marcus laughed. "They'll stay a while. Some of them will be here until August, I imagine."

"I'll talk to Juan, see if we can work something out, but I'm not hopeful."

Marcus's heartbeat picked up speed. "I could visit you." His mouth was suddenly dry. He drained the last of his coffee, then headed into the kitchen to pour himself another cup.

There was a pause. "Will you come back here to live, do you think?"

It was a question Marcus had asked himself a

lot in recent weeks.

"No clue, not yet. Let me get through the summer first." He hesitated, then plunged ahead, his heart racing. "I started writing a book."

He caught Nick's sharp intake of breath. "Seriously? Am I in it?"

Marcus laughed. "You will be—when I get to that part. But it's not that kind of book. It's more of a… self-help guide. Something along the lines of 'This is what Marcus did. Don't be like Marcus.'"

There was a pause. "I read your article."

"Oh." There was a tightness in his chest, and his mouth dried up again.

"So did a lot of your friends."

"Oh." *What friends?* Marcus was dying to ask what had been said, but he didn't dare. He had a fair idea anyway.

"Let's just say… opinion is divided into three camps. There's the Who-gives-a-fuck? camp, the Good-for-him camp, and—"

"Let me guess. The He's-fucking-delusional camp."

"Pretty much."

Just as he'd suspected. "And which camp are you in?" When Nick didn't reply, Marcus's chest constricted even further. "I see. You haven't believed a word I've said, have you?"

"Hey, you said you haven't got a problem," Nick retorted. "In fact, back in New York you were *telling* me you didn't have a problem before I even opened my mouth."

"I told you. I'm doing okay."

"I'm sure you are. All I'm saying is, I've seen some fine men fall prey to it, men who thought they could handle it. Hell, if the events of *my* life had happened in a different order, there but by the grace of God…"

Marcus's stomach churned. "You're talking about the past."

"Yeah. And let's remember something here. I saw what a sorry state you were in. I told you to make a break. I was surprised as fuck when you did. But if you think I'm going to believe you can just walk away from all that?" There was silence for a moment. "Sorry, Marcus. I shouldn't have said that. It's just that when you didn't call…"

"You concluded it was a case of same shit, different location, is that it?"

Another pause.

Marcus couldn't contain his ire a second longer. "You know what? It *is* possible for someone to say, 'Hey, I'm done with this.' Because if it wasn't, what the *fucking use* is a twelve-step program, or AA, or anything like that?"

"Can we change the subject?"

"Fine by me." He was *this close* to disconnecting.

"How far have you got with the book?"

"I've written about seventy thousand words so far."

"Jesus, that's huge. Wow."

Marcus strove to breathe evenly. "Before you get lost in admiration, it's seventy thousand words of a mess. It needs sorting out, chunks cutting, rewriting…" And rewriting. And more rewriting.

"Are you gonna publish it?"

Marcus hadn't gotten past the cathartic exercise writing afforded him. "We'll see when it's done." It was only then he realized the good place he'd been in had vanished from under his feet like quicksand. His stomach was clenched, his throat tight.

This is not *helping.*

"Sorry, Nick, but I'm going to have to cut the conversation short. I just realized I need to go to the store before it closes." He wasn't lying. He really did need to go shopping—just not right then.

Nick's voice was quiet. "I've upset you, haven't I?"

No shit.

"You just made me think about things I haven't thought about for a while. And before you say it, that's not because I've been avoiding them. I really had left them behind."

Yeah right.

"I don't think they're all that easy to walk away from. Christ, I'm sorry. Maybe it's not such a good idea Juan and I coming to see you."

Aw fuck. But before Marcus could tell him he'd be welcome anytime, Nick plowed ahead.

"I'll leave you to your groceries. Enjoy the oils. I hope they help in those moments when you might need them." Nick disconnected.

Shit.

What cut him to the quick was that one remark. *I've seen some fine men fall prey to it, men who thought they could handle it.*

It didn't take a genius to work out he was talking about Marcus.

He doesn't believe me. Did I really expect anything different? Why should he go against the tide of popular opinion? But that was what hurt. He *had* expected

Nick to be different.

The lure of a stroll was stronger than ever, if only to clear his head and settle his stomach.

Marcus got up and went into the kitchen to compose a list. The store was about fifteen minutes away on foot. He grabbed his wallet, then raided the net hanging from a hook in the closet where Mom kept neatly folded plastic bags. He put on his leather jacket and stuffed the bags into his pockets, one on each side.

When he reached the end of the driveway, he turned right onto Land's End Road. He maintained an easy stroll as he ambled along the dirt verge that lined the road. Not a sidewalk to be seen, just houses scattered here and there, and shady spots where lush green trees met in graceful arches above the road, providing cool relief from the late afternoon sun's glare. There was little traffic, and that made the birdsong around him all the more noticeable.

As he approached the intersection with Wildes District Road, his phone buzzed in his pocket, and the thought briefly crossed his mind that it was Nick.

I don't want to talk to him. His stomach roiled. *But if it wasn't for Nick, I wouldn't be where I am now.* He pulled out his phone, and his anxiety crumpled at the sight of Jess's name. "Hey, sis."

"Mom said you're at the house in Cape Porpoise."

"Yeah, they said I could stay here a while." Except he figured there would come a point when he'd have to leave, and despite his insistence to Nick that all was well, he wasn't ready just yet.

"Damn. I bet it's great up there right now."

That wistful catch in her voice tugged at his heart.

"Sounds quieter than Boston does." He could hear the dull roar of traffic in the background.

"Are you okay? Thought I'd ask, since you missed my birthday. You know, the big one."

"I sent you a gift, didn't I?" For the second time in less than an hour, his chest tightened. He'd been in no state to attend her family party, not in April. Apart from a bottle of champagne, he'd sent her a mug with the words *I am 39+* on it, plus a drawing of someone giving the finger.

She snorted. "You should've seen Mom's face when she saw it." There was a pause. "And you haven't answered my question."

Damn that sixth sense Jess always seemed to possess when it came to his moods.

"I'm fine. You still coming here on the Fourth?"

"Yeah."

Despite her obvious yearning to be where he was, she didn't sound all that enthusiastic. He turned right onto Main Street, and suddenly there was more traffic, sidewalks, and properties. Boats sat in front yards wherever he looked. "What's wrong?"

She huffed. "Never could hide anything from you, or Chris, for that matter." Another pause. "I'm worried about Jake."

"There's nothing wrong, is there?" His nephew had just finished college.

"He's gotten real quiet lately."

"Isn't he home now? I know graduation is next month. Maybe he's thinking about the future. Does he know what he wants to do next?"

Jess sighed. "I don't think it's that. Every

time I ask him what's going on, or if he's worried about something, it's as if he can't get away from me fast enough. Whatever it is, he won't talk to me about it. Maybe… maybe he needs a guy around… To talk to…"

Marcus got the feeling he knew where this was going. "He *has* got two uncles, right? Chris is older than me, wiser…" *And not such a fuck-up.*

"Chris is dealing with his own issues."

Yet more guilt flushed through him. *I've been a selfish bastard.* It seemed his siblings were struggling, and he was MIA.

"This vacation might be what we all need, you know," Jess remarked. "Are you *sure* you're okay? You've been on my mind a lot lately."

"I'm fine, I promise." A little white lie, but hey, he was getting there, right? "And I'll tell you what. If Jake wants to talk, then fine, we'll talk. But I'm not going to push."

"Thank you." Her voice was warm. "It's at times like this I wish I hadn't made such a mess of my life. Maybe then he'd have a dad."

Marcus knew how often Jess kicked herself about Jake's origins. He'd been the product of a drunken encounter at a party, and the guy concerned did *not* want to know. Nor had he been interested in whether Jess did or didn't keep the baby.

Fuck him. She was better off without him.

"Are you dating at all?"

She snorted again. "What—and risk the Gilbert curse come crashing down on my head?"

He laughed. "That's just Chris being an ass. There's no such thing."

"Oh yeah? Name me *one relationship* in our

family that stayed the course."

"Easy. Mom and Dad. It's their golden wedding anniversary this year. That sounds pretty curse-proof to me. *And* Aunt Carol."

"Uncle Jon died!"

"Sure—when he was seventy-seven. They almost made it to sixty years of marriage."

"And what about Rob? Susan divorced him. Lisa? David divorced her. Chris? Rachel left him."

"What about me?" he fired back. "Haven't seen any sign of the curse in *my* life, have you?"

"You don't count."

He let out a dramatic gasp. "Excuse me?"

"Hello? The curse requires that you're in a *relationship*? Not sure if you've ever come across one of those." That sounded more like his sister.

The last thing on his mind was a relationship. Bradbury's was ahead on the right. "Okay, I'm at the store. If I keep talking to you I'll be home by the time I realize I've forgotten something."

"Then I'll let you get on with it. I'll see you on the Fourth."

"I *will* talk to Jake, okay? If you think it'll do any good."

"Thank you." Another pause. "Hey, Marcus? If I need to come up there before the Fourth... just me... would that be okay?"

"Why would it *not* be okay?"

"Oh, I don't know. I mean, having me around might cramp your style."

He laughed. "No style to cramp. All I'm doing is walking and writing." Besides, the only people he saw on a regular basis were the people who ran the store, and the mailman, who had to be at least sixty years old.

Never mind a relationship—the last thing I need right now is a distraction. And guys definitely came under that heading.

"Sounds perfect. I might see you soon then. Love you." She disconnected.

Marcus went into the store, removed his list from his pocket, and grabbed a cart. He liked the place: there was everything from the basics to craft beers, wine and liquor, pastries to tempt anyone from the straight and narrow path of healthy eating, and a deli that catered to all tastes. Plus, the folks who ran it were always polite: he got a smile and a greeting every time he went in there.

He headed for the produce section, where he picked up a bag of apples and another of grapes, before going to check out the bananas.

"So what's the deal with green bananas?"

It took a second or two for him to register the guy standing next to him was addressing Marcus. He was young, maybe in his mid-twenties, with wavy brown hair that strayed into gorgeous pale blue eyes, a lean kind of guy who wouldn't have seemed out of place on a surfboard. He had to be a summer visitor: Marcus didn't recall seeing him before at the store. *Because fuck, I'd have noticed.* He wore a T-shirt, and whatever was printed on it was obscured by his denim jacket.

Marcus resisted the urge to lower his gaze.

He gave the guy a polite smile. "Are you talking to me?"

The guy pointed to the bananas. "So, is the deal you take 'em home and wait for them to ripen? Is it a good idea to buy some green and some yellow?

That way, you can eat some right away and the others will be ready by the time you need 'em."

Marcus resisted the urge to say "whatever." He reached past the guy, grabbed a bunch of bananas, placed them in his cart, and hurried away.

Why do some people feel the need to start conversations with strangers? It wasn't something Marcus had ever done—except when he was hooking up with guys in gay bars, of course. But this wasn't a gay bar, it was a grocery store, and the guy didn't know Marcus from Adam.

Not that Marcus would have *minded* knowing him. If he'd run across him in a bar in New York, it would have taken him less than a nanosecond to react with a sexy line. And it would have been no time after that before one of them had a dick between their lips.

He went over to the magazine rack, and peered at the covers. On the front of one magazine there was a guy fishing with a line, and he had to smile. *Lord, how old was I the last time I did that?* Going out in Dad's boat, spending all afternoon trying to catch a fish, just him, Dad and Chris on an idyllic hot summer's day during the long summer vacation.

Maybe I should take it up. Marcus was sure he could rent a boat somewhere in Cape Porpoise. There were boats everywhere, and he'd bet even money there was fishing gear lurking in a closet back at the house.

"Wouldn't you know it? The one magazine I want, they don't have."

Marcus sighed inwardly. Maybe ignoring this guy wasn't the way to go. "Which magazine are you looking for?"

"*Out.*"

Marcus blinked. Then he noticed the guy had taken off his jacket, revealing his T-shirt. Across his chest were the words *Yes, I am, and no, you can't watch.* Then he caught sight of the rainbow enamel pin on the jacket the guy clutched in his hand.

Fuck, he's not exactly subtle, is he?

Marcus cleared his throat. "Ask them to get it for you. They'll order it if they can." He could have added that he didn't think for one second the store would have a gay magazine on their shelves, but that would have given the game away. Marcus was too long in the tooth to fall for the guy's ploy.

Not going to give him the satisfaction.

He walked away, heading for the cash register. He didn't have everything on his list, but there was no way he was going to hang around, just in case the hot dude decided to strike up another conversation.

Because *fuck yeah*, he was hot. It was a delicious thought to look at that barely-there beard and mustache, and imagine their owner rubbing them against Marcus's—

No. No. No. Do not *pass go. Do* not *hook up with hot guy.*

There were limits to Marcus's willpower, and it had been months since he'd gotten laid. But sex was a distraction he could do without.

One of those oils Nick sent is supposed to help with focus. That was what Marcus needed. He did *not* need the sexy lean frame and gorgeous blue eyes of the guy who seemed determined to check him out.

Chapter Four

June 15

When his alarm went off, Seb wanted to throw his phone against the wall. It was four freakin' a.m. He rolled onto his back, his morning wood tenting the sheet. He had half an hour to get to the pickup point. After a shower, coffee, and more coffee, that left no time to deal with his hard-on.

Fuck it. There's always time to deal with a hard-on.

Seb threw back the sheets and went into the bathroom in search of the bag where he'd stashed his lube. Then he slipped back beneath the comforter, bent his legs, planted his feet on the mattress, and slicked up his hand. He closed his eyes, knowing exactly who he'd see behind them—the guy from the market.

God, you are one big tease, you know that?

The only decent-looking man for miles, and he was straight. Okay, Seb didn't know that for sure, but the evidence was definitely there. Seb's graphic tee had drawn no comment, and as for his mention of *Out?* Christ, that had been *inspired.* The guy's lack of reaction kinda nailed it though. He wouldn't have known *Out* magazine if someone smacked his ass with a rolled-up copy of it.

Seb slid his hand a little faster along his hard shaft at the thought of landing his hand on the guy's firm, bare butt with a sharp slap. So what if he was straight? Seb could dream, right? And Market Guy checked *all* Seb's boxes. His dark hair was longer on top, but that silver at his temples and the sides where it was shorter had caught Seb's interest in a nanosecond. *Gimme a silver fox any day.* The guy's firm jawline and upper lip were covered in scruff, mostly gray but peppered with black. He had good lips, the kind Seb could imagine sliding his dick between, watching it emerge glistening and pink, only to bury it again in a tight throat. His brows were heavy and dark, giving his blue eyes a sultry gaze that had almost unraveled Seb right there in the store. And as for the rest of him…

Seb tugged on his cock, trying to picture Market Guy naked. He wasn't some muscle-bound hunk, but he wasn't a wimp either. *Just right.* The kind of guy who'd be freaking *perfect*, kneeling between Seb's spread thighs, fucking him with slick fingers while he sucked on Seb's dick—

Warmth coated Seb's belly, and he shuddered, his body jolting with each drop that pulsed from his slit. He lay there, relishing the afterglow.

So what if the guy was straight? He was gorgeous, and Seb envisioned making frequent withdrawals from his spank bank while he pictured him in that black tee and black leather jacket. Not to mention those tight jeans that showed off his long legs and toned thighs.

You're not off the hook, God. This is so *not fair. You bring me to this god-awful spot, then dangle a delicious guy in front of me before you yank him away.* Seb was not into straight guys. *Been there.* It was always the same.

Some bi-curious guy would demand to fuck or be fucked, and Seb would oblige. *Hey, never turn down a willing ass or a nice dick, right?* Then the guy would wake up the next morning full of remorse and recriminations. Life was too short for that shit. Give Seb a man who rolled over, kissed him, maybe indulged in a good morning wank or fuck, then went on their way.

His chest tightened. *And where has* that *got me?*

Alone, that was where.

Seb got out of bed and headed for the shower. He had no time for regrets. He had lobster to catch.

Seb leaned on the railings at the end of the pier, contemplating the ocean. Behind him to the right was the Cape Pier Chowder House, and to the left was the grassy headland where visitors came to watch the boats in the harbor. He rested his forearms on the top rail, holding his insulated mug in both hands. The sky was that strange ethereal mix of twilight colors that always preceded dawn. Four-thirty had come and gone, and there was still no sign of Tim. Not that Seb was concerned—he knew Tim would get there eventually.

He gazed out over the calm water. Maybe he was being unfair to Cape Porpoise.

As he watched, the sun came up over the

islands in the bay, tingeing the tops of the trees there with gold. Seagulls were already spiraling overhead, their cries harsh against the quiet of the morning. It was beautiful. And after all, *this* was why he'd stayed in Maine, right? This was why he lived in Ogunquit. So what if the view from his window was of more houses? Seb knew he didn't have to go all that far to be confronted with the rolling ocean, miles of sand, and a vast expanse of sky. For the next couple of months, the view out of Gary's window was way better than his own back in Ogunquit.

"You figure on workin' today, yow'un?"

Seb snapped to attention. Tim sat below him in a small rowboat, his eyes filled with obvious amusement. He had to be going on forty, but the wrinkles made him appear older. He wore a zipped-up thin jacket beneath his bright yellow oil pants, a baseball hat on his head.

Seb grinned. "Hey, Tim. Long time no see. And I'm not so young anymore."

Tim snorted. "Lord, but you grew tall. Get your ass in here." He paddled the boat closer to the wooden ladder a few feet away.

Seb climbed down, stepping carefully into the rocking boat. "You got oil pants and muck boots for me too? There were none at Gary's."

"On the boat." He looked Seb up and down with obvious approval. "You wore layers. Good job."

"Some things you don't forget, apparently." Seb hunkered down on the wooden slat bench, and Tim sculled out into the bay.

"He's gone to his sister's then," Tim commented as he rowed. He grinned. "Sucks to be him." Then his smile faded. "How was he?"

"Suffering." Seb finished what remained of his coffee.

Tim nodded gloomily. "That'd be right. Not sure which is worse—the pain from his injuries, or havin' to stay with his sister." His eyes widened. "Shit. I forgot she's your aunt."

Seb chuckled. "You're safe. I know what she's like."

Tim had moored the thirty-six-foot lobster boat close to a buoy. That hadn't changed one bit. Even at a distance, Seb spotted the paint peeling in places, but she was a sturdy craft. "Good to see the *Liza Jane* is still going strong."

Tim laughed. "She'll outlast me, I reckon."

The first time Seb had met him, Tim had to have been about twenty. "You were doing your apprenticeship last time I was here."

"Yup. Got my license last year."

Seb gaped. "It's taken you that long to get a license?"

Tim cackled. "Apprenticeship lasted two years. But it can take years, even decades, to get a license. You have to wait for lobstermen to retire before they let someone new in. And we're not talkin' just one lobsterman retirin' neither. A whole *heap* of 'em."

They reached the boat, and Tim dropped the anchor. Seb climbed the metal ladder and clambered over the side onto the deck, Tim following. He recognized the barrels of bait, the crates piled up, the hooks and grapples everywhere, even the barrels of fuel lashed into place.

It was as if he'd never been away.

He glanced at the plastic-coated traps piled up in the stern. "Hey, he got rid of the wooden ones."

"'Bout ten years ago." Tim tapped the top of one of them. "This is the regulation now. Gotta have a biodegradable hatch so lobsters can escape if the trap gets lost in the ocean." He headed for the bow. "I'll get your oilskins and muck boots. Got a barvel for ya too." He paused. "Do I have to remind you of the rule?"

"I remember. Don't step in the rope." He was liable to get caught in a flying line and dragged overboard.

Tim smiled. "You always was a good kid. When Gary told me you were comin', I wondered how you'd turn up. Glad to see you remembered how to dress." His eyes sparkled. "Read somethin' in a magazine t'other week. Some dub talkin' 'bout lobster fishing. He was sayin' how lobsters practically climbed into his boat. I laughed so hard I wet myself. There was a picture of him standin' on the wharf. Jeezum crow, I reckon if you added up the price of everything he was wearin', you'd get no change out of seven or eight thousand dollars." He unzipped his jacket. "I've got a fifteen-dollar Carhartt shirt and three Carhartt sweatshirts under here. He wears all that to go fishin'? What a gaumy dub. One day aboard the *Liza Jane* would pretty much ruin it all. When the top layer gets caked in salt, bait and grease, I just take it off and put on another one. Christ, the most expensive thing we wear is muck boots, and they cost about a hundred." He cleared his throat. "Okay, enough jarrin'. Sun's up and we got work to do."

And just like that, Seb's day began, and he stepped back in time.

Some things hadn't changed: the sound of the waves slapping against the hull; boots squeaking on the wet deck; the whine of the winch as it drew up a trawl; and the soft *chug* of the engine. There were the smells too, taking him right back—gasoline fumes and motor oil. Then there was the wet spray that slipped under his collar, the feel of the sun on his face, dazzling him as it sparkled on the water.

He'd forgotten how fast he had to work. Tim steered the boat, while he prepped the bait. Then as they reached each buoy, Tim leaned over to grab the line with a hook, and Seb used the winch to haul up the eight traps connected to the trawl. They emptied the catch into a crate.

Seb had never forgotten the clicking sound of lobster claws.

Tim held up a gauge. "This is how we decide which ones are keepers. You measure from the rear of the eye sockets to the beginning of the tail. The minimum it can be is three-and-a-quarter inches, and the maximum is five inches. The shorts get thrown back, along with the oversize ones. We figure they're stronger producers."

"Does anything else get into the pots?"

"Yuh. One time there was this fish that looked like it was something prehistoric." He picked up a lobster in his gloved hand and pointed to a triangular notch cut into the flipper. "That shows she's carryin' eggs. The v-notch shows she's a breeder. Can't keep those. You do that, and they slap a fine on you of over a thousand dollars." He tossed her back into the ocean.

Seb peered into the crate. "You can tell if a lobster is male or female? They all look the same."

Tim cackled. "All you gotta do is lift up their skirts." He turned the lobster over to reveal its underside. "Look at the swimmerets here. If they're hard, it's a male. If they're soft and feathery, it's female. The females have wider tails too."

He picked up a lobster, and even with Seb's limited experience, it appeared odd. The shell appeared rotten. "What's wrong with that one?"

"Shell disease. Can't be sold on the live market, but it can be sent to the processors—the meat's still good. Used to be, shell disease was found in southern Massachusetts and Rhode Island, but it's creepin' north into Maine." Tim scowled. "Yet another thing makin' it hard to earn a livin'."

They got into a pattern. Tim lifted each hatch and they sifted through the catch. Once it was emptied, Seb took a prepped bait needle, which resembled a giant metal skewer, and threaded the bait onto a string inside each lobster trap. Each newly baited trap would fly off the stern one by one. Then it was on to the next buoy, the next trawl of eight traps.

Tim nodded in satisfaction. "And now they'll sit on the bottom overnight, and tomorrow we get to do it all over again."

The lobsters were in a milk crate. Seb and Tim went about the next task of slipping rubber bands over their claws with a pair of pliers. He got nipped once or twice, and he let out a yelp. "They have a wicked bite."

Tim hooted. "You get used to it." Then all the lobsters were placed in a tank.

By noon, they were done. Tim steered the boat to the wharf on the bank across from where he'd picked up Seb that morning. The lobsters were packed into pallets, unloaded and weighed. All in all, it came to three hundred and fifty pounds.

"Not a good day," Tim muttered as he stuffed the receipt for the catch into his pocket. "Gary told me to hold onto all the receipts so you don't have to bother with 'em. I get twenty percent. Let's hope we have better luck tomorrow." He snorted. "I come across far too many dubbers who think lobstermen earn a packet. If Gary brings in six hundred pounds, that works out at about a thousand dollars. What folk don't see is the three hundred or more dollars he paid out for bait, or the repairs on the boat that cost an arm and a leg." He gestured to the *Liza Jane*. "Come on, I'll take you over to the other side."

"You don't have to do that. I can walk from here." Langsford Road would take him back to Pier Road and Gary's place.

Tim grinned. "You'll prob'ly be achin' like a son of a bitch tonight. Just be ready in the morning, same time, same place." He pointed to Seb's oil pants. "Wanna keep hold of those?"

"I might as well." Seb went back to the boat and exchanged muck boots for his own. He grabbed his jacket, then gave Tim a nod. "See you in the morning."

Right then he could almost hear the shower calling his name, and maybe the bed too.

As he strolled along Langsford Road, he realized he was starving. Bed could wait. He walked past the fish and lobster wholesalers, noting the cars in the lot. Business appeared brisk. Then he caught sight of a familiar face heading his way.

Market Guy wore the same jacket. In one hand he carried a set of binoculars. Seb knew the instant the guy recognized him: he came to a halt in the middle of what little sidewalk there was.

Seb gave him a cheerful smile. "Hey."

Market Guy scrutinized him, an up and down study from head to foot. "That's a different look." His lips twitched.

Shit. The oilskins.

"I've been out hauling traps." Seb smirked. "Just so you know, this isn't something I make a habit of wearing."

"Hey, what you choose to wear is none of my business." Those blue eyes sparkled. "I think I prefer the tee though. Even if it *was* about as subtle as a train wreck." Then he smiled. "I'll let you get on your way." He strolled past Seb, close enough that he caught a whiff of—

Was that sandalwood?

On impulse, Seb spun around and called after him, "Excuse me?"

The guy stopped and turned, gazing at him, his eyebrows arched.

"You live around here?" Seb asked. "Because if you do, there's a chance we could bump into each other again, seeing as I'm gonna be staying here a while, and if that's gonna happen, I think I'd like to know the name of the guy I keep running into." He took a breath.

Jesus, that was corny as fuck. I have never sounded like such an idiot.

Market Guy clearly thought so too—there

was definite amusement in those cool eyes. He studied Seb for a moment, as though deciding on a course of action. At last, he spoke. "My name's Marcus Gilbert, but I don't live here—I'm just staying here too."

Seb beamed. "Good to meet you, Marcus. I'm Seb Williams."

Marcus gave him a polite smile. "And now that we've gotten that out of the way, I'll leave you to enjoy the rest of your day." He turned around and kept on going.

It was only then that Marcus's words sank in.

He noticed my tee.

Now *that* was interesting.

Chapter Five

June 20

Marcus stepped into the shower. Of all the alterations that had been made over the years, this had to be his favorite part of the house. The tub had been taken out of the bathroom, and a walk-in shower created, complete with a tiled bench. Compared with the poor water pressure of his shower in New York, the jets felt amazing. He washed his hair, rubbing his fingers over his scalp, inhaling the invigorating scent of the shampoo.

When his dick jerked, Marcus glanced down at it. "Well, good morning," he murmured. "I'll get to you in a minute." He turned his face toward the shower head, eyes tight shut, enjoying the warmth and the feel of the water on his body. Jerking off in the shower had to be the best way to start the day.

Well—*almost* the best way.

Maybe it was a sign that his batteries were finally recharging, because Marcus couldn't remember the last time he'd woken up horny. He knew exactly where to lay the blame for this—that lean, sexy… lobsterman. Marcus had to admit, seeing him in the oilskins had been a revelation. He'd had him pegged as a loafer, a surfer dude, someone who spent his days on the waves and his nights drinking beer.

Maybe he's nothing like that at all. Marcus

remembered his grandfather talking about the men who trawled for lobster. He'd had nothing but admiration for them. So perhaps Marcus was doing the guy a disservice.

His name is Seb. Marcus smiled to himself. *He made sure to tell me that part.* He hadn't meant to hurry away, but running into Seb had caught him unawares. *I'm not here to hook up with a hot guy, remember? I'm here to get my life back on track.* Because sooner or later—probably sooner—the idyllic bubble he found himself in was going to burst, and he'd have to return to reality.

The only problem was, he had no idea what that reality would be.

He filled a cupped palm with bodywash and proceeded to clean everywhere. He placed his foot on the bench and slid soapy fingers through his crack and over his balls before tentatively pushing a single finger into his hole, wincing at the burn. His douche was stowed away in his toiletries bag, gathering dust, it had been that long since he'd used it. For a man who couldn't go a day without sex in some form or other, it was hard to believe it had been almost three months since he'd enjoyed the feel of another man's body against his.

Except that was looking back with rose-colored glasses, and he knew it. Sex had taken on a new dimension, a way of releasing tension, relieving stress, and ultimately had created even more of that stress.

When was the last time I really let myself go and enjoyed it? Just sex, no… enhancements.

He sat on the bench, his legs spread, and wrapped a slick hand around his shaft. Marcus put his head against the wall and closed his eyes, casually sliding his hand back and forth.

Fantasy shower sex was *way* safer than real-life shower sex any day.

Seb straddled his hips, his hands on Marcus's neck and nape as they kissed while Seb lifted himself slowly, only to sink back down, until Marcus's dick was buried in tight heat.

Fuck, that felt amazing.

Marcus grabbed hold of Seb's ass, prying his cheeks apart, stretching his hole, and Seb rocked faster, riding him harder now, bouncing on Marcus's hard cock. Marcus kissed Seb's nipples, flicking them with his tongue, and loving how Seb's body tightened around his shaft.

"You like that."

Seb regarded him with wide eyes. "Fuck yeah. Don't fucking stop."

Marcus stroked Seb's back, then slid his hands under Seb's ass, helping him to bounce harder, faster, his own orgasm advancing. Seb put his hands on Marcus's shoulders, using them to lever himself up and down, his cock so fucking hard and straight, pointing up at Marcus.

"Put your arms around my neck," Marcus demanded. When Seb did as instructed, Marcus looked him in the eye. "Now hold on tight and lean back." He gripped Seb's hips, forcing him down onto his dick.

"Oh fuck, right there." Seb's breathing quickened, his eyes wide, his chest rising and falling, the muscles in his stomach contracting. "Fuck, you keep hitting it like that, and I'm gonna come."

Marcus smiled. "Then come. Shoot all over me. I want to feel it."

Seb threw his head back, his hands locked around Marcus's neck, his mouth wide. "Fuck me. Fuck me." And then a cry fell from his lips as he shot his load, creating an arc of spunk that pulsed from his cock.

The sight of him coming hands-free, and the feel of his body so fucking tight around Marcus's dick was the final push. Marcus came inside him, his arms enveloping Seb, holding him against Marcus's chest.

Kissing Seb while his cock throbbed inside him was the hottest thing Marcus had imagined in a long time. He shot hard against the tiled wall of the shower, so hard that he swore he could hear bells ringing in his head. Tremors shook him as the last drops swirled away with the water.

Except there *was* a bell ringing.

Marcus launched himself off the bench, flipped off the water, and opened the shower door, listening.

There it was again. *Fuck.* That was the doorbell, and it was way too early for the mailman. Marcus grabbed a towel, wrapped it around his hips, and stepped out onto the rug, still dripping.

"Marcus?"

What the hell?

He opened the bathroom door. "Jess?"

"Hey," she called out. "I came in through the French doors. They weren't locked." There was a pause. "I haven't come at a bad time, have I?"

He laughed. "I just finished my shower. Give me a sec to put on some clothes. You wanna be useful? Make some coffee." Then it hit him. "Do you know what time it is?" It wasn't even six-thirty.

Jess snorted. "Sure I do. It was still dark when I left Jamaica Plain. And I would have been here even earlier, except I hit a lot of traffic on the 95. My GPS said it would take me an hour and forty-three minutes. I want my money back. That bastard lied."

He laughed. "Maybe it would take that long in the dead of winter, but not in the summer on the weekend when everyone is heading up to their summer place." He rubbed himself down briskly, then went into his bedroom to grab his jeans and a T-shirt.

By the time he reached the kitchen, the smell of freshly brewed coffee filled the air. Jess was sitting at the breakfast bar, two plates out, each filled with a couple of pastries. She grinned. "I picked these up on the way. Figured I'd bring breakfast to make up for my very early arrival."

Damn, it was *so* good to see her.

Marcus held his arms wide. "Get over here." Jess was off the stool in a heartbeat, and in his arms for a hug. He clutched her to him, disconcerted to find he was trembling.

Jess broke the hug, put her hands on his upper arms, and stepped back, staring at him. "What is it? What's wrong?"

He stroked her cheek. "I think I missed you."

"That's good, because I missed you." Her eyes sparkled. "Now pour the coffee."

Marcus went over to the cabinet and removed two cups, then carried them to the coffee pot. "You still like it with way too much creamer?"

"I started drinking it black a year ago. Which bedroom are you using?"

Marcus grinned. "Guess."

She laughed. "Well, you're a little too big for those beds in the attic now, so I figure you're in the master bedroom, the one with the door that leads onto the patio. You always did like that room, even when you were a kid." She studied him for a moment. "You look good."

"I feel good," he admitted. "This place has been a godsend for me." He brought over the two cups and joined her on the stool next to hers. "When you asked last weekend if you could come down before the Fourth, I didn't realize you meant *this* weekend."

"I did ask Jake to come with me, but he said he had things to do. Not all that surprising, really. What twenty-two-year-old guy wants to spend the weekend with his mom and his uncle?" She shrugged. "He'll be here in a few weeks anyway."

"Exactly two weeks today. I guess when everyone arrives, I'll be relegated to the attic room again." He grinned. "Want to keep me company? It'll be like old times."

She guffawed. "I am *not* sharing a bedroom with my brother. I'd rather sleep out in the yard."

"Actually, I was thinking of staying in the summerhouse." At least that would give him a place to retreat to, if it all got too much.

Think positively. It's going to be fine.

All he knew was, the Fourth had seemed such a long time away when he'd first arrived at the house, and yet here it was, almost upon them.

But I'm better than I was then.

He sipped his coffee. "Do I have the pleasure of your company for just today, or are you staying till tomorrow?"

"Would that be okay if I did? Stay, I mean. I put a bag together, just in case. It's in the car."

Marcus frowned. "Hey, it's *your* family summer home too. You stay as long as you want.

Mom and Dad always said we should feel free to do that."

"I just didn't know what you're doing, if you're working…" She gave him a sideways glance. "But I *am* concerned."

"Don't be." He glanced at the pastries. "These look good. In fact, I think just *looking* at them, I've gained five pounds."

Jess laughed. "Are you kidding? You could always eat anything. I used to *hate* you for that." She smiled. "Not really." She sipped her coffee. "Could we go for a walk after this? It's such a beautiful day. I'd like to stroll down to the dock and sit and stare at the ocean. I've missed that."

He arched his eyebrows. "Did Boston suddenly move inland when I wasn't looking?"

Jess hit him on the arm. "Idiot. And it's not the same. Okay, it *is* the same ocean, but…" Her eyes lit up.

"I get it." He felt the same way. There was something about the view from the tip of Cape Porpoise that brought his childhood back to him. How many times had *he* walked there in the past few months? "Sure. We can do that."

He'd walked the same route for the past four days, unsure of the reason why. It had occurred to him briefly that his subconscious had played a part in that.

Was I hoping to see Seb again?

"This was a good idea," Jess murmured as they gazed out over the bay. "I'd forgotten how beautiful this place is. It's funny how life gets in the way." She sighed. "I can't remember the last time I was here."

"Same here. I don't think it's changed much." Boats were moored close to the dock, water slapping against their hulls, ropes creaking as they loosened and pulled taut. The slight breeze carried the growl of an engine starting up somewhere, and there were voices raised as people called to one another from boats as they passed each other. Birds circled high in the air above them, their shrill cries shattering the tranquility.

Jess leaned against the bench, her arm draped over the back of it. "Can we talk now?"

"About what?"

"Whatever's going on that you're not telling me. Like, why you came here. Why you're not in New York, working." She peered at him. "Did you lose your job?"

"No," he assured her. "I still have a job. I'm just taking… I suppose you could call it a sabbatical. A mental health break."

"Okay," she said, drawing out the two syllables. "Are you able to share what led up to you *needing* this break?"

Jesus, how the fuck do I answer that?

He stared at the sunlight glinting on the calm water. "I got into a cycle of corrosive behavior, is the simplest way of putting it." He sighed. "Which I know doesn't tell you anything, but this really is difficult for me."

She reached across and took his hand in hers. "You were there for me in my darkest days. You were the brother I turned to when I found out I was pregnant. And you were amazing."

"All I did was listen," he protested. "And maybe give a few practical suggestions." He'd been twenty-one, in his final year at college, when a seventeen-year-old Jess had called him in tears. They'd talked for two hours on the phone, and he'd been the one to assure her Mom and Dad would not freak.

"Okay, then *I* can listen now. Or is it so bad that you can't even tell me?"

He didn't know what to say. *I can't tell you, because I'm so scared you will never look at me the same way again* wasn't an option. The fear almost choked him.

"I was under a lot of pressure. Deadlines to meet, copy to write, more deadlines, more copy… I had my own ways of relieving my tension, and I do *not* want to get into those."

Her lips twitched. "For Christ's sake, I'm forty years old. If we can't talk about sex—because that's what I'm guessing is at the root of this reluctance to share—then we are truly lost." She tilted her head to one side. "Does it help if I tell you I don't believe for *one nanosecond* that my big brother is a virgin? Fuck, you live in New York. You're gay. You're a good-looking guy. And believe it or not, I do know what goes on among gay men. Some of my best friends are gay, and their stories make my jaw drop."

He laughed. "I'm sorry. I keep forgetting. In my head you're my little sister, the five-year-old kid I chased through the trees at the back of the house, growling I was going to eat you when I caught you."

"And you *still* wouldn't catch me walking out there." She rubbed her thumb on the back of his hand.

He guessed he could be honest about some of it. "Okay, you were right. I did a lot of hookups to relieve my stress. That wasn't the problem. It was something that came about because of the sex, and far from helping my situation, my stress levels grew. I know this is vague, but I really can't talk about this."

"You're scaring me." Her shoulders seemed tense, and her lip trembled.

"All you need to know is that I pulled my head out of my ass, and realized I had to do something. So I did. I called Mom and Dad, and told them I needed to get out of New York for a while and decompress. Dad was worried about the work situation, so he suggested taking a break from it, and he gave me a loan. Not a huge amount, just enough to keep me from going under for a few months, until I felt ready to go back." A lot of his anxiety had lifted right there.

"And are you ready? To go back?"

"I'm not sure. There are days when I wake up, the world is bright, and I feel like I can do anything. But there are also days when I think about what will come next, and it scares the shit out of me." He breathed deeply. "I started to write, mostly as a means of getting everything in my head out onto paper. Well, virtual paper. Only, it grew, until I knew I had to finish it, because there are guys out there who are in the same situation I was. They're being fed so much disinformation, and they need to know the truth." That was way more than he'd intended saying.

"How much have you written?"

"Enough to publish it as a book. When it's finished."

"Can I read it?"

He pulled his hand free of hers and drew back, his breathing rapid. "No." He'd never thought about that part. Maybe publishing it under a pseudonym was the way to go.

She nodded. "Because if I did, then I would know whatever it is you're too scared to share with me. Jesus, Marcus. You have to know I'm imagining all kinds of horror stories here."

"Don't. I really am okay. I'm in a much better place." He smiled. "Geographically as well as mentally. At least now you know why I didn't feel I was the best person for Jake to talk to. Chris is much less of a fuck-up than I am."

She took a deep breath. "Jake hasn't said anything, and I haven't pushed, but I get the feeling you are the *perfect* person for him to confide in." Her eyes met his.

Ah. "I see."

"It's just a feeling," she said. "Little things I've noticed, things I've picked up on... But... something tells me there's more to it than him not wanting to tell his mom he's gay, or bi, or whatever. We've always been able to talk about everything. So whatever is going on, it's more than his realizations about his sexuality. I could be wrong, of course."

"Maybe it's something about moms. Some vibe they pick up on. Mom knew about me, after all. I think Chris was more shocked than she was."

Jess laughed. "Oh my God. I remember."

"You were fourteen and you didn't even bat an eye. He was twenty-one and stared at me as if I'd grown a second head. I think the first words out of his mouth were, 'But you can't be gay. You play football.'"

They laughed.

Marcus took her hand. "I'm sorry I can't tell you more. I guess the truth is, I don't want you to see what I became. I'm scared you'll look at me and see me as someone else." Christ, he was shaking.

Jess gaped at him. "Marcus, if you came to me and told me you'd just murdered someone, I'd go get a shovel." Her lips twitched, and then they were both laughing. "Love you, okay?"

"Love you too."

Jess's eyes sparkled. "So… any hot guys staying in Cape Porpoise this summer? Is there the prospect of a little summer fling?"

"I wouldn't know. I'm not looking." It wasn't a lie. He hadn't been looking when Seb had struck up a conversation at the store. But Seb definitely came under the heading of hot guys,

"Well, you should. Just because *I'm* not getting any, doesn't mean *you* can't. That way, I get to live vicariously through you." She grinned. "And you know what? I'm going to take my big brother out for lunch. Someplace where we can see the ocean while we eat."

"I'd like that."

Her eyes were warm. "Thank you. You could've told me to butt out, but you didn't. And if anyone asks too many questions while they're staying here, *I'll* tell them to butt out. I've got your back."

The first thought to cross his mind was a question.

Would she feel that way if she knew the truth?

Chapter Six

June 21

It had only been six days, but *Lord*, Seb was tired. He did the math: there were ten weeks left until school started. *Fuck.* He hadn't even scratched the surface. Levi's remark about being buff by the end of it had one drawback that Seb could see—he'd be too exhausted to do anything about the line of guys waiting to drool over him.

Okay, that's an exaggeration. He'd never be *that* tired, and a *line* of guys? In his dreams.

He'd celebrated the start of summer vacation with a night at Maine Street, and if he'd known that would be the last time he'd get off for almost three months, Seb would have foregone Grammy's birthday party, and spent the whole weekend in as many different positions as he could imagine.

I can imagine quite a lot.

Maybe that was why it was eight o'clock on Sunday morning, and he was still in bed, enjoying the luxury of not having to get up. *What is there to get up for?* All the shit he hadn't done during the week because he was too tired? He'd made himself some coffee and taken it into the bedroom. Then he lay under the comforter, scrolling through his phone and drinking coffee.

When his phone buzzed and he saw Levi's

name, Seb smiled. "Hey. Welcome to my only day off of the week."

"You're still with us then."

"What did you think I'd do—fall overboard? Get eaten by a huge, radioactive lobster?"

Levi chuckled. "So how was it, the first week?"

"Tim—that's the guy who works with Gary—said after two days that we could start working properly. When I asked what he meant, he said, 'Well, you've had a couple of late starts to get you into the swing of it.' *Late*? I was on the dock by *four-friggin'-thirty*. *Then* he tells me Gary is usually out on the water by four."

"Four a.m.?" Levi sounded horrified.

"Yup. So the last four days, we've been out there before dawn." There *was* one benefit to that— Seb got to watch the sun come up over the ocean, and the sight never grew old.

"How's it going?"

Seb stretched beneath the sheets. "What gets me is the uncertainty of it all. We can have a huge haul one day, and not enough to cover fuel the next. The thing is, Tim's been doing this long enough, he knows the ocean. He knows the best places to go. Of course, so does everybody else. We spend a lot of time dodging the traps that aren't Gary's."

"How do you know they're not Gary's? Don't all traps look the same?"

Seb cackled. "You can't see traps on the bottom of the ocean—you see the buoys they're attached to. Every lobsterman has their own color of buoys."

"So how are you coping with the early

mornings?"

Seb snorted. "I'm not cut out for this. Only time I usually see *that* hour of the morning, is when I've stayed up all night."

There was a pause. "Have you been keeping up with local events?"

Seb knew Levi well enough to know it was a loaded question. "What's happened? What have I missed?"

"It was on the news last night. Police busted a party. Teenagers mostly. A lot of them are students at your school, the report said."

"Busted for what? Did the neighbors complain about the noise?"

"Nah, the kids got busted for possessing pot. A large amount, by the sound of it. Plus, they were drinking. The cops said in a statement that other drugs had been found. Seems like nothing changes, hmm?"

It didn't take a genius to work out Levi was thinking about his mom.

"Schools *are* trying to make a difference, you know?" Seb said in a gentle voice. "There's a program in Maine to educate the kids about drugs, and another to help those kids already experimenting with booze, pot, and other drugs." The staff at the school had all gone through training.

"I'm sure there are a ton of programs out there. But if the message is only *Don't do drugs*, then they're not working. The message is not getting through. I'm seeing this more and more in the stuff I post for work. They start on pot, but they don't stay on it. They move on to better and harder stuff. Before you know it, they're addicts. And we all know how society treats addicts, right?"

The bitterness in his voice tugged at Seb's heart. "It still hurts. I get it."

"I'm sorry, but you don't. You *know* where your mom is. You might not *want* to know, given her opinions, but she's still around. I have no fucking clue whether my mom is alive or dead." He made a choked sound. "I'm sorry I brought this up. Let's talk about something else."

Seb could do that. "You would be amazed at what time I go to bed."

"Go on. Amaze me."

"Well, the first day, I took a nap once I'd finished work. Except I soon realized it didn't help. All that happened was I didn't sleep at night. So I forced myself to stay awake. We work from four till noon and when I come home, no more naps for me. Then the moment my head hits the pillow, I'm out like a light. There are some nights when I'm in bed by eight."

Levi laughed, and the sound sent a flush of relief coursing through Seb. "Okay, I'm amazed. Have you met any of the locals yet?"

"Apart from Tim—who doesn't do a whole lotta talking if it's not about lobster—I've spoken to precisely one guy." *But what a guy.*

Levi let out a wry chuckle. "Why am I not surprised it was a guy? Dare I ask… Was he a *hot* guy?"

"Fuck, yeah. Except the jury is out on whether he bats for our team. My first instinct was no." But after that remark about Seb's shirt, he wasn't so sure.

Oh, come on. You're just hoping, that's all, because

you want him to be gay.

"So what are you doing with the rest of your Sunday?"

Seb cackled. "I have some really exciting things planned. First there's the laundry. Then I get to shop for groceries. *Then* I get to clean."

"Wow. You have so much excitement crammed into a few hours. But to be honest, I think some of those can wait. It's a beautiful day. Why don't you go outside?"

"I'm outside six days out of seven. On the ocean. In a boat."

"That's not what I mean. All you see of Cape Porpoise is from the boat. So go for a walk. You're gonna be there for a couple of months. You get one day off a week. You get afternoons too, by the sound of it. Take a look at the town. Take photos. Get to know your surroundings. If all you do is work with Tim, shop for groceries, and then spend the rest of your time in that house, you'll go nuts." He paused. "You're not meant to be a solitary person. You need people. And you're not gonna find them inside those four walls. So get out and meet people. *Talk* to people. I've seen you charm little old ladies five minutes after you opened your mouth."

Seb snorted. "You wouldn't say that if you'd heard me in the store a week ago."

"What do you mean?"

"I struck up a conversation about bananas. It was all I could think of."

"Did it work?"

"Nope. He probably thought I was an idiot. And of course, the *next* time I ran into him, I was wearing oilskins. I mean, nothing says sexy like a bright yellow fucking oilskin, right?" Thank God he'd changed out of the muck boots.

"Would this be the one guy you were talking about?"

"The same."

Levi snickered. "Then you'd better work on your lines in case you meet him again."

Chance would be a fine thing. "Well, it's been a week and there's been no sign of him."

"Have you been *looking* for him?"

Seb snorted. "Levi, you know me *way* too well."

He laughed. "I'll leave you to enjoy the rest of your Sunday. Don't work too hard this week."

"Hey, if I don't work hard, Gary will have my ass. I'll talk to you soon." Seb disconnected, and tossed the phone onto the bed. His heart went out to Levi. *It must hurt him something awful.* Seb wondered where Levi's mom was. There was always the possibility she was dead, but surely Grammy would be notified if that happened. *He lost his mom, and she lost her daughter.*

Thank God they had each other.

Seb glanced toward the window. Levi was right—it was a beautiful day. Too damn nice to be stuck inside doing laundry. *I could combine a walk with the groceries. That'd work.*

It would—*after* he'd gotten rid of his morning wood.

Seb grabbed the phone, pulled up one of his favorite porn sites, and reached for the lube. Except it wasn't long before he'd abandoned the porn and closed his eyes to focus on Marcus.

Because Marcus was *way* hotter than the guys

on that small screen.

Seb walked along Langsford Road, drinking in the sights and smells. Boats were moored along both sides of the channel of water that separated the two banks, their masts reaching into the sky, their white hulls mirrored in the rippling water. Chains rattled and flags snapped in the stiff breeze. Chatter could be heard as boats passed on their way in and out of the bay.

Seb had to admit Levi had nailed it. It was far too beautiful a day for doing laundry.

The plan was to head for the spit of land at the end of the road, do a loop, and work his way back to the store. Langsford's Lobster and Fish House was up ahead. It occurred to Seb maybe a little lobster salad would be perfect for his Sunday dinner. Not that he was gonna buy a live one, no sir. He had enough recollections from childhood of the smell that filled the kitchen when lobster was boiling. Better to buy it ready-cooked.

Then he spied a couple of people up ahead outside the fish house, and his breathing hitched at the sight. *Marcus.*

Except Marcus was with a woman. They were laughing, and the way she touched his arm and watched him spoke volumes.

Damn. Guess he's gonna stay relegated to my spank

bank after all.

Seb knew when to back off. It was a pity. He'd been anticipating a little flirting if the occasion presented itself, but he wasn't about to flirt with a straight guy. He watched as the woman went into the shop.

Do I keep on walking? Or turn around and go back before he sees me? What was it about Marcus that made him so damn skittish?

Stupid question. Marcus ticked *all* Seb's boxes: hot, sexy as fuck older guy, not too tall, silver among the black...

Down boy. Seb was imagining silver on Marcus's chest, running his fingers through it, trailing them down to his pubes. He hoped to God the man didn't shave.

Doesn't matter if he does. He's straight. It was too much to hope he was bi.

God was having *way* too much fun at Seb's expense.

Then Marcus saw him, and that was the end of that. Seb walked towards him, with as much nonchalance as he could muster.

Marcus gave him that same polite smile. "Good afternoon. No hauling today?"

"I do get one day off." He glanced at the shop. "I thought about getting some lobster for dinner. Which might seem weird, considering how I spend my week."

"I don't think it's weird at all." Marcus gestured to the gray cedar shakes that covered the shop, buoys strung up as decoration. "I like all these different colors."

Seb pointed to a buoy with orange and yellow

bands. "That's Gary's. He's my uncle."

Marcus peered at the sign beside the shop. "Steamers?"

"Clams," Seb told him. "Delicious dipped in clam broth, butter, cider vinegar, and with a couple of slices of garlic bread."

Just then, the woman came out of the shop, a bag in her hand. Marcus laughed. "That doesn't look like a live lobster to me."

She opened her eyes wide. "He pointed to a tank of live ones and asked me which one I wanted. I just couldn't."

"So what did you get instead?" Marcus asked.

She beamed. "They sell them ready cooked. Look at this." She opened the bag and Marcus peered into it.

"That is one big lobster. There must be a lot of meat in those claws."

"Can I see?" Seb asked.

The woman gave him a quizzical glance. "You want to look at my lobster?"

Marcus laughed. "This is Seb. He catches them." He gestured to her. "This is Jess."

Seb gave her a nod, then peered into the bag. "Oh my God."

"What?" Marcus and Jess exclaimed at the same time.

"I know that lobster! I caught him yesterday."

Marcus gaped at him. "You can tell it was one of your catch just by looking at it?"

Seb grinned. "No, but the look on your face was priceless." Marcus rolled his eyes.

"I was more impressed you knew it was a male," Jess remarked. "Do you live around here?"

"I'm staying here for a couple of months. My uncle runs a lobster boat. But he went and broke his pelvis, so I'm helping out."

"We've caught Seb on his one day off," Marcus told her. He gave Seb his attention. "Out for a walk?"

"I was taking a stroll before I headed to the store. Gotta get my groceries before bed."

"I imagine you have to be up really early to go out on the boat. What time do you go to bed?" Marcus inquired.

"If I can get by on six hours' sleep, nine o'clock. It *should* be closer to eight."

"Do you like lobster?" Jen asked suddenly.

"Not when they nip me with their claws," Seb replied with a grin. Marcus laughed.

"Well, we're having lobster salad for dinner. Why don't you join us?"

Judging by the way Marcus jerked his head to stare at her, the suggestion was as much a surprise to him as it was to Seb.

"You don't know me." And Seb did *not* want to be forced to see the pair of them together. That would be rubbing his face in it.

She smiled. "You seem to be the only other person Marcus has met in this place, apart from the mailman."

"I couldn't possibly," Seb protested.

"See?" Marcus interjected. "He doesn't want to."

Jess had a glint in her eye that told Seb she could be a handful. "I won't take no for an answer. Besides, I want to make dinner for my big brother before I leave. I promise we'll be finished in time for you to go to bed at a ridiculously early hour. Plus, I spied a rather nice bottle of white wine in the kitchen back at the house. I bet it would go great with lobster."

"I *was* going to get some lobster for tonight," Seb admitted. He'd taken in one vital fact from everything she'd said.

Brother? Well, what do you know about that?

She beamed again. "See? Now you don't have to. *I'll* make the salad, and *you* can talk to my brother and keep him out of the kitchen. Works perfectly."

Seb glanced at Marcus. "Does she always get her own way?"

Marcus let out an exaggerated sigh. "Always. Resistance is futile."

Seb got the idea Marcus wasn't all that enthused about the prospect. "Look, it's a wonderful invitation, but—"

"Please." Jess locked gazes with him. "I'll be offended if you say no. And you wouldn't want to offend me, right?"

Seb winced. He looked at Marcus. "Ooh, she's good."

Marcus rolled his eyes. "You have *no* idea."

The thing was, Seb didn't want to say no, not now he knew the whole situation. "Okay. What time, and where?"

Her eyes gleamed. "Sixteen Land's End Road, and make it five o'clock. That way, we can let Marcus loose in the liquor cabinet, and see what amazing cocktails he can concoct." She bit her lip. "Can you get there on foot? I wouldn't want you to drink and drive."

Seb laughed. "Have you seen the size of Cape

Porpoise? You can get *everywhere* on foot. Okay. Five o'clock. I promise not to come in my oilskins," he added, glancing at Marcus.

"See you then." Marcus grabbed Jess's arm and tugged her away. Seb watched them, smiling to himself when the conversation grew animated.

He wasn't going to tell me Jess was his sister. He had to have known how it looked. And she let the cat out of the bag. His instincts told him the slip had been deliberate. Seb had a feeling he was going to like Jess.

That same feeling told him he'd like her brother a whole lot more.

Chapter Seven

"I still don't know why you invited him," Marcus grumbled as he took a final glance around the living room to see if he'd missed anything. Jess had thrust a duster into his hand, and had even told him to dust the ceiling fan.

She thumped a cushion on the couch into submission. "He seems nice. I *loved* that bit about recognizing the lobster. He's got a good sense of humor. *And* he's gay."

Marcus blinked. "You can*not* know that. You spoke with him for less than five minutes." It didn't matter that Marcus was fairly certain of it.

"Did you see his T-shirt?"

"I wasn't looking." That wasn't a lie. He'd been doing everything he could *not* to look at Seb's chest—or anywhere lower, if it came to that. Not to show that he was interested in the slightest. Except he was. "If it was the one that says *Yes I am, and no, you can't watch*, I've seen it. He was wearing that the day I met him."

She grinned. "Yeah, I've seen that one too. *This* one said *I'm not gay but my boyfriend is*. How could you miss that?" He didn't bother replying. "You should see some of the stuff the guys at work wear. And that's another reason how I know he's gay. Out of the five guys who work in my office, three are gay. You get a sense for these things after a while. So let's look at the facts. He's good-looking. He's funny. He's into guys." Her grin widened.

Aw shit. "No. Get that idea out of your head right this second."

She gazed at him, those blue eyes wide and innocent. "What idea?" *Yeah right.* "Make yourself useful. Go check the liquor cabinet for supplies while I deal with Pinchy."

He stared at her. "You know how to get the meat out of the lobster?"

Jess shrugged. "Sure, it's easy."

"I'm impressed." He recalled their parents taking them out to dinner when they were in their teens. They'd ordered shrimp, and Jess's plate after she'd attempted to peel off the shells had resembled the aftermath of an explosion.

"I just pick up my phone, type *how to get the meat out of the lobster*, and watch the video." He rolled his eyes. Jess gave him a meaningful stare. "So, about Seb… Does he know you're gay?"

"No."

"Are you going to tell him?"

"No."

Her eyes twinkled. "Can I at least drop hints?"

He narrowed his gaze. "*You* are going to behave this evening, you got that?"

"Sure. I'll behave." She grinned. "Badly."

Marcus was starting to get a sinking feeling about this.

When the doorbell rang, Jess called out from the kitchen, "Can you get that? I'm a little busy right now."

"Who's winning? You or the lobster?" he yelled back. He took a last glance at his reflection. He'd gone with a dark gray T-shirt and jeans, aiming for low-key and relaxed. Then it occurred to him that his efforts were all for Seb.

No. Don't go there.

"The door, Marcus!"

He hurried to open it. Seb stood there in jeans, flip-flops, and a denim jacket over a tee, a large white box in his hands. "I'm not too early, am I?"

"You're fine." Hell, he was a damn sight more than fine. "Come on in." Seb walked ahead of him into the living room, and Marcus tried not to stare at Seb's ass.

Seb's very firm-looking, *delectable* ass.

"Stay out of the kitchen," Marcus told him. When Seb frowned, Marcus grinned. "Jess is fighting with the lobster. I think it's winning."

"I heard that!" she hollered. "Hey, Seb. Marcus will get you a drink. I'll be out in a sec with snacks."

Marcus peered at the box in his hands, and Seb instantly held it out. "One of my best friends was raised by his grandmother, and I spent a lot of time around their place growing up. Grammy drummed into me that you never turn up empty-handed."

Marcus peered inside. "Is this chocolate cheesecake?" He resisted the urge to drool.

"Good choice?"

"Perfect choice. Thank Grammy for me when you see her next. Let me take it into the kitchen." Marcus paused. "Look, I know Jess said cocktails, but there's beer too. I made sure I picked some up from the store."

Seb grinned. "You're a lifesaver. I don't mind a glass of wine, but I'm not a cocktails kinda guy."

"I'll grab us a couple of bottles." Marcus hurried into the kitchen, stopping short at the sight of the clean countertops. "Wow. This looks better than I anticipated."

Jess glanced up from her task of tipping cooked pasta into a colander. "What did you expect?"

He cackled. "Carnage." He deposited the box on the countertop. "Seb brought dessert. Chocolate cheesecake."

Her eyes glittered. "Ooh, we like Seb."

He opened the fridge and took out two bottles of beer. Then he grabbed the opener and removed the caps.

"There's a bowl of chips. Take that too."

Marcus did as instructed, then went back to their guest. Seb was standing by the window, his jacket in his hand, staring out at the yard. "This is my favorite spot to drink my morning coffee," Marcus told him. "I get to watch squirrel antics."

Seb peered over his shoulder at Marcus and smiled. "Squirrels are cute." Then he turned, and Marcus had to smile.

"You changed your shirt."

Seb's eyes gleamed. "You noticed."

"You don't do subtle, do you?" Seb's T-shirt was black, emblazoned with *Let me be perfectly QUEER.* The lettering was white, apart from queer which was larger than every other word and done in rainbow colors and glitter.

Seb took the bottle Marcus proffered. "Jesus, this one is tame compared to some of the ones I wear when I go out." He grinned. "I have a collection."

"Why does that not surprise me? If this one is mild, what are the others like?"

Seb waggled his eyebrows. "They're great for breaking the ice." He took a swig from the bottle, then smiled. "By the way, you've got good taste." He tapped the label with his finger. "This microbrewery makes some great beers. I only discovered it recently."

Marcus was still intrigued about Seb's tees. "What are your top three T-shirts?"

"That's a tough one." Seb rubbed his sparsely bearded jawline. "Okay, number three would be *Gay men suck, but only if you ask nicely.* Two would be *Does this dick in my mouth make me look gay?*"

Marcus was almost choking with laughter. "I'm not sure I want to know what number one is."

Seb's eyes sparkled. "It's just a plain white tee with four words in black." He paused. "It says, *Come in me bro.*"

Marcus tried not to cover the rug with beer. "Christ, I'm so glad you didn't wear that one." When Seb gave him a quizzical glance, he explained. "My sister works with three gay guys. She'd be ordering them as Christmas gifts in a heartbeat." He gestured to the couch. "Please, have a seat." Marcus placed the bowl of chips onto the table next to it.

Seb sat and gazed at his surroundings. "This is a beautiful house." He inclined his head toward the yard. "I love all the trees."

Marcus joined him at the other end of the couch. "If you walk through them, you'll find a creek. My parents drummed into us about keeping away from it when we were kids." Marcus looked at the cozy living room. "This house has been in my family for years. Every summer we'd be here. So many good memories." He took a drink from his bottle. "Trawling for lobster... Is it hard work? I imagine it would be."

"I've only been at it a week." Seb sighed heavily. "And I've got a lot more weeks to come."

"What about when you're not trawling for lobsters? What do you do?"

There was that grin again. "Guess."

Marcus swallowed another mouthful of beer. "Oh, that's not fair."

"Why not?"

"If I say something stupid, I either offend you, or I make myself look like an asshole."

Seb's eyes sparkled. "I'll be gentle. You get three guesses."

Marcus went with his gut. "You're a professional surfer. You're going to be one of the big names in Olympic surfing."

Seb laughed. "Hey, I like that. But no."

"Musician? You play in a band?"

"That sounds great, except I can't play a single instrument and I can't hold a note. So no. One more try." Seb took a long drink from his bottle.

Marcus was all out of ideas. "Artist." It was a stab in the dark.

Seb cackled. "Not even close. I teach junior high."

He blinked. "No shit."

Seb's lips twitched. "I'm not sure whether to be amused or offended by that reaction."

"I'm just trying to picture you in the classroom, in a suit…"

"A suit? Oh hell no." Seb raised his feet off the floor and peered at his flip-flops. "I'd wear these if they'd let me. But *no*, dress has to be 'professional' or 'appropriate'," he air-quoted. "I wear dress pants and a button-up shirt. They'd like it if I wore a suit or a sports jacket, but it's not required. Jeans are a definite no."

Jess walked into the room, a glass of wine in her hand. "Dinner is all done. I thought I'd join you two and sit a spell." She smiled. "I'm not interrupting anything, am I?" She sat in the armchair by the window.

Marcus gave her a hard stare. "Of course you're not. We're just chatting."

Jess sipped her wine. "So, Seb, Marcus says you're a visitor to Cape Porpoise. Where do you live?"

"Not that far from here, in Ogunquit."

Her face lit up. "I've been there. There was this great candy shop—"

"Harbor Candy," Seb interjected.

"That was it. And I remember another place, farther along the coast, I think. I used to stand and watch the taffy-pulling machine in the window. I could have stood there for hours."

Seb nodded, smiling. "That's the Goldenrod, in York Beach."

"I took Jake—that's my son—there to show him. Except he was more interested in the wrapping machine in the corner window."

"If you went there, you probably went to the Nubble Lighthouse too."

Jess beamed. "Yes! I took Jake there too, when he was little." She frowned. "Now, what was the name of that place at the lower end of the Nubble parking lot? It sold the best ice cream." Her eyes widened. "Brown's. That was it."

Seb nodded. "It's called Dunne's now. And the choice of flavors *still* makes my head spin." He narrowed his eyes. "Except they don't have the Danish custard flavor that Brown's had."

"Bummer." She cocked her head to one side. "And are you single?"

Oh my God. Marcus cleared his throat. "I think that comes under the heading of 'None-of-our-damn-business'?"

Seb waved his hand. "It's okay. I don't mind her asking. Yes, I'm single."

"Do you know Machine or Jacque's Cabaret in Boston?"

Seb frowned. "I've never been to Boston, and I don't recognize those names. Should I?"

"They're gay bars."

Seb's lips were twitching again. "And you think I keep a list in my head of every gay bar in the country? That's almost as funny as asking me if I know a friend of yours in Boston because he's gay."

Jess flushed. "I see what you mean."

Marcus had to work hard not to laugh. *Score one to Seb.*

"What do you do in Boston?" Seb asked.

"I work for an interior design company. I'm the secretary, gofer, coffeemaker, delivery girl on occasion… They call me their right-hand woman."

"And what about you?" Seb asked Marcus.

Before Marcus could open his mouth, Jess got in first. "Marcus is a copywriter."

Seb grinned. "So *you're* the one who's responsible when I see an ad and rush out to buy something I didn't need in the first place."

Marcus chuckled. "Probably."

"He's very good at his job." Seb could hear the pride in Jess's voice.

"I'm sure he is. So when you're not staying here, where do you live?"

"New York."

"City boy, huh? Must seem very quiet here."

"Trust me, I don't mind that at all." In fact, Marcus wasn't sure he wanted to return to all the noise and bustle.

"Marcus is writing a book," Jess blurted out. He glared at her, and she glared back. "Well, you are."

Seb's eyes were wide. "I'm impressed. Fiction, non-fiction…?"

"Non-fiction. I'm not even sure if I want to publish it when it's finished. And please, don't ask me to tell you what it's about, because you'd be snoring within seconds, it's so dull." Anything to get off the subject.

"So how did you two meet?" Jess inquired.

Marcus gave her another stern glance, but she

was steadfastly ignoring him.

"We bonded over bananas," Seb said with a straight face. Then he laughed. "Not really. I have a terrible habit of talking to complete strangers, and Marcus happened to be on the receiving end."

"Then he did it again, only this time it was about magazines," Marcus added.

"I meant to ask that day, only, you hurried off before I got the chance. You were looking at a fishing magazine. Are you into fishing?"

Jess snorted. "When he was ten years old, maybe. He used to go out in our dad's boat—him, my dad, and our brother—and they'd sit out in the bay all day long, Marcus with this cute little fishing line."

"Did you catch anything?" Seb asked, his eyes bright.

"Once or twice, I think. I'm sure we caught some mackerel." Marcus smiled. "I told my dad I wanted to catch a lobster."

"Maybe you should take it up while you're staying here," Seb suggested.

Marcus stared at him. "That's what I was thinking about when I saw that magazine. I'm sure Dad's fishing gear is around here someplace." He sighed. "The boat is long gone."

"Maybe Seb can find a boat, and you can both go fishing." Jess's seemingly innocent suggestion wasn't fooling Marcus for a second.

"I'm certain Seb is way too busy to go fishing," Marcus said in a firm voice. "Besides, he spends his days out on the water—he might not want to spend his free time out there as well."

"And then again, he might." Seb grinned. "I

can't remember the last time I did that. It would be a nice change to be in a boat and *not* chasing my tail, trying to do three things at once." He drank some more of his beer. "And I think I can find us a boat."

"That settles it," Jess announced with a smug smile.

"No, it does *not*." Marcus cleared his throat. "Is it time to eat yet?"

As soon as Seb left, he was going to have words with his sister.

"That was delicious," Seb said with a smile.

Jess snorted. "Anyone can put together a salad."

"Yeah, but I've never had lobster salad that had pasta in it."

"You liked it though?" She looked a little anxious.

"I loved it. Besides, you drowned it in garlic mayo so as far as I'm concerned, you're golden."

She beamed. "See? *Some* people *like* a lot of mayo." Seb got the feeling that was a dig at Marcus. She got up from the table. "I'll fetch dessert." Jess walked away from the dining table and into the kitchen.

"I'm sorry about Jess," Marcus said at once in a low voice.

Seb bit his lip. "What did you say about *me*

not doing subtle? Your sister could give lessons." It hadn't taken him long to work out Jess was trying her hand at a little matchmaking. It would have tickled him, except Marcus's reaction made it clear he wasn't happy about it. Seb sighed. "She didn't come right out with it, but it was kinda obvious."

"What—the fact that I'm gay? What gave it away?"

Seb couldn't hold back his smile. "I *think* it was when she suggested I visit New York next year in June, to watch the Pride parade with you."

Thankfully, Marcus saw the funny side too. He burst into laughter. "Yeah. She's about as subtle as a sledgehammer."

Seb shrugged. "Hey, she means well. I should be flattered, right?" He stilled, his eyes wide in mock horror. "Unless she does this with every guy she meets?"

Marcus shook his head. "You're the first, thank God."

Seb was confused as fuck. Talk about mixed signals. It was as if Marcus was two separate men, at war with each other. One minute he was charming and funny, the next…Seb prided himself on being pretty good at reading guys, but Marcus was an enigma.

"Thank you for reacting so politely," Marcus said at last. "You're right, she means well. It just doesn't occur to her that two gay men might not be interested in each other."

Okay, *that* felt like Marcus was closing the door on any chance of them being anything more than acquaintances. *Message received. Backing off.*

Seb didn't want to back off. He was already

hooked.

Jess came out of the kitchen, carrying two huge wedges of cheesecake. "I checked. There's vanilla ice cream in the freezer if you want some to go with that." Both Seb and Marcus nodded. "I'll bring out the tub." She disappeared back into the kitchen.

"Ice cream with cheesecake is the best. Pity it's not chocolate, but hey, nothing wrong with vanilla." He locked gazes with Marcus, unable to help himself. "You a fan of vanilla?"

For a moment, it felt as if Marcus wasn't going to respond. Then he smiled. "I'm more a Moose Tracks guy myself." He licked his lips. "I prefer something that's more of a mouthful. And maybe harder to swallow."

Maybe that door wasn't as tightly shut as Seb imagined.

Then Jess came back in, and *damn*, Marcus shut down faster than Seb could draw breath.

It was seven-thirty before he knew it. Seb thanked Jess for the meal, and both of them for the company. "You want me to find a boat so you can go fishing?" he asked as he put on his jacket. He could do that much for Marcus.

Jess opened her mouth to speak, but shut it again when Marcus fired a glance at her. He returned his attention to Seb. "Yes," he said at last. "But on one condition."

"What's that?"

Marcus looked him in the eye. "You have to come too. I wouldn't want to be out on the water alone. If you get the boat, I'll bring food, rods and lines, bait…"

Seb smiled. "Deal. I'll even give up my next Sunday for you. After that it's going to get busy around here, what with the Fourth the following weekend."

"Okay. Next Sunday then."

Seb said goodnight to Jess, and Marcus accompanied him to the door. Seb held out his hand. "I know Jess kinda steamrollered you into inviting me, but I had a good time. Thank you."

"You're welcome." Marcus shook it. "Hope it's a good week for you." Marcus opened the door, but before Seb could pass through it, he said, "Not that I mind *what* you wear, you understand, but… which tee were you thinking of wearing next Sunday?" He smiled. "Just so I'm prepared."

Seb rubbed his chin. "Maybe my new one?"

Marcus arched his eyebrows. "Dare I ask what's on it?"

He grinned. "Mean gays suck. Nice gays swallow."

"Oh God."

Seb laughed. "Relax. I'm yanking your chain. I'm not gonna wear one of my precious tees out where the salt water can ruin it. You're safe." He paused. "Well, fairly safe." He bade Marcus goodnight, then strolled along the dirt driveway that led to the road.

I don't know what to make of him.

There was one thing Seb was sure of—he wanted to get to know Marcus Gilbert a whole lot better.

Chapter Eight

June 22

Seb ached like a son of a bitch. The haul had to be the biggest he'd seen yet. *About time we had a decent day.* He waited by the *Liza Jane* while Tim had the catch weighed. Judging by Tim's smile, he was a happy bunny too.

"Six hundred and fifty pounds, yow'un," he said as he headed back to the boat. "That should put a smile on the ol' bastard's face."

Seb cackled. "If Gary smiled, his face would crack." He pulled off his muck boots and grabbed his flip flops from his bag. The oil pants were already gone.

"Let's see what tomorrow brings."

"Hey, you know where I can get a boat? A friend wants to go fishing on Sunday." Maybe a *friend* was a slight exaggeration. Lord knew, Seb wanted to get real friendly with Marcus, preferably when both of them were naked, but that was looking about as likely as the next Pope being called Betty.

Tim narrowed his gaze. "You're not taking *this* boat out."

Seb snorted. "I wasn't even gonna ask. One, it's too big, and two, I couldn't take it out without a license. I'm not *that* dumb. I just wondered if Gary had another boat someplace that I could use. Small enough for two guys to go fishing in."

Tim cocked his head to one side. "How far out you figure on going? Because if you're gonna stick close to shore, there's the *Little Liza*. She's a lot smaller than this one, and she doesn't guzzle fuel like the *Liza Jane* does. Plenty of places to fish close to shore, especially if this friend of yours wants to catch a striper. He got a license yet?"

"He needs a license?" As if Seb would know that.

Tim nodded. "You gotta register over't the town hall. Costs two bucks. But if he's going after stripers, he can only catch one. You *could* catch a shitload of mackerel though. If you like mackerel. Some folks don't." His eyes gleamed. "You startin' up your own charter business?"

"Yeah, sure. I'm gonna give up teaching for it." Seb rolled his eyes. "Like I said, he's just a friend. He hasn't done this in years, so I said I'd help him out."

"That *all* he is? 'A friend'?"

Seb wasn't sure how to take that. Gary had no issue with him being gay—Seb didn't know about Tim. It wasn't exactly something they'd discussed.

Tim waved a hand. "Relax. You're safe. I'm not one of them holy rollers, out to save your soul. Got a cousin who's into guys." He shrugged. "He's all right. And it's none of my beeswax what you do with your tackle. But if you're gonna do it in the boat, make sure no one sees ya. You get arrested, Gary will kill us both."

"Why will he kill *you*?"

"For lettin' you use the damn boat. And clean up when you're done." He smirked. "I don't wanna be steppin' into that boat and slippin' on something."

Seb almost choked. "I don't think that's gonna be a problem. He really is just a friend."

"*Sure* he is." Tim gave a gleeful grin. "But if I look out and see that boat a-rockin', I won't be in the least bit surprised. I'll tell you the best places to go. Just bring the boat back in one piece, that's all I ask."

"Thanks, Tim."

He waved his hand again. "We're good. Now get your ass home, and I'll see you tomorrow mornin'. Let's see if we can get more than six hundred and fifty pounds."

Seb said goodbye and started the stroll back to Pier Road, weary but grinning.

Sex in a boat. Sounds kinda interesting. Then he huffed. *And it ain't gonna happen, so quit thinking about it. Save it for the spank bank.*

June 28

Marcus couldn't believe his eyes. He stared at the boat tied to the pier. "Oh my God, I'm in a time warp." He handed the rods down to Seb, who stowed them beside the wooden console. Marcus did his best not to stare at Seb's ass as he bent over, but *damn*, it was hard work.

And speaking of hard... Marcus grabbed the cooler bag and held it in front of him.

Seb gave him a quizzical glance. "Excuse

me?"

He pointed to the 1969 Boston Whaler Seb was standing in. "My dad had a boat just like this. Christ, this thing is older than I am. And it's still going?" The boat was a sixteen-footer. The gel coating on the blue interior seemed like it had seen better days, but the console, the bench toward the stern, and the center seat looked good. A large tank sat in the bow in front of the console, a hatch on top. "What's that for?"

"That's the live well," Seb told him. "Tim says if you want to catch a striper—that's a striped bass to you city folk—the best way is with live mackerel. So the first thing we gotta do is catch some mackerel. We keep 'em in there."

"We're going to feed the mackerel to another fish? What about keeping some for us?"

Seb laughed. "Hey, if there's any left at the end of it, you get mackerel too. In fact, you might get a lot of mackerel."

Seb's words sank in. "I know what a striper is. Do you have any idea how many summers I spent here?"

Seb arched his eyebrows. "Are you gonna stand there, or are you getting in the damn boat?" He held out his hand for the cooler.

Marcus handed it over. "There's the lunch, as promised." He willed his erection to wilt. *Jesus, this was why I jerked off this morning. Fat lot of good* that *did.* One look at Seb waiting on the pier, tall and lean, those worn jeans tight across his ass, and Marcus's libido roared into life.

Down boy.

Seb grinned. "Got any beer in there?" He

placed the square bag between the benches.

"There might be a few beers in there, as well as water." He'd brought the micro beers Seb had liked so much. "Plus snacks. I had no idea how long we were going to be out there so I came prepared." He was buzzing. "I can't tell you the last time I did this." He glanced at the sky, shading his eyes. "And it's such a beautiful day." Not a cloud to be seen, and if it hadn't been for the stiff breeze off the ocean, he could have said it was warm. The temperature had to have been heading for the high sixties.

"Then let's stop wasting it talking, and get out of here."

Marcus got into the boat and Seb gestured to the bench toward the stern. "You can sit there. I'll steer." His eyes gleamed. "You say you haven't been fishing in years, but you probably have more experience at line fishing than I do."

Marcus buffed his nails on his T-shirt. "I'll teach you everything I know." Then he grinned. "That'll take about a minute." He peered at the wooden bench. "Dad's boat had seat cushions. I think my mom made them."

Seb guffawed. "I don't think Gary knows what a seat cushion is." He switched on the engine, then untied the rope.

Marcus hadn't expected it to be so loud. "Guess I should have brought ear muffs," he yelled.

Seb cupped his ear and shouted, "You say something?" He laughed. "Once we find a spot I'll turn it off and we'll drop anchor." He glanced at the rods lying beside the console. "Do these belong to your dad?"

"Yeah. I even found the old fishing hat he

gave me when he first took me out." Marcus removed the floppy green hat from his bag, lures fastened around its band.

Seb's eyes widened. "Oh my God. That is so cute. Put it on."

Marcus gave him a mock glare. "Sure. Then you whip out your phone and take a picture of me looking like an idiot."

Seb cackled. "And who am I gonna send it to? I'm not likely to post it online. 'Hey, look at this guy I took fishing.'"

Marcus sighed. Seb had a point. He put on the hat. "There. You've seen it."

Seb bit his lip. "I've seen worse." He reached into his own bag, pulled out a baseball hat, and stuck it on his head. "There. Just no laughing when I take it off. Hat hair is a bitch."

Marcus could have told Seb his hair begged to be mussed against a pillow, or tugged from behind while—

Christ, I really need to stop thinking with my dick.

"I promise." He was in such a good mood. He'd been looking forward to this all week. Marcus wasn't sure whether it was the promise of time spent out on the water, or time spent with Seb that was most alluring.

It didn't matter how much he tried not to think about Seb—the lean, hot guy still managed to slide into his thoughts. And there had been moments when the idea of stripping Seb bare and fucking him through the mattress seemed like a perfectly reasonable course of action.

One night couldn't hurt, right?

Except Marcus had the feeling one night with

Seb would not satisfy him.

Then he remembered he was supposed to be avoiding distractions.

Yeah right. At this rate, it'll take until Rapture to finish the damn book.

"Got another couple!" Marcus hoisted the glistening mackerel from the water.

Seb laughed. "We've already got too many. Throw 'em back." The well was full. "How about we try for a striper?" He cocked his head. "You like it cooked whole or in fillets?"

"My mom always cooked it whole." Marcus glanced at him. "Do *you* know how to fillet a bass? Because I don't."

"Nope. Never done it."

"Well, there's always Jess's method. It seems to work for her." When Seb gave him an inquiring glance, Marcus grinned. "Watch a YouTube video on it."

He laughed. "Pick a rod, we'll bait it with mackerel, then we'll cast it out and see what turns up." Tim had gone over the basics with him on Friday. He hooked a fish on the end of the line and lowered it into the water. Then he handed the rod to Marcus. "Let the line out, and let it swim around." He sat on the bench by the console, and inclined his head to the rear seat. "Sit. This might take a while."

He grinned. "It's time to play the Baiting Game."

Marcus groaned. "Oh, that's bad." He leaned against the back of the bench, but was on his feet a heartbeat later, reeling in the line. "I've got one!"

"Fuck, that was fast." Whatever was on the end of Marcus's line was certainly tugging on it, the rod flexing. Marcus reeled faster, and from the water burst a large, wriggling— "Fuck, it's an ocean death snake!"

Marcus dropped the conger eel onto the floor of the boat, where it thrashed, its huge mouth wide, its black eyes glassy. "What do I do?"

"Throw the fucker back in!" Seb yelled.

Marcus attempted to pick up the writhing eel. "It won't stay still long enough for me to grab it," he remonstrated.

"Here—you grab its body, and I'll unhook it and throw it back." Between them, they wrestled the unwieldy eel off the hook, and Seb flung it over the side.

Marcus's eyes danced with amusement. "'Ocean death snake'?"

Seb gave him a sheepish grin. "It's what I called them when I was a kid." He opened the well. "Lemme get you another mackerel." He baited the line again, and Marcus let it out. They sat, staring out at the calm waters, the sunlight sparkling on the ripples. "So, you got any other brothers or sisters, apart from Jess?"

"I have a brother, Chris. I'm the middle one."

"The second son, eh?" Seb grinned. "Then it's true what they say." When Marcus arched his eyebrows, Seb continued. "Guys with older brothers are more likely to be gay."

"According to whom?"

Seb gave him a wide-eyed stare. "NBC. They did a feature on it."

"Oh, then it must be true." He rolled his eyes.

"And now that I think about it… I've got no brothers and three sisters."

"Which sounds a more plausible argument for growing up to be gay," Marcus said with a smile. "Do you see much of them?"

Seb's stomach quivered. "Nope. Can we change the subject, please?"

Marcus's face tightened. "I think I just hit a nerve. I'm sorry."

His throat thickened, and his cheeks grew hot. "You've got nothing to feel sorry for, okay? It's not *your* fault I have a homophobic bitch for a mom, and that my sisters seem to have come out of the same mold. I'm better off without them." He studied the horizon, unwilling to meet Marcus's gaze, forcing himself to not think about them.

A gentle hand squeezed his shoulder. "No, it's not my fault," Marcus said quietly, "but I can still regret asking a question that brought you pain."

Seb turned his head. Marcus's eyes were warm. Seb let out a sigh. "Gonna guess your upbringing was nothing like mine, if Jess is anything to go by."

"I think you'd be right. I was luckier than you. I have a supportive, amazing family." He bit his lip. "My Aunt Carol was the only one who struggled when I came out, but she rallied eventually. When I was growing up, we spent our summers here in Cape Porpoise. There was not only my immediate family, but my cousins Lisa and Robert. They're older than me. I wish you could have seen the house back then. Packed to the rafters with people. I remember one summer—I think I was seventeen—all you could hear was laughter. Lisa had two kids by then: Ashley was six and Matt was four. And Robert's son Josh was nine. Jess was thirteen. She and I spent that summer playing with them on the beach in Kennebunkport, helping my dad repair our tree house out back so they could play in it…"

There was a lump in Seb's throat. "Your family sounds awesome."

Marcus gave a wry smile. "I might not find them so awesome next weekend. They're coming here for the Fourth. I've just gotten used to having the place to myself, and I'm about to be invaded." He stiffened. "Seb. Something's taken the bait."

Seb grabbed the net as Marcus lurched to his feet. "Keep a tight hold and reel it in slowly." Something thrashed in the water several feet away. "I hope it's not another conger eel." Marcus reeled it in, and Seb peered into the water. "Oh, that's a beauty." He lowered the net, and when he raised it, a large striped bass wriggled in it.

Marcus beamed. "Biggest thing I ever caught." Seb lowered the net to the bottom of the boat, and removed the hook from the fish's mouth. "Look at that." Seb loved the note of awe and pride in Marcus's voice. Then Marcus frowned. "It's still alive."

"And it could stay like that for hours, so we're gonna put it out of its misery, okay?" Tim had prepared him for this. "If you don't wanna watch, look away now." He reached into his bag for the spikes and wire Tim had given him. Within seconds, the fish was brain dead, so that meant it didn't feel any more pain. Then Seb lifted the gills and made a couple of cuts, then another to the tail, so it could bleed out. He pointed to the bucket in the bow. "Take off that lid." He'd filled it with ice from Gary's freezer. Then he lowered the bass into the icy water and popped the lid back on.

"I'm impressed." Marcus's brow furrowed. "That was always the part I hated whenever Dad caught anything. His method wasn't so… humane."

Seb grimaced. "I can imagine. I asked Tim to show me the best way to kill a fish so it doesn't suffer. He says fish are just like us. They have a central nervous system too." Marcus gazed at him thoughtfully, and Seb frowned. "What?"

"Nothing. It's just…" Marcus smiled. "I think I have a handle on you, and then you go and say something that shows me I still have a lot to learn about you."

That sort of implied he *wanted* to learn more, which Seb found intriguing. *What's going on here?* It was so *easy* to be around Marcus, so comfortable, as if they hadn't just met a week ago.

He glanced at the bottom of the boat. "Ew. I think the first thing I do when we get back to land is clean this up. Fish blood and guts everywhere…"

"I'll help," Marcus responded promptly. "After all, it was my fish that made all this mess, right?"

Seb grinned. "I guess I know what *you're* having for dinner tonight."

"Correction. What *we're* having for dinner."

He blinked.

"Look, you got us a boat, you caught half the mackerel in there, you saved me from the ocean death snake…." Seb laughed. Marcus gazed at his catch. "I do have an ulterior motive."

"Oh really?" Seb was dying to know.

"Well… we've got a lot of mackerel here. We *could* throw them all back or…" Marcus gave him a coaxing smile. "You could come back to the house with me and help me clean and gut them all before I put them in the freezer. That way, dinner would be my way of saying thank you."

Seb tilted his head. "Do you *know* how to gut and clean mackerel?"

"No, but there's bound to be—"

"—a YouTube video on how to do it," Seb concluded, laughing. Not that he minded the idea of spending more time with Marcus. Gutting fish wouldn't have been his first choice of activity, however. "Fine. Besides, I love bass."

"I've got steak fries in the freezer," Marcus told him.

Seb shook his head. "Bradbury's do the most awesome corn and clam chowder sauce, and I can make a salad."

"Deal." Marcus's eyes twinkled. "And we've got beer to go with it. We didn't drink any."

"You got any of that wine left? That would be great with fish." When Marcus arched his eyebrows, Seb gave him a mock glare. "So I like wine over beer. Bite me." *Preferably on my ass. And leave marks.* He took a moment to rein in his libido. Ass-biting would definitely *not* be on the menu.

"Can we go in now? My butt is numb from sitting on this bench so long."

Seb burst into laughter. "Sure." He wiped his hands on an old towel he'd brought along, pulled in the anchor, then started the engine. As he steered toward the pier, one thought dominated all the rest.

I want to know you better, Marcus Gilbert.

Chapter Nine

Marcus glanced down at his soiled tee and jeans, and grimaced. "Now I'm glad I wore my oldest clothes. I must look nasty."

Seb bit his lip. "Oh, I wouldn't say that." He sniffed. "Jesus, I reek of fish guts. I'd better go home. I need a shower and some clean clothes before I sit down to eat."

"You don't need to do that. I can shove your clothes in the washer and by the time you leave tonight, they'll be dry. You can have a shower here. I'll find you a pair of sweats and a clean tee that should fit you." He gestured to his own clothing. "Trust me, I'll be doing the same."

Seb looked at the remaining mackerel in the bucket at his feet. The bass was already filleted, cleaned and in the fridge. "How about I finish up here, while you grab a shower? It won't take me long to prepare these."

"Okay. And while *you're* in the shower, I'll go to Bradbury's and get the sauce. Corn and clam chowder, I think you said? Plus whatever else we need for this salad you're going to make. Think about it while I'm showering." He got up and left the kitchen, heading for the bedroom. Once inside the bathroom, he stripped off his clothing. It felt as though his hair was full of salt. Marcus left his clothes in a soiled heap and stepped into the shower enclosure.

Not going to think about Seb. It was getting to be a habit, especially first thing in the morning. He deliberately pushed such delicious thoughts from his head, ignoring his rising cock, and concentrated on getting clean. By the time he'd rubbed his hair dry, put on clean clothes, and sauntered back into the kitchen, Seb had finished, and all the mackerel had been placed in the freezer.

Seb grinned. "That's a lot of mackerel you got in there. Any idea how you're gonna cook it? Grammy used to make this great dish. I'll see if I can get the recipe."

"I'll take your clothes if you're ready for a shower."

Seb immediately stripped off his T-shirt. Marcus tried not to stare, but that was always going to be a losing battle. It was obvious Seb took care of himself. His stomach was toned and flat, and there was definition in his chest and upper arms. The hair on his pecs was light brown, and there was a definite treasure trail leading down into his jeans—and as Marcus gazed at it, Seb lowered the zip.

Christ.

"Oops. Guess I forgot I'd gone commando."

The sight of that dark fuzz drew Marcus like a moth to a flame. Seb had gone low enough to reveal the base of his dick, and judging by the way he filled his jeans, it was a long, fat cock.

The effort it took to raise his head…

He looked Seb in the eye. "I'll get you a towel." And then he was out of there.

He really doesn't do subtle, does he?

He went into the bathroom to the cabinet

where he kept the towels. The first one he saw was a hand towel, and it drew a smirk. *I could always give him that. It might just about cover him.* But that was his libido talking. Marcus grabbed a bath towel and went back to the kitchen.

"Here." He held it out. "I'll put your clothes in the washer with mine. Just chuck them out of the bathroom."

"Nah, you can have 'em now." And before Marcus could protest that Seb *really* didn't need to do that, he took the towel and placed it on the countertop, turned his back on Marcus, and lowered his jeans, revealing a firm bare ass.

Oh dear Lord, would you look at that?

Marcus's dick responded, straining against his zipper. Seb bent over to shove his jeans down to his ankles, and Marcus's face felt as if it was on fire. His fingers ached to reach out and touch, to stroke those firm, inviting cheeks covered in a soft down. Then Seb straightened, and Marcus held his breath.

Please don't turn around. Please don't turn around.

He was only capable of so much willpower.

Thankfully, Seb wrapped a towel around him, then scooped up the jeans and T-shirt from the floor. He handed them to Marcus, then inclined his head toward the countertop. "I made a list of what I'd need."

"Hmm?" Marcus was mesmerized by the bulge in Seb's towel.

Seb's eyes twinkled. "For the salad? You asked me to think about what I'd need."

"Oh. Yeah." Salad was the last thing on his mind right then, except for maybe tossing it.

Do not go there. Stop it. Right now.

"Marcus?" He blinked. Seb was gazing at him with obvious amusement. "Wanna show me where the shower is? I smell like the *Liza Jane* after a long day."

"Sure." Marcus led him through the bedroom into the bathroom. He pointed through the glass door. "There's shampoo and bodywash, and I put a fresh washcloth out for you." He cleared his throat. "You've already got a towel. If you need anything else, tell me now because I'll be going out to the store."

Seb's eyes gleamed. "You're not gonna stay and wash my back?" He grinned. "Or any other parts that might need special attention?"

Marcus narrowed his gaze. "You don't do subtle at all, do you?"

Seb laughed. "You're learning." He glanced into the shower. "I think I've got everything I need." Then he did a slow up and down glance. "Well— almost everything."

Marcus got out of there as fast as he could. He started the washing machine, then grabbed the tablet from the kitchen countertop and pulled up a simple recipe for cooking bass. He made a list, grabbed one of his mom's plastic bags, and got out of the house.

As he drove to the store, his mind was not on the road.

Would it have been so bad to get in there with him? No one says we have to fuck. I could have washed his back. Except Marcus knew he was deluding himself. One glimpse at that ass and he didn't want to help Seb wash it—he wanted to clean it with his tongue, and he wouldn't be able to stop himself from going further.

Marcus forced himself to concentrate.

'So what were you doing at the time of the accident, Mr. Gilbert?'

'Well, officer, I was thinking about cleaning a hot guy's hole with my dick.'

It was going to be a long evening.

Seb grabbed the avocados, cherry tomatoes, and cucumber. "I'll get to work on these. What are you doing?"

"Combining the lemon rind, juice, olive oil, thyme, oregano, salt and pepper, to drizzle over the fish. It takes less than fifteen minutes to bake in the oven." Marcus grated the lemon rind into a glass bowl.

Seb grinned. "Then I'd better get moving." He sliced through the dark green-purple skin of the avocado. "How's the writing going?"

"It's okay." Marcus's non-committal tone made it clear he didn't want to discuss it.

"How long have you been a copywriter?" Seb figured it was a safer topic.

"Fifteen years."

"And you're still doing it? You must be good."

Marcus shrugged. "It's a lot of pressure. More than there used to be. The job's getting more difficult."

Seb coughed. "There are always ways to relieve stress."

Marcus arched his eyebrows. "And I can guess how *you* do that."

"Hey, my weeks can be pretty stressful too. So I live for the weekend when I can go to Ogunquit. There are two bars where I hang out a lot. I dance my feet off, kiss as many guys as I can, and let it all hang out." Okay, so he did a lot more than kiss, but he was trying to tone it down a little. His earlier attempts at flirtation had sent Marcus scuttling out of the bathroom like a cat with its tail on fire.

"I bet the guys line up for you," Marcus commented, squeezing juice into the bowl.

"I don't go without." He snorted. "Except for now, of course."

Marcus's eyes sparkled. "*Now* I get the oh-look-Gee-I-went-commando routine. Would *I* be helping to relieve the stress of lobster hauling?"

Seb couldn't hold back on his grin. "I thought that might be a possibility." *Okay, maybe the flirtation actually worked.* He sliced the avocado into cubes. "You telling me you don't do hookups, over in the Big Apple?"

"Not *everyone* is into hookups."

Seb would have believed him, if he hadn't seen a familiar bottle containing even *more* familiar blue pills in Marcus's bathroom cabinet. He shouldn't have peeked, but knowing Marcus was also on PrEP told him one thing—they were both active.

"So who is this Grammy you've mentioned a couple of times?"

Seb knew evasion when he heard it. "She's a

formidable lady. She raised Levi—her grandson—mostly on her own when her husband died. Levi is one of my closest friends, and I spent a lot of time with him when I was growing up. So did most of our friends. For some of us, Levi's was our second home. For me, it was my family." He cackled. "You don't wanna get on the wrong side of Grammy. She looks like butter wouldn't melt, but she's got a wicked tongue, and she doesn't take shit from anyone."

"Sounds like she and my aunt Carol would get along," Marcus observed.

"Is she coming next weekend?"

"No, she's in a care home in Boston, but my cousins will be here. More victims of the Gilbert curse, or so Jess would have you believe."

"What in the hell is the Gilbert Curse?"

Marcus laughed. "Apparently, we're not fated to stay with anyone for too long." He snorted. "Bullshit. Mom and Dad are doing just fine."

"Have *you* survived it so far?"

"As Jess pointed out only a couple of weeks ago, I don't count. You need to be in a relationship first."

Seb put down his knife and stroked his chin. "What is this word of which you speak, 'relationship'?" That raised a laugh. "Have you ever had one?"

"Two or three. Longest one lasted two years and no, it wasn't the curse. The split was amicable." Marcus glanced at him. "What about you?" He laid the fillets on a baking sheet, and drizzled the lemon and herbs over them.

Seb said nothing for a moment, slicing the cherry tomatoes in half. He was conscious of

Marcus's gaze. Finally, he sighed. "If you'd asked me a few weeks ago, I'd have laughed and said 'who needs a relationship?'"

"That implies you wouldn't say it now. So what's changed?"

"I think I decided to be honest with myself." He paused. "I have kind of a reputation with my friends. When I was growing up, I knew a lot about sex before I ever got the chance to experience any of it. I guess a lot of that was retaliation. My mom told me I was a deviant, and that I was going straight to hell, so I basically said 'Okay, point me in the right direction, because Hell has to be better than here.' College was *all* about the sex."

"She paid for your education?"

Seb snorted. "Yeah right. No, my grandparents did. They set up a trust fund to pay for my education. And believe me, I got an education."

Marcus slid the tray into the oven. "I'm trying to marry up these two images in my head. Teacher—and sex fiend." He grinned.

Seb laughed. "Sex fiend? Wow. Not sure if I should be insulted. But you're right. They don't go together. I have to be *so* careful. No photos online. No videos. I'm not even on Grindr. I don't want an ex-student finding me on there and telling the school. Not that an ex-student is *likely* to be on Grindr—I haven't been teaching *that* long. And not that I'd be interested in an ex-student. One, it would be weird. And two, I'm not into younger guys."

Marcus coughed. "I take it you prefer older guys?"

Seb locked gazes with him. "Oh yeah. Have to tell you, I never imagined coming to Cape

Porpoise and finding a guy who ticked *all* my boxes."

Marcus leaned against the fridge. "Would I know this guy?"

"You might." *Come on, Marcus. Take the bait.*

Marcus cleared his throat. "Do you enjoy teaching?" He poured wine into two glasses, and pushed one carefully toward Seb.

Damn it. He doesn't wanna play. Seb shrugged. "It has its good days. But I'm getting a bit tired of entitled brats. Seems to be a growing number of them."

"Did you always want to teach?"

Seb laughed. "I went through college with no clue as to what I would do after. Then I saw a couple of old movies that inspired me to become a teacher." He took a sip. "Hey, this is nice."

"I'm intrigued. Which movies?"

"*Dead Poets Society*. You ever see that one, with Robin Williams?"

Marcus almost choked on his wine. "I thought you said it was old? Christ, I was thirteen when that came out. I remember it."

Seb waggled his eyebrows. "I rest my case."

That earned him a mock glare. "What was the other movie? Although now I dread to ask."

"*The Ron Clark Story*. I think I was just into my teens when I saw it. A sweet movie about a teacher who leaves a nice safe job to go teach disillusioned and difficult kids in New York. It was based on a true story. I'm not sure it's *that* easy to get kids out of trouble and onto the right path. But any film that makes teaching look like fun? All credit to it."

"And *is* it fun?"

"Sometimes, but I didn't get into it for the shits and giggles. There was a line from *The Green Mile* that stuck in my head. Tom Hanks's character explains he and Brutal went into Boys Correctional. 'Get 'em young was our motto.' Maybe if I do a good enough job in junior high, they won't *need* steering onto the right path when they reach high school—they'll already be on it." Seb shook his head. "There are *way* too many distractions for kids these days." He threw all the ingredients into a bowl, then combined the olive oil, lemon juice and cumin for the dressing.

"What distracted *you* when you were at school?"

Seb grinned, reaching for his glass. "Boys." The wine was cold and delicious.

Marcus arched his eyebrows. "I'm sure you distracted a great many of them too." He smiled. "You certainly distract me."

"I do?" Seb put down his glass and took a step toward him. "I must be doing something right then."

Marcus narrowed his eyes and took a step back. "Seb…"

Seb took another step. "Yes?" He was close enough to feel warmth radiating from Marcus's body.

It wasn't close enough, not for what he had in mind.

"Something you want?"

He bit his lip. "Can I be blunt?" Because being subtle sure as shit wasn't working.

"I'd be surprised if you were anything else."

Fuck it. "You, Marcus. I want you. Any way I can get you."

Marcus stilled, appearing a little dazed. He took a deep breath. "Then I'm going to have to disappoint you. You're a distraction that I don't need right now."

Seb wasn't entirely surprised by the revelation, but he *had* allowed himself to hope.

"I came here to get into the right head-space to write my book. *And* sort out my life. I'm better than I was, but I'm not there yet. I need to be mindful of where my head is at, so I'm not going to jump into *anything* that would risk me backsliding."

"And does that include jumping into bed with me?" As if he didn't already know the answer to that.

Marcus regarded him with warm eyes. "I like you, Seb. I really do. And if we'd met a year or two ago, we wouldn't be about to eat right now—I'd already be fucking you on the kitchen table, because I wouldn't be able to keep my hands off you." His lips twitched. "I can do blunt too."

"No shit." Seb gave the table a wistful glance. "My timing apparently sucks."

Marcus chuckled. "I'm not saying never, okay? I'm just saying *not now*."

Seb let out a sigh. "Thank you for being honest." Despite the letdown, he preferred to know.

"I'm sorry. If it's any consolation, you're one of the hottest guys I've ever met. And if it had been any other time… What I *really* need right now is a friend."

Something in Marcus's voice touched him. "It's okay. I'll back off. I'm not gonna make this awkward for you. And I can be a friend."

Marcus shuddered out a breath. "Thank

you."

"For what?"

"Reacting the way you did. You're still here, for one thing."

Seb grinned. "That's because you're feeding me, and I know what's for dinner."

Marcus laughed. He raised his wineglass. "Thank you for today too. I loved it, being out on the ocean again after such a long time. You made it an enjoyable experience."

Seb clinked glasses with him. "You're welcome—friend."

He trusted his instincts, and right then they were telling him there was more to Marcus than met the eye. It didn't matter that his hole tightened at the thought of Marcus bending him over the table and plowing into him.

It's not gonna happen.

Well—not in real life, at any rate. Marcus couldn't dictate what happened inside Seb's head.

Chapter Ten

Seb glanced at his phone. It was already eight-thirty. He'd stayed way longer than he'd intended at Marcus's place, and it had been a real wrench to leave. Seb had been telling him stories about Grammy, such as the time she'd caught him stealing apples from the tree in the back yard, and had taken a broom to his ass. Or the time he'd stayed over, and she'd threatened to cover his mouth with duct tape because he and Levi had been talking till the early hours and they'd made far too much noise.

Marcus had laughed his ass off, they'd drunk a few beers, Seb had changed back into his own clothes, and had left in a good mood, despite the earlier rejection.

Hey, look at me, the grown-up.

There were other stories he could have told, but Seb was in no mood to share *them*. Marcus didn't need to hear how Grammy had cuddled him on the couch, fed him cookies, and wiped away his tears. His throat still tightened when he remembered her words.

"We don't get to choose our family, more's the pity. So all I'll say is this. If that culch of a mom of yours wants to be number than a hake and not see you for the shinin' boy you are, that's her loss. You got family under this roof, y'hear?"

Then he recalled how he'd gotten onto the topic of Grammy in the first place, and he speed-dialed Levi.

"Why aren't you asleep?" Levi demanded. "Don't you have to be up at the crack of dawn?"

Seb snorted. "I'm usually on the water by the time dawn shows her sorry ass. I need something from you."

"I am *not* driving over there to give you a massage, you got that? Ask the hot guy who might not bat for our team to give you one."

"Yeah, about him…" It had been a week since he and Levi last spoke, and Seb needed to bring him up to speed.

Levi made a choking sound at the other end of the line. "Fuck. He's gay, isn't he? I swear, if you fell into a septic tank, you'd climb out of it smelling of roses. How do you do that? Just *happen* to run into a hot daddy who turns out to be gay? You're not getting *any* sleep, are you?"

"Whoa there, Usain Bolt. Not so fast with the assumptions, all right? And can I just say…. Septic tank? *Ew.* Yes, Marcus is gay. But… he's not interested, okay?"

Crickets.

"Levi? You still there?"

"I take it Marcus walks with a white stick, or a dog. Because why the fuck would he not be interested in *you*?"

Seb smiled. "You're great for my ego, you know that?"

"How do you know he's not interested?"

"Because I made a move and he turned me down. Not sure what's going on with him—because *something* is—but right now, nailing my ass is not on his agenda."

"Sure he doesn't just need more persuading?"

Seb rolled out a heavy sigh. "I'm backing off, okay? No more flirting. Because if my best moves got me nowhere, I'm flogging a dead horse. Now… remember that recipe of Grammy's for mackerel?"

Levi went quiet for a moment. "You called me to get a recipe? *Now* it all makes sense. Who are you, and what have you done with Seb?"

He laughed. "I took Marcus fishing today, and we caught a shit ton of mackerel. I wanted to give him the recipe. I always love that meal whenever Grammy makes it."

"I'll get it off her tomorrow and email it. She's asleep."

"Is she okay?"

"She's fine." Another pause. "You like this Marcus, don't you?"

Seb never could hide shit from Levi. "Yeah, I do. Because apart from the fact that he's hot as fuck, he's also a really nice guy. I'm sorry it's worked out this way, because… *dayum*… but he needs a friend." *And not even one with benefits.*

"You're good at that." Levi's voice was warm. "And for the record, I know how tough it is when you're really into someone, and they don't want to know. At least, not in the way you'd like them to."

There was an ache in Seb's throat, and he yearned to ask who it was that Levi burned for, but he didn't dare. If Levi wanted to share that, he'd come right out with it.

"So… what are your plans for next weekend?" Levi's bright tone felt forced.

"*This* weekend still has a few hours left. Not

that *I'll* see 'em."

"It's the Fourth next Saturday, you doofus. You're not working, are you?"

Seb snorted. "Are you kidding? The wharf is gonna be swarming with tourists."

"You could always come here. You know you'd be welcome."

Yeah, Seb knew. "Thanks for the invite, but to be honest? I think I might just veg out on the couch and watch TV. A couple of days chillin' sounds awesome right now."

"And speaking of chilling… you need to sleep, so I'll let you go to bed. Sweet dreams, dude."

"Thanks, Levi." Seb knew exactly what to do to ensure he fell asleep within seconds, and it involved lube, a towel—and thoughts of a sexy guy with silver hair at his temples and a sultry gaze that made Seb go weak at the knees.

See you in my dreams, Marcus.

If he was lucky.

June 30

Marcus peered at his shopping list. He wasn't buying a lot of groceries, just making sure he had the basics for when the hordes descended. Mom and Dad were due the following day, then more would trickle in over Thursday and Friday. He'd spent most of the day cleaning, not that the house was dirty in the first place, but he knew his definition of clean differed widely from his mom's.

If she couldn't eat off it, it wasn't clean.

He stopped by the produce and scanned the available fruit. If memory served, Mom preferred to keep the fruit bowl overflowing, rather than buy snacks.

We're going to need a lot of fruit.

"So what's the deal with green bananas?"

He turned to find Seb standing behind him, grinning. "I have the strangest feeling of déjà vu." There was no suggestive tee this time, only a plain white one under his plaid jacket. Marcus pointed to it. "How very... Maine."

How does he do that? Seb could wear something as plain as jeans and a tee, and yet be a poster boy for Sexy AF.

A boy you don't want, remember? Looking at Seb's slim frame, Marcus was finding it difficult to recall his excuses for turning Seb down. Because he *did* want him.

Seb's eyes twinkled. "Have they started arriving yet?"

"Mom and Dad drive up tomorrow. I'm not sure when Jess is getting here. And no one else has been in touch. They'll just turn up."

"But how many is 'they'?

Marcus rolled his eyes. "I wish I knew. There could be as many as thirteen adults and two kids under that roof if they all show up. Which is why the washer and drier have been running nonstop all day. Every piece of bedding in the house has been through them." He affected a heavy sigh. "I'm worn out. I've been trying to work out who sleeps where, but I gave up. They're all going to have to double up, that's the only solution. And they can fight it out as to who they share a bed with."

Seb laughed. "You can't fit fifteen people around that dining table."

"Ah, but there's *another* table in the garage, and more chairs. Big family gatherings?" He waved dismissively. "We've got this." Except the nearer he got to showtime, the more nervous he became.

What the hell is wrong with me?

It had been a while since he'd been around so many members of his family. They were an intuitive bunch, so Marcus couldn't afford to let his guard slip. He knew Mom and Dad would have questions, and he wasn't sure how to handle them.

"If it all gets too much, you can escape to my place," Seb said suddenly. When Marcus blinked, he held up his hand. "It's just an idea. There's a huge couch and it's comfy. The place is small, but it's peaceful. Any time you wanna get out of the house, call me. Or text me the word HELP and I'll call you and make it sound like an emergency, if you need an excuse."

Marcus tilted his head to one side. "Do I look as if I need an escape plan?"

Seb nodded, his eyes bright. "Man, you've got panic written all over you. I thought your family was okay?"

"They are," Marcus protested. "Just… not in huge numbers." A comfortable warmth surged through him. "Thanks for the offer. If it gets too much, I might take you up on it." He sighed. "I'd better get going. Right now it feels like I'm about to feed the five thousand."

Seb's eyes lit up. "Oh. I've got that recipe I told you about. The one for mackerel." He grinned. "If you're gonna feed the five thousand, what better than fish, right? I'll text it to you. It's real easy."

"Thanks, Seb." What impressed Marcus more than anything was the complete lack of flirtation, even when Seb had offered his house as a refuge. *He promised he'd back off, and he did.* Respect was a very appealing trait.

"You're welcome." Seb grabbed a bunch of green bananas and put them in his cart. "I'll let you get on with your shopping. And Happy Fourth of July, for when it gets here. Yours will be a damn sight busier than mine."

Marcus squeezed Seb's shoulder, unable to resist the urge to connect with him. "It was good to see you."

Seb's eyes were warm. "Ditto." Then he walked away, heading for another aisle. Marcus drank in the sight of those long legs and that firm butt.

Maybe I've got this all wrong. What harm would it do? It would just be sex, right? And he wants it as much as I do. No strings, just for the summer.

Then he shoved down hard on such thoughts. He couldn't think about sex with Seb when his parents and the rest of the Gilbert menagerie would be upon him before he knew it.

That offer of an escape route was *such* a temptation.

July 1

Marcus opened the front door as soon as he heard a car engine. Mom waved at him from behind the wheel, and he gaped. "He let you drive?" Dad *never* let Mom take the driver's seat. Then he got a good glimpse at his dad, and his chest tightened.

Dad seemed *tired.*

Marcus dashed out to the car and opened the door for him. "Hey. Are you okay?"

Dad waved a hand. "Don't you start. I've had enough of that from your mother. I only let her drive to shut her up."

"Did it work?"

Dad rolled his eyes. "What do *you* think?" He inclined his head toward Mom. "She keeps saying I need to think about stopping driving. Hell, I'm only seventy-five."

Mom walked around to Dad's side. "He's being stubborn, as usual. He saw the doctor yesterday, and the diagnosis was he needs to stop doing so much and slow down. Stupid old fool never listens though."

Marcus couldn't miss the love in her voice, however, which wasn't bad going after almost fifty years of marriage.

"What's he been doing?"

Dad glared at him. "I *am* here, y'know. And all I've been doing is gardening."

Mom snorted. "*All*, he says. He only decided to re-landscape the entire yard, and it's almost an acre. I told him to get someone in to do the job, but did he listen?"

Marcus held up his hands. "Okay, can we cease hostilities for a moment?" He turned to Dad. "*You* are not going to lift a finger while you're here, all right? You're going to sit out in the yard, read, sleep, eat—and relax." Then he gave Mom a hard stare. "And *you* are going to do exactly what *he* does. We are all old enough and big enough to take care of ourselves, *and* you two."

Mom blinked, her mouth opened and closed, but she said nothing.

Marcus gave a satisfied smile. "Now we've got that settled, let me get your bags."

"I've popped the trunk," Dad told him.

"I don't suppose you know who's coming?" Marcus inquired as he walked around to the rear of the car.

"Robert called last night to say Josh couldn't make it. He's gone camping for the weekend with friends from his college days. I think it's some kind of reunion. And Robert's not coming either."

"Aw. That's a shame." Marcus liked his cousin Robert. He had fond memories of flying a kite with Robert one summer, when Marcus was about eight years old. Robert had just graduated from college, but had found time to play with his young cousin.

"Matt called to say he can't make it either. Apparently he has a new girlfriend, and her parents have invited him to spend the weekend with them." Mom's eyes sparkled. "I say new—they've been dating almost a year now, so I think it's serious." She darted a glance at him, and Marcus steeled himself for The Question. *'So are you seeing anyone?'* When nothing else was forthcoming, he grabbed as many bags as he could manage, and headed back inside. Dad followed, and Mom locked the car.

The moment she crossed the threshold, she sniffed. "You've been cleaning. I can smell that lavender furniture polish." Dad went into the living room and immediately opened the French doors to the back yard.

Marcus put down the bags and kissed her cheek. "Does it pass inspection?"

Mom arched her eyebrows. "How long did you spend cleaning the place? I was imagining three months' worth of bottles and God knows what else."

He wasn't listening—he was preparing a list in his head of all the room permutations. "You and Dad are in your usual room. Do you have any idea where you want to put everyone?"

"We'll take a look at the room situation when I've made us all some tea." She peered at him expectantly. "There *is*—"

"Yes, there's tea. I got Earl Grey, chamomile, peppermint, and green tea. Oh, and there's breakfast tea too."

Mom stroked his cheek. "Thank you." She went into the kitchen, and Marcus picked up the bags and carried them into the master bedroom. All his belongings had been packed into his suitcases and bags, ready for the move to the summerhouse. Although the total number of adults had been whittled down to ten, it still made sense for him to sleep out there.

"Marcus?" Mom appeared in the doorway, her hands on her hips. "Why is my freezer full of mackerel?" Her lips twitched.

"Ah. Yes. Well... I went fishing."

She widened her eyes. "Seriously?"

He nodded. "A friend took me out, and we caught a striped bass. What you see is what's left of the bait."

Mom raised her eyebrows and crossed her arms. "A friend? Here in Cape Porpoise?"

"I met him a couple of weeks ago. He's staying here to haul lobster for his uncle who had an accident."

"And does this friend have a name?"

Marcus bit his lip. "You might be retired, but you haven't lost that teacher voice, have you? He's called Seb. And he's also a teacher when he's not working on a lobster boat."

"What's he doing for the Fourth?"

Marcus didn't think Seb was doing anything except chilling. "Why do you ask?"

"Well, I thought you might like to invite him to join us for dinner on Saturday," she said nonchalantly.

Marcus wasn't fooled. "He's just a friend."

Her eyes widened again. "Did I suggest he was anything *other* than a friend?"

He didn't deign to respond to that. "He might have plans," he protested.

"Then why don't you call him and find out? It's not as if one more mouth to feed would be a hardship." Her eyes sparkled. "I've already decided on dinner for Saturday, thanks to you."

Marcus had a sneaking suspicion he knew

what was coming. "Oh?"

She smiled. "Mackerel, seeing as there's enough to feed a small army—or a house full of Gilberts."

"Seb sent me a recipe for mackerel."

"Excellent. Then if he agrees to join us, he can help *you* cook it." That smile grew sweeter. "Well, you did say I wasn't to lift a finger this weekend, didn't you?"

Damn, she's good.

"Fine, I'll call him."

"Do it now. Strike while the iron's hot."

Marcus shook his head. "And you say *Dad* is stubborn?" He pulled his phone from his jeans pocket and glanced at the time. Seb would be done for the day by now. He hit *Call.* Mom didn't move from the doorway.

"Escaping already? Wow. That was fast."

Marcus laughed. "Hey. My mom would like to invite you to dinner on Saturday, but before you say anything, there's a catch." Mom gave him a mock glare.

"Uh-oh."

"You know all that mackerel we caught, gutted and cleaned? She wants us to cook it."

Silence.

"Seb?"

"That has to be the most unusual invitation I've ever received. Well, almost, but you don't wanna know about that. Okay. Thank your mom, and tell her I'd love to. One thing—just how many people are we cooking for?"

"Including you? Thirteen, two of which are children."

"Good thing I'm not superstitious then. What time Saturday?"

Apparently his voice carried. "Tell him to come over as early as he likes," Mom said. "That's in case he needs to *escape* from something." Her eyes glittered. Then she turned around and walked away.

Aw shit. At seventy, Mom's hearing was as sharp as ever.

"Oops. Did I just drop you in it?"

Marcus chuckled. "Forty-four years old, and she still makes me feel as if I'm just a kid. You sure you want to do this?"

"Hey, I've got nothing else to do, and your mom sounds like she'd be a lot of fun."

It wasn't the first word that sprang to Marcus's mind. "In that case, I'll see you Saturday. And if you call to say you can't make it because a mutant lobster bit off your foot, I'll say bullshit."

Seb laughed. "Damn. I'd better think of another excuse. See ya." He disconnected.

Marcus pocketed his phone, smiling.

Guess who's coming to dinner?

Chapter Eleven

July 3

By Friday afternoon, everyone had arrived. Marcus had been hugged to death, and he was already growing tired of answering question after question about why he wasn't in New York. He knew concern lay at the root of the interrogation: Lisa had asked him more than once if he was okay, and his brother Chris had come out to find him in the summerhouse, ostensibly to inquire whether he had a HDMI cable. Marcus knew better—Chris was checking up on him.

A HDMI cable, for Christ's sake. Chris was the techie of the family. As if he'd turn up unprepared.

Once the logistics of who was sleeping where had been worked out, calm was restored. His cousin Lisa had the luxury of a room all to herself, and his niece Sarah didn't have to share her sofa bed with anyone. Not that the others complained—they were accustomed to family gatherings at the house.

Mom had told them all there'd be a visitor Saturday, and that prompted another round of questions about Seb's age, occupation, and marital status. Jess provided them with more info, and that clearly piqued their interest. *What is it with Gilberts and their all-consuming need to matchmake?* Maybe it was his age. Maybe his family was worried he'd have no one to lean on when he got old and gray. Marcus chuckled to himself. *Already halfway there*. The only one of his siblings and first cousins not to show considerable amounts of gray was Jess, and Marcus suspected that was down to frequent visits to her hairdresser. Jess did *not* intend to go like Mom, who'd been going gray by the time Marcus put in an appearance when she was twenty-six.

"Uncle Marcus!" Sophia dashed into the backyard where he'd gone in search of a little peace. "Will you play Sorry with me and Alex? No one wants to play."

He wasn't her uncle, of course—strictly speaking, she was his first cousin twice removed—but Ashley's nine-year-old daughter and eleven-year-old son referred to him as such. It made life much simpler. Sophia was a bundle of energy who wore everyone out.

I suppose it'll soon be the turn of Mike, Sarah, and Jake to produce the next generation. Except that it was too soon to be thinking about that. They were still in their early-to-mid-twenties, and so far none of them were in a relationship. *That I know about.* Marcus didn't keep tabs on them, relying on his mom or siblings to pass on any news.

Lisa and Ashley were taking care of dinner, Chris was doing God knew what with the TV in the living room, and Dad was snoozing in his big armchair in the den. Mom was getting into some serious weed removal in the front yard, and Sarah was helping. His nephews Jake and Mike had gone for a run down to the wharf, and he suspected Jess was keeping out of everyone's way in the room she shared with Ashley.

Looks like I drew the short straw.

"Sure. How about you and Alex come into the summerhouse? We can play there."

"I'll go get the game." She dashed off again.

Marcus didn't really mind spending time with the kids. At least they weren't going to ask awkward questions. Then he reconsidered.

They're kids. Awkward questions are a given.

Sarah and Ashley cleared the dishes from the table, Lisa went to make coffee, and Dad leaned back in his chair with a contented sigh. "I could get to like this not-doing-anything activity." He seemed more relaxed than he had on arrival. Then he straightened. "Okay. Tonight, I want everyone in the living room at eight o'clock. Including the kids." He rubbed his hands together, smiling gleefully. "Chris and I have a surprise for you."

Jess rolled her eyes. "I am *not* playing charades again. You always come up with movies I've never heard of."

Dad gave her a mock glare. "That's because you watch crap movies." He addressed the rest of the table. "I gave Chris all our summer home movies from years ago, and he's converted them. He's going to hook his laptop up to the TV and we're going to watch them tonight."

Marcus stared at Chris. "You converted his Super 8s? How long did that take?"

Chris sighed heavily. "Don't ask. I thought he had a couple of them. He turned up with a box full."

"Who's on them?" Mike asked Dad.

"Me and your grandmother, your dad, your aunt and uncle, your great aunt Carol, her kids…."

"Hey!" Lisa called from the kitchen. "This *kid* is fifty-five."

Dad waved his hand. "Life is too short to be wasting breath using terms like first cousin once removed, okay? Especially when I want to hold onto as much breath as I can. If you're younger than me, you're a kid."

"So were these filmed in the fifties, sixties…?" Jake grinned.

Jess smacked the back of his head. "I wasn't born until 1980, you little shit." Then she winced as Mom fired a glare at her, before inclining her head toward the small table where Sophia and Alex sat.

"Little pitchers?" Mom said, her eyes gleaming.

Mike snorted. "I was seven the first time I said the word shit. Mom handed me a bar of soap— you know, the whole wash-your-mouth-out routine? Then Dad said, 'where do you think he heard it? That would have been *you*, last week.'" He grinned.

Chris coughed. "The things you say nowadays would make your mom's eyes pop out. Good thing she's not around to hear them, right?"

There was a moment of awkward silence. Chris's marriage had only recently hit the rocks, so it still had to be pretty raw.

Dad cleared his throat. "We got plenty of popcorn in the house?"

Marcus laughed. "Not enough for this many.

There are maybe one or two bags in the cabinet."

"Then you're going to Bradbury's to get more," Dad informed him.

He arched his eyebrows. "It's six-forty-five. They close at seven."

"Then you'd better drive," Dad said with a grin. "Your car is blocked in, so you'll need to—"

"We can take mine." Jake got up from the table. "Come on, Uncle Marcus. I'll drive you."

Marcus followed him out of the room and waited while Jake grabbed his car keys from his jacket that hung in the hallway. They hurried out to Jake's car, and he pulled out of the driveway.

"Want to remind me how to get there?" Jake asked with a chuckle.

"Turn right at the end of this road, then follow it to the end. Bradbury's is on Main Street."

Jake sped up the road, and when they reached the store, Marcus left him in the car and dived through the doors. He didn't bother wasting time checking on flavors, just grabbed as many boxes as he could carry, and rushed to pay for them before they finished for the day.

The lady at the cash register smiled as he packed them into a brown paper bag. "They're not all for you, are they?"

Marcus merely grinned. He went out to where Jake sat, his phone in his hands. Marcus got in, and reached over to place the bag on the back seat. "I got multi-pack boxes. That should keep us going. And if anyone wants fancy flavors, they're out of luck. It's butter or nothing."

"Butter works for me," Jake murmured, his eyes locked on the screen.

Marcus was in no hurry to get back to the house. It was the first chance he'd had to be alone with Jake, and mindful of Jess's request, he meant to make the most of it. "You okay, kiddo?"

Jake let out a soft laugh. "You still call me that." He pocketed his phone. "I'm fine."

When he made no move to switch on the engine, Marcus took that as a sign. "Sorry you and Mike drew the short straw and got one of the couches. Mind you, Sarah got the other one."

He shrugged. "It's okay."

Except it didn't *feel* like it was okay. Maybe Jess was right.

Marcus studied him. "Anything you want to talk to me about?"

Jake gave him a puzzled glance. "Like what?

"Oh, I don't know. Maybe you've got something on your mind. Something you can't tell your mom." It was as far as he dared go.

Jake blinked, then gave a hard, obvious swallow. "No. Nothing I can think of."

Marcus wasn't buying it. "I know it's been awhile since I've seen you, but... I get the feeling something is not quite right. You've just finished college. You should be turning handsprings. Or is it a case that you don't know what to do next?"

Jake sagged into the seat. "I've put out a few applications. We'll see what comes of those. And... I've just got a lot going on, okay?"

Marcus looked closely at him. The dark circles under Jake's eyes concerned him. "Didn't you sleep well last night? Did Mike keep you awake wanting to talk? I bet you haven't seen each other for a while." Marcus could remember summers when they were little. The two cousins were almost inseparable every time they got together.

"We didn't talk all that much. We were both tired."

"At least you have someone to go running with."

Jake stared at the side of the store. "Uncle Marcus…"

"Just Marcus, okay?"

His lips twitched. "It makes you feel old, doesn't it?"

Marcus chuckled. "You got that right." He waited, trusting his instincts.

Jake gripped the steering wheel. "You were right. There *was* something I wanted to talk to you about, only…" He swallowed. "Jesus, this is hard."

"Why did you want to talk to me in particular? Is it because you felt I'd understand?"

Jake drew in a deep breath. "Because I thought you of all people wouldn't judge."

"I'm hardly likely to do that, am I? What does your mom call me? 'The rainbow sheep of the family'?" Relief flooded him to hear Jake laugh. "So… what's up?"

Jake didn't look at him. "I know *why* this is so fucking difficult." He froze.

"It's okay. Your mom's said much, *much* worse," Marcus reassured him.

He snorted. "Yeah, why don't I find that hard to believe?" He shivered. "I guess… I'm scared you'll look at me differently, once you know the truth."

Christ.

Marcus fought to repress his own shudder. "I

know exactly how you feel. Not going to say more than that, because I can't right now, but trust me, Jake… I *do* know where you're coming from."

Jake turned his head to meet Marcus's gaze, and his eyes widened. "You do, don't you? I can… sense it somehow." His breathing hitched. "Have you ever been in love?"

Marcus sighed. "I *thought* I was, once. It turned out to be more of a case of being in *lust* with someone."

"I wouldn't know about that." Jake bit his lip. "I'm still a…" Another swallow.

Marcus caught up fast. "Hey, nothing wrong with being a virgin, all right? And don't let anyone rush you into doing something you don't want to do. *You* choose when the time is right, okay?" He cocked his head. "But that's not what this is about, is it?"

Jake shook his head. "I'm in love with… someone, and… oh fuck, it's never gonna work, and that's what torments me."

"Does this someone love you?" Marcus was careful to avoid pronouns.

"I haven't dared ask. Too scared." He put his head against the rest and closed his eyes. "What if… what if I tell them how I feel, and…"

Marcus's throat tightened. Whatever was eating away at Jake was plainly much bigger than the fear of coming out, and Marcus felt so fucking *useless*.

He took a couple of deep breaths. "Look… I don't know what it is you feel you can't tell me, but… If you ever want to talk, call me." He removed his wallet from his pocket and handed Jake one of his business cards. "My cell number's on here. Anytime, okay? And Jake." He cupped Jake's chin, holding his head still. "I will never judge you. There is *nothing* you can tell me that will make me love you less, or think differently about you."

Jake's eyes glistened. "Thank you," he whispered. Then he shivered. "I think we'd better get back, before Granddad sends out a search party."

Marcus got the message. *Talk over.* "Come on then. Let's go watch movies of me, your mom, and your uncle Chris when we were kids."

Jake switched on the engine. "Do they have subtitles? Because movies with sound weren't around then, were they?" He smirked.

"Just for that, you don't get popcorn. And you *definitely* don't get one of my beers."

"Aw," Jake wailed as he turned onto Main Street.

"Yup, that's me. Mean ol' Guncle Marcus."

It took Jake a second to react, but then he laughed. "Fuck, that's even better than rainbow sheep of the family." They headed for the house.

Marcus fell silent, his mind on Jake.

I wish I could help. What could be so bad that he couldn't share it? It couldn't be worse than what lay so heavily on Marcus's heart.

Oh God, he hoped not.

Chapter Twelve

July 4

Seb took one look at the house and was glad he'd left the car at home. The driveway was full of vehicles, every inch of space taken. He was disconcerted to find his mouth was dry, and there was a fluttery feeling in his stomach.

What have I got to be nervous about? Just gonna meet a houseful of Marcus's relatives, that's all. Why should it matter? He'd never meet any of these people ever again. At least he already knew Jess, so there'd be one friendly face. He hoped Marcus had explained the situation, because if she tried her hand at matchmaking again, things were likely to get real awkward.

He marched up to the door but as he drew close, it opened. A woman with short wavy gray hair, and blue eyes reminiscent of Marcus's stood there. "You must be Seb." Her pale blue top and the glass beads around her neck picked out the color of her eyes.

"Mrs. Gilbert?"

"Call me Sandra." He held out the sturdy bag to her, and she glanced inside at the two bottles of wine. "Oh, how kind of you." She took it with a smile. "Come in." He crossed the threshold and was immediately hit by the sound of laughter. "Happy Fourth of July."

"Happy Fourth to you."

"You just missed lunch." She gestured toward the living room. "It's a madhouse in here." She rolled her eyes. "My great grand niece and nephew found Twister in a closet, and somehow persuaded us it would be a good idea to play it."

Seb blinked. "They got *you* playing Twister?" He couldn't picture it. Sandra *oozed* dignity.

She laughed. "No, just some of the more flexible among us. Which includes Marcus, although I think he's regretting it now."

Seb *had* to see this.

He followed her to the living room and paused in the doorway. The couches and chairs had been pushed back to the outside of the room, and the Twister sheet was in the center. Two little kids sat on the floor next to it with the spinner. Seb tried to gauge how many adults were actually playing. It was a sea of tangled arms and legs, but there appeared to be five grownups.

Then he saw Marcus, and grinned. "You having fun?" Marcus looked kind of precarious.

He also looked hot, which was *not* fair. The dark blue buttoned shirt was a tight fit, and the short sleeves clung to his muscular upper arms, just like those black jeans clung to his thighs. Marcus's feet were bare, and why this should have sent a shiver of desire through him, Seb had no idea.

So, so *not fair.*

Marcus rolled his eyes. "Did you ever see *Bill and Ted's Bogus Journey*?"

"Yeah, when I was a kid."

"Remember the scene where they challenge Death to a game of Twister? That's about to be me any second now." He glanced at the rest of the people contorted on the sheet. "For God's sake, nobody fart, okay?" Raucous laughter rang out. One of the players glared at him.

"Aren't there supposed to be two teams of two people?" Seb commented. "You've got one too many bodies on there."

"Hey, did no one actually read the rules?" A guy who was probably about Seb's age carefully disentangled himself, straightened and backed away, his hands held up. "I'm out then. I couldn't hold that position a second longer anyway."

"Uncle Marcus, it's your turn." The little girl spun the dial. "Right hand yellow," she called out. Marcus bowed his head and peered at the remaining circles.

"Come on, Uncle Marcus, you can do it," Seb shouted encouragingly.

Marcus jerked his head in Seb's direction, his gaze narrowed. A second later, he collapsed with a yelp, taking everybody else with him and creating an undignified heap on the floor.

"Aw, Marcus." That came from another young guy. "We could have won that."

Marcus pointed at Seb. "Blame him. He distracted me."

Seb gaped at him. "Yeah, right. You did that on purpose."

"Now we have to start again," the little girl said in a plaintive voice.

There was a chorus of "No!" and Seb burst out laughing.

Marcus got up off the floor and walked over to him. "Hey." He leaned in and whispered, "Great timing." Then he straightened. "I'd better do the introductions. You'll need to take notes because this gets complicated." By now the adults had retreated to the couches, chairs, and various floor cushions. "Everyone, this is Seb."

A chorus of "Hi, Seb," filled the air, and he raised his hand.

"You've met my mom." Marcus pointed toward the window. "That distinguished-looking gentleman over there is my dad."

The white-haired guy waved at him. "Hi Seb. I'm James. Thanks for joining us today."

"Thank you for the invitation."

"And the handsome guy sitting next to him with the glasses? That's my brother Chris. The gorgeous young lady sitting at his feet is my niece Sarah, and next to her is my nephew Mike." One by one they nodded at Seb. Marcus pointed to the other side of the room, to a lady with white short, cropped hair. "This is my first cousin Lisa, next to her is her daughter Ashley, and next to Ashley is my other nephew, Jake. The two little Tasmanian devils are Sophia and Alex, Ashley's kids."

Sophia giggled.

"And you already know me," came a voice from behind him.

Seb whirled around and smiled when he saw Jess. "Hey." He held out his hand, but Jess ignored it and pulled him into a hug.

"I've made punch," Sandra said, beside him. "Would you like some?"

Seb glanced at Marcus. "How lethal is it?" he asked in a stage whisper. That got a chuckle from the adults.

Marcus grinned. "Put it this way. After two glasses, I agreed to play Twister."

Seb rubbed his hands together. "I'm in. Bring it on." Sandra laughed and headed for the kitchen.

Alex tugged on Seb's jacket sleeve. "Are you the lobster man?"

That was cute. "I guess so." Alex had hair exactly likes Seb's had been at that age, long, wavy and unruly.

"He's here to help me make tonight's dinner," Marcus told Alex. "Seeing as he helped me catch it."

"But you'll stick around for the fireworks, won't you?" James asked.

"Mike brought fireworks," Marcus explained. "Pyrotechnics must be in the genes, because his dad used to do the same thing years ago. It's sort of a Gilbert family tradition." He gave Seb an earnest glance. "Can you stay?"

"It's not like I have to be up at dawn Sunday, right? So yeah, I'd like that. I love fireworks."

"Great." Sandra handed him a glass.

Seb took a sip. "Wow." He glanced hastily at Sandra. "A good wow. What have you got in this?" It tasted as if there was a *lot* of booze.

Marcus laughed. "She won't tell. It's a secret recipe."

"And it'll stay that way," Sandra added. "You'll get it when I'm gone—*if* I don't decide to take it with me to my coffin. I'm not sure the world is ready for the Gilbert."

Marcus sighed. "Yeah, she named it too." He inclined his head toward the kitchen. "I got all the ingredients on that list you sent. We're in charge of the fish, Ashley volunteered to do the vegetables, and it's ice cream for dessert."

"I want to play twister again," Alex demanded. He tugged on Marcus's T-shirt. "Will you play, Uncle Marcus?"

"Only if Seb does," Marcus replied, his eyes glinting.

"Yeah, he looks like he'd be really... flexible." There was an equally mischievous glint in Jess's eyes. Marcus fired her what had to be a warning glance, but Jess grinned at him.

"You don't have to play," Sandra said in a firm voice. "Don't let them bully you into it. You're a guest."

"I don't mind. I haven't played this in years." Seb took off his jacket, kicked off his shoes, and walked over to the sheet. "Who's spinning?"

"Me," Sophia piped up. "There's a competition too."

He frowned. "What kind of competition?"

"I heard my mom talking about it," Sophia confided. "She said Uncle Marcus was gonna get the prize for the most swear words."

Seb couldn't hold back his smile. "Oh really?" *Out of the mouths of babes.*

This promised to be a lot of fun.

Ten minutes later, he and Marcus were entangled on the sheet, and Seb was doing his best to keep his feet and hands in the circles. He was close enough that he could smell Marcus, that same scent he recalled from the last time he'd been in the house.

It had given him a hard-on last time too.

"Seb?" He jerked his head to look at Sophia, and she spun. "Left hand blue."

Seb shifted his hand, to find himself with his arms behind him, his knees bent, feet apart, his butt hovering over the sheet. Marcus had his hands on either side of Seb's waist. One false move, and he'd pin Seb to the sheet.

"I think I saw this on *Sex and the City*, season two," Jess commented, her eyes twinkling. She bit her lip. "Can I point out this game isn't *supposed* to be R-rated?"

Marcus's lips were inches from Seb's. "The last time I was this close to someone?" he whispered. "There were no clothes involved."

"You're not allowed to say things like that," Seb ground out, keeping his voice quiet. "Not when I'm wearing my tight jeans." Besides that, it wasn't fair. Marcus couldn't say *back off* one minute and then tease him the next.

"Uncle Marcus. Right hand blue."

Marcus peered at the circles. "I can do that."

Seb wasn't so sure. "Only if you're a contortionist."

"No, really, I can do it." He shifted his hand, gravity took over, and he collapsed on top of Seb, both of them laughing.

"Hey kids," Ashley called out in a bright voice. "Let's go into the back yard and play ball. It's too nice to be indoors."

"But we're *playing*," Sophia wailed.

"Yeah, well, I think we've played enough." Ashley glanced at Seb, her eyebrows arched.

Seb pushed Marcus off him and gaped at her. "Hey, don't look at me." Marcus got up off the floor and held out a hand to Seb. He hoisted Seb to his feet.

"So, Seb." Chris's eyes sparkled. *"How* long have you known my brother?"

"Three weeks tomorrow," Seb replied promptly. When Marcus's eyes widened, he grinned. "What can I say? Some people are memorable." Jess handed him his glass of punch, and he raised it. "Happy Fourth of July, everyone. I'll do my best not to poison you all this evening with my cooking." That brought on more laughter.

Jess launched herself across the room into the space on the couch vacated by Ashley. "Sit here, Seb." She patted the seat cushion.

Seb glanced at Marcus and whispered loudly, "Help me." Everyone laughed.

"And if Jake moves onto a floor cushion, Marcus can squeeze in next to Seb," she added. Jake was off the couch and onto a cushion in a heartbeat, grinning.

Seb gave Jess a hard stare. "Stop it."

"Stop what?" she asked, her eyes wide.

"You *know* what," Marcus said, inserting himself into the space between Seb and the arm of the couch. Lisa got up and headed for the kitchen, not bothering to hide her smile.

Sandra sat on the arm of James's chair. "Marcus says you're a teacher, Seb."

He nodded. "At Wells Jr High along the coast. I was a student there."

"So you grew up in Maine?" Chris asked.

At his feet, Sarah rolled her eyes. "No, Dad. He grew up in New Hampshire and came in by bus every day."

Sandra cleared her throat. "You'll have to forgive my granddaughter. She's doing a Masters in

Sarcasm."

Seb loved the banter. Being around the Gilberts was turning out to be an unexpected joy, and he couldn't think of a better way to spend the Fourth, unless it was with his friends. He wondered what they were all doing, and his chest grew tight. With the exception of Levi, he hadn't been in touch with any of them since Grammy's party.

Why would I call them? To tell them how much lobster we brought in? That'd make for great conversation. Besides, calling them would only remind him that they couldn't get together, and that would sour his mood. He took another drink from his glass, enjoying the warmth that spread through him.

Marcus's thigh touched his, but given the close proximity, it was hardly surprising. Jess hadn't shifted along the couch, despite Lisa creating more room, and Seb saw the move for what it was. Marcus hadn't told her to budge up either.

What the fuck is going on here?

"Was there any mackerel left?" Dad inquired, his legs stretched out on his recliner. "I'm keeping my fingers crossed for leftovers tomorrow." Dinner was over, and everyone had gone into the living room to wait until the skies were dark enough for the display. Mike and Jake sat on the floor, sorting through the huge box of fireworks and discussing which ones they'd set off first. Through the open window came the sound of music as Cape Porpoise celebrated the Fourth.

Marcus grinned. "You liked it." Seb had been right: it was a simple but delicious dish.

Dad arched his eyebrows. "*Liked* it?" He peered at Seb. "Can you give Sandra the recipe? I'm not usually a big mackerel eater, but that was tasty."

Seb beamed. "Grammy has another recipe too, where you dip the fish in cornmeal, and then fry it in bacon fat."

Across from them, Chris groaned. "Oh my God, I want it for breakfast. Is there any mackerel left for tomorrow morning? We *have* to try that."

Laughter rippled around the room. Marcus leaned into Seb. "You did well."

Seb chuckled. "*We* did well. It was a joint effort."

Mike got up. "Jake and I will go set things up outside. We'll call you when we're ready." Then they headed out of the French doors.

"Is it difficult to catch a lobster?" Ashley asked. She shuddered. "Those claws give me the shivers."

Sarah snorted. "I notice you didn't say that last year when we had lobster. In fact, you ate more than—"

"Okay, okay, don't remind me. And I was comfort-eating, all right? Rick had just left me for that... that..." She huffed out a breath. "Do you know what you're letting yourself in for, Seb, getting involved with a Gilbert? There's a curse, you know."

Marcus froze. *What the fuck?*

Seb cleared his throat. "Okay. If you mean

the Gilbert curse, yes, I know all about it. Only...
I'm not exactly involved with Marcus."

"But he'd *like* to be," Jess whispered to
Marcus. Seb jerked his head so fast to stare at her,
Marcus swore he'd have whiplash.

Then Seb relaxed. "Is matchmaking a Gilbert
trait?" His lips twitched.

Dad laughed. "I think you've nailed it, Seb.
We can't help ourselves. I was just the same, when
my sister Carol met her husband John. She was
seventeen. The first time she brought him home, I
was the annoying little twelve-year-old brother who
asked if they were going to get married. John didn't
know where to look."

Jake poked his head around the French door.
"Fireworks, anyone?"

And that was the end of *that* conversation.

Everyone got up and filed through the doors
into the backyard. Marcus could already hear
fireworks in the distance. It wasn't long before the
first rockets *whooshed* into the night sky, and
starbursts of color erupted from them high above
their heads. Jake set off more fireworks, and soon the
air was filled with *bangs* and *cracks,* a riotous display of
color and sound that took Marcus back to his
childhood.

Seb leaned in, his mouth close to Marcus's
ear. "You're a very lucky man. You have an awesome
family."

"Even when they make assumptions?" He
still couldn't believe Ashley had said that.

Seb smiled. "They love you, that's obvious.
They're only looking out for you." He stared up at
the sky, the bursts from the fireworks reflecting on

his face, lighting him in red and green and gold.

Marcus gazed at him, his mind turning an idea. He knew his opportunities to write would be curtailed for the rest of the month. Unless he took steps to physically remove himself from the house, work would be next-to-impossible, a constant stream of interruptions.

So much for avoiding distractions. And taking all *that* into account… why the fuck was he concerned about any distraction *Seb* would provide?

I'm looking at this all wrong, aren't I?

Except Marcus knew there was more to pushing Seb away than avoiding distractions. There was a whole lot of fear wrapped around that prospect, and Marcus wasn't sure he was ready to confront it.

It's just sex, right? No stress, just two guys enjoying each other.

Maybe it *was* time.

Then he reconsidered. *That's making a rather large assumption, isn't it? I told Seb I wasn't interested. I told him to back off. He did. So how is he going to feel if I suddenly turn around and say 'hey, I've changed my mind'?*

There was only one way to find out.

He needed to be honest with Seb—and be prepared for a letdown.

"Marcus?"

He blinked. Seb was staring at him. "Did you say something?"

Seb grinned. "Where did you zone out to? You missed the end of the fireworks." The rest of the family was going back inside.

No time like the present.

"I was thinking about you, actually."

Seb lifted his eyebrows. "Oh? And what were you thinking?"

"I was toying with the idea of giving you a ride back to your place."

Seb smiled. "You don't need to do that. I can find my own way home. I'm a big boy."

Marcus swallowed. "And what if I want to discover just how big a boy you are?"

For a moment Seb didn't move. "But you said—"

"I said I wasn't saying never, remember?"

"And what about me being a distraction? You needing a friend?"

Marcus glanced toward the house, ensuring they were out of earshot. "Are you *really* trying to talk me out of wanting to fuck you all night long?"

Seb's pupils enlarged, and his breathing hitched. "Jesus."

Marcus moved closer. "Because we can make that happen," he said softly. "Just say the word."

"Your family—"

"—won't worry if I stay the night at your place." He grinned. "I'm a big boy too."

Seb's eyes gleamed. "Prove it."

Chapter Thirteen

"What did you say to Jess?" Seb asked as he opened the front door. "Apart from asking her to help you move about three cars so you could get yours out. We *could've* walked here, y'know."

Marcus speared him with a look. "Spend time walking, or get here quicker—which option would *you* have gone for?"

Seb bit his lip as he switched on the light. "Good point."

"And I told her to make sure Dad didn't lock the side gate, so I can go around the house to the summerhouse where I'm sleeping. Oh, and not to wait up for me." He had plans for Seb's ass that could take all night to come to fruition.

Seb came to a dead stop. "Hey, wait a sec. You can't be sleeping there if we're fucking all night. Unless that was just a ruse to get me out of there."

Marcus was too keyed up to waste breath talking. When Seb closed the door, Marcus spun him around and shoved him against it. Teeth, lips and tongues clashed as Seb responded to his kiss with a hunger that matched his own. It was brutal, almost primal, and promised so much.

"About fucking time," Seb muttered, before grabbing Marcus's head and opening for him, their tongues in play as Seb rocked against Marcus's body.

Marcus broke the kiss. "Hey, at least I waited till you closed the door."

"As if anyone would be looking." Seb had one hand on his neck, stroking him, while the other rubbed over his chest, his fingers grazing Marcus's nipples through the thin cotton.

Holy fuck. Marcus's need reached white-hot, his arousal spiraling by the second.

"Fuck, it's been three weeks," Seb murmured between kisses.

Marcus nuzzled Seb's neck, loving the shudders that coursed through him. "Does that count as a long break for you?" *God, he smells good.*

"Fuck yeah. Longest I ever go without is a week."

Marcus claimed Seb's mouth again with another ravenous kiss. "Try three months." He reached behind Seb, slid his hands lower, and squeezed the tight ass he'd been fantasizing about. "This is mine tonight."

Then he caught his breath as Seb insinuated his hand into the back of Marcus's jeans and nudged a finger through his crack. "Does the same apply to me?"

Marcus couldn't be *that* lucky. "Are you vers?" When Seb merely grinned, Marcus raised his eyes heavenward. "Hallefuckinlujah." Then it was back to kissing, only now he slid his hands under Seb's tee, encountering warm, smooth skin, and Seb got busy with the buttons on Marcus's shirt. Seb leaned in to kiss his bared chest, and when he teased Marcus's nipple with his tongue, it was one sensation too many.

"Okay, where's the bedroom?"

"Don't you want the guided tour?" Seb batted his lashes.

"Bed," Marcus ground out. His dick was so hard, he could've cut glass with it.

Seb dragged him across the room to a door. He flung it open and Marcus propelled him toward the bed. When Seb's legs backed up against it, Marcus stopped. "Okay. Serious stuff time." His heart was hammering, and the thought of getting Seb naked consumed him, but this was important.

Seb looked him in the eye. "My last test was the day before I met you. All clear."

"Mine was back in April, before I left New York. All clear too."

"And I'm on PrEP. So are you," Seb commented.

"How do you—"

"I saw it in your bathroom cabinet." When Marcus arched his eyebrows, Seb mimicked him. "Oh, come on. You've *never* been in someone's house and peeked in the cabinet? Or been in a guy's bedroom and not been tempted to look in the nightstand drawer?"

Marcus stilled. "You should be careful. You might find something you don't expect."

"You know what *you're* gonna find when you get these jeans off of me?" Seb's eyes gleamed. "My hole, waiting for you to fill it."

Marcus laughed. "Yeah, you don't do subtle at *all*. So I'm topping?"

"After three months, I'd say your need is greatest. And being subtle isn't gonna get my ass pounded." His eyes met Marcus's. "We're good to go bare? Because I trust you." Marcus nodded, and Seb's face lit up. "Then fuck me."

Marcus shoved him backward onto the bed, then covered him with his body, grinding his hard shaft against Seb's equally solid dick as they kissed. It would have been funny, the pair of them rolling on the sheets as they tried to combine kissing and undressing, but neither of them was apparently in a laughing mood. The air was charged with a sexual electricity that made the hairs on Marcus's arms stand on end. Their mingled staccato breaths only served to ramp up the intensity, and by the time they were both naked, Marcus's need had never been greater.

Seb lurched toward the nightstand where a bottle of lube sat, grabbed it, dropped it onto the comforter, then straddled Marcus's hips. *Fuck, the heat of him...* Marcus stroked Seb's ass cheeks, and Seb bent over to kiss him. Marcus cupped his nape and deepened the kiss as Seb rocked back and forth, his hot bare dick sliding against Marcus's.

"So you didn't lie," Marcus murmured, breaking their kiss.

"Hmm?" Seb's hands were on his neck and shoulders, gentle as a whisper.

Marcus wrapped his hand around Seb's dick and gave it a leisurely tug. "You *are* a big boy." It was a long, cut cock, widest at the base, and nicely tapered at the head.

Seb laughed. "Yeah, but look what *you* have to play with." He reached behind him to free Marcus's dick, and slapped it against his hole. He rocked, letting it slide through his crease. "I don't know whether to suck it, or have a sword fight."

Marcus's breathing hitched. "Suck it, baby."

It had been way too long since he'd felt a warm, wet mouth on his shaft.

Seb grinned. "Whatever you want."

Whatever else Marcus had been about to say was lost when Seb tugged him to lie diagonally across the bed, his legs wide on either side of the corner, before shifting lower, his fingers holding Marcus's cock steady. Seb locked gazes with him as he licked up Marcus's length.

Marcus groaned and lowered his head to the bed. "Fuck. Oh yeah." Seb's slow, sensuous glides up and down his shaft sent shivers through him. It was no good. He had to see. He propped himself up on his elbow and placed his hand lightly on Seb's head.

It seemed that was all the encouragement Seb required. He sped up his movements, pausing to suck on Marcus's balls and drag a moan from his lips. Then it was back to sucking his dick again, only now he swallowed it to the root.

"Oh fuck." Marcus kept his hand on Seb's head and thrust up, pumping into Seb's mouth, his hips bucking. Seb slowed, tugged on Marcus's balls, and with each upward glide of his tongue on Marcus's shaft, Seb looked into his eyes.

That was so hot, it was a wonder Marcus didn't spontaneously combust.

Seb rested his arms on Marcus's thighs and got into serious bobbing mode, the heat and wetness driving Marcus toward the edge. "Fuck, you're good at that."

Seb was off his cock long enough to grin. "It was my major in college."

Marcus could believe that. "Give me that dick," he croaked.

Seb was off the floor in a heartbeat, and they lay on their sides, each cradling the other's ass as they sucked and licked. Seb tugged on Marcus's balls as he took him deep, and Marcus groaned around Seb's fat cock. He felt for the bottle of lube, slicked up a couple of fingers, and slid them into Seb's tight pucker.

"Oh yeah, fuck me."

"As you wish." Marcus sucked on that gorgeous dick as he fingered Seb's hot little hole, loving the way Seb's body sucked him in. "I want to fuck you so bad."

Seb writhed on his fingers, moaning around Marcus's shaft. When Marcus added a third finger, Seb pulled free of his cock with a shiver. "Want you in me."

Marcus couldn't wait a second longer.

"Stand up." Seb scrambled off the bed, and Marcus grabbed his thigh. "Foot on the corner," he demanded as he slicked up his dick. When he had Seb where he wanted him, Marcus wrapped his arm around Seb's chest, aimed his cock at that enticing hole, and plunged right in. Then with both arms enveloping Seb to anchor himself, he kissed Seb's neck as he drove his dick home, slamming into Seb's body.

"Yeah, fuck me, Daddy," Seb moaned.

Marcus's hips snapped forward as he settled into a rhythm, each thrust punctuated by the slap of flesh against flesh as he nuzzled into Seb's neck. "You like being fucked by Daddy?" He wasn't into Daddy/boy scenes, but some instinct told him Seb wasn't either. Seb *was* into older guys, however, and if he got off on it, Marcus would play along.

The tightness around his shaft increased, and Marcus grinned. "Oh yeah, you *do* like it." Then Seb did it again, and Marcus groaned. "Jesus, when you do that, I can't think straight."

"Then don't think—fuck."

Marcus finally saw the light. Here was a gorgeous man with an appetite for sex that matched his own. He wanted it hard, he wanted it rough—and Marcus was just the man to deliver.

He withdrew virtually all the way out, then slammed into Seb's ass. "Like that?"

"Christ, yeah."

Marcus tightened his grip on Seb's body and rocked his hips back and forth, and with each forward motion the impact rippled through Seb's ass cheeks. Then he slowed, and Seb cried out, "God, don't stop." He stretched back, slipped his arm around Marcus's neck, wound his fingers through Marcus's hair as if to keep him in place, then turned his face toward him.

It was a plea to be kissed, and one Marcus couldn't ignore.

They kissed while Marcus pumped his hips, his body slamming against Seb's ass, one hand on Seb's throat, the other on his nape. "Is this how you like it?"

"Fuck yeah."

He slowed, filling Seb's hole with long, leisurely strokes of his dick, Seb's moans increasing. Then it was back to pounding his ass. The mirror on the closet door afforded the perfect view of Seb's rock-hard cock, bobbing stiffly with each thrust. A shudder ran through Seb and Marcus propelled him down to the mattress on his hands and knees. "I need to get deeper."

Seb's only response was a mumbled "Oh fuck," as he tilted his ass higher.

Marcus straddled him, one knee on the bed, the other leg bent with his foot flat on the mattress, aimed his cock, and drove it all the way home.

Not deep enough.

He crouched over Seb, his arms braced, his weight on his hands, both feet planted firmly on the bed. Then he mounted him, plunging his cock into Seb's loosened hole. Again and again he fucked into him with long, deep strokes, bowing his head now and then to meet Seb's upturned face to exchange kiss after kiss.

"Don't stop," Seb pleaded. "Feels so good."

Marcus took his mouth in a brutal kiss. "Time for you to do some of the work." He withdrew his shaft and lay down. "Face the other way and ride it. I want to watch your ass swallow up my cock."

Seb spun around and sat astride him, guiding Marcus's dick to his hole. He sank all the way down onto it, then let his arms take his weight, his feet on the mattress as he bounced on Marcus's cock. "Oh, that's it, fuck yourself on it," Marcus moaned. Sweat coated his chest already, and there was a fine sheen of perspiration on Seb's back. The muscles in Seb's arms flexed as he rode Marcus's dick faster and faster, a soft cry punching the air each time he impaled himself on it. The slick sound of his cock sliding in and out only added to the heat.

It was mesmerizing, watching his glistening shaft slide into Seb's hole, but it wasn't perfect. Then Marcus realized what was lacking.

He eased his dick out of Seb. "On your back, baby, and grab your knees."

Seb dropped onto the bed and drew his knees up to his chest. Marcus knelt at his ass and speared his cock into that welcoming hole. Then he leaned over to kiss Seb, his hips pumping. Seb looped his arms around Marcus's neck and drew him close, both feeding each other gasps and grunts as Marcus fucked him, not holding back.

Seb placed his feet on Marcus's chest, his eyes widening when Marcus sucked on his toes. "Fuck, that feels amazing." Marcus picked up the pace, his body smacking into Seb's ass with each thrust. Then he dropped to the bed beside Seb, lifted his leg high into the air, and drove into him once more. He slid one arm under Seb's neck, holding Seb's leg captive against his chest with the other as he alternated between quick, short thrusts and long, slow glides into him while they kissed.

"Fuck," Seb gasped. Marcus's dick slid out of him. "Put it back." Marcus filled him to the hilt, and Seb cried out, "Yeah, fuck me."

"Like that?" Marcus plunged his cock deep.

"Yes!"

He withdrew almost all the way out, then thrust back in, hard. "Like that?"

"Yes!" Seb reached for his own dick and tugged.

Marcus slowed, cradling Seb in his arms, changing the pace from frenetic to sensual. Their kisses were unhurried and exploratory, as if they were only now discovering each other. Seb seemed in no hurry to reach the finish line, and that was fine by Marcus. He rocked gently in and out of Seb's body, stroking and caressing him.

Seb gazed into his eyes. "We went from Fingerville to Poundtown, but I'm really enjoying this diversion."

Marcus leaned in and kissed him. "I think we've just come to the end of the detour. Ready for more?"

Seb's eyes sparkled. "How do you want me?"

"Ride me again? Only, face me this time." Marcus cupped his cheek. "I like seeing your face while I fuck you."

Seb shifted to straddle him, and Marcus guided his cock back to where it belonged. Seb sank all the way down, then leaned back on his arms, his legs bent, and began to ride. He rocked his hips, his dick slapping stiffly against his belly.

"Something else I like doing while I fuck you," Marcus announced.

"What's that?"

"Kissing you. Come here."

Seb knelt astride him and leaned over to kiss him, and when their lips met, Marcus thrust up into Seb's warmth, his hands on Seb's ass. "This my hole?"

"Yours," Seb confirmed, his breathing becoming shallow as their bodies slapped together.

"You make me so fucking hard," Marcus said with a groan.

Seb cradled his head and they kissed, a deep, lingering kiss that sent heat flooding through him. Marcus jackhammered Seb's hole, his tongue exploring Seb's mouth while he lifted him up and down, his hands on Seb's ass, helping him bounce on Marcus's shaft before going so fucking deep inside him.

Seb stared into his eyes as they fucked, and Marcus couldn't look away. "You feel so good," he whispered. "You are so fucking sexy when you moan." He claimed another kiss, his dick driving into Seb faster and faster, both of them moaning.

"Getting close," Seb cried out.

Marcus freed his shaft and gently nudged Seb onto his back once more. "Me too." He grabbed Seb's feet and drew them up to his chest. "I liked it when you did this." He applied a bit more lube, gripped Seb's knees to anchor himself, then slid into Seb's body as though he fucking belonged there. He paused to lean down and kiss Seb, then it was back to sheathing his cock in Seb's warm channel. Seb's hand was a blur on his shaft, and Marcus quickened the pace, spearing into him with short, quick thrusts, his hips rolling as he drove them both closer to their goal.

"Gonna come," he moaned.

Seb reached for him, his long legs capturing Marcus, his arms locked around Marcus's neck. "Come in me, come in me," he whispered, his eyes wide, his chest and face flushed.

Marcus buried his dick in Seb's ass and shot hard. Seb kissed him and held him as Marcus pulsed into him, shaking with each jolt of pleasure. When he was done, Seb curled his fingers around his own dick and tugged, once, twice, three times, before spurting warmth onto his belly. Marcus slid his hands over Seb's chest in a gentle motion, and when Seb was done, he carefully eased his spent shaft from Seb's body and lay on his back beside him, sighing.

Seb rolled onto his side and propped himself

up on his elbow. "Have I worn you out already?"

Marcus laughed. "I've got how many years on you? Eighteen? Allow me more than thirty seconds of recuperation, if you please."

"I think I need to warn you." Seb ran a finger through Marcus's damp chest hair. "You might run out of cum before I run out of energy."

"Then maybe I need to warn *you*." Marcus cupped Seb's bearded chin. "You won't be getting much sleep tonight. I've got three months of catching up to do."

Seb's eyes sparkled. "Bring it on." Then he let out a contented sigh. "This has to be the best Fourth ever. Two lots of fireworks…"

"Two?"

He grinned. "Yeah. The ones your nephews set off—and the ones *you* set off when you plowed my ass. Not to mention the stars I saw when I came." Seb teased Marcus's nipple with his thumb and forefinger. "Think you can do it again?"

The way Marcus's dick was already jerking, he thought that highly likely.

Chapter Fourteen

July 5

Seb stirred, surfacing through several warm, cozy layers to emerge from a restful sleep. The room was still in semi-darkness. It took him a moment to realize something was different. Then he became aware of the arm laid across his waist, the hand pressed to his chest, and the warm breath that stirred his neck.

I could get to like this.

Marcus was curled around him, his breathing even and deep. Seb lay in his arms, enjoying that delicious, sated feeling he always got after really good sex. Not that he usually got to enjoy it for long. His hookups were brief, and if he stayed a night with a guy, he was out of there as fast as he could the next morning, because more often than not, that was how the other guy wanted it. But this was bliss. Nothing to get up for. No work. And the prospect of more to come.

That last thought prompted his hole to tighten, bringing back memories of Marcus taking him again and again, until they'd both declared themselves exhausted. Even the prospect of waking Marcus for a morning ride gave him a moment's pause.

I might wait a bit. Say, an hour or so?

Marcus stirred, stroking Seb's belly. "Morning," he murmured. He trailed his fingers lower, until they reached Seb's already stiff dick. "Christ, are you always hard?"

Seb gave a soft chuckle. "What can I say? I'm twenty-six. My powers of recovery are phenomenal." There was something he'd been meaning to ask as soon as they'd gotten through the front door, but Marcus had derailed him with that kiss. "Can I ask you something?"

"I'm a captive audience. Ask away. Just don't expect coherence. I haven't had my coffee yet."

"What changed your mind?"

"Hmm?"

"I thought I was a distraction."

Marcus's sigh stirred his hair. "Do you know how long my family will be staying in Cape Porpoise? Probably until the end of July. Not *all* of them, mind you, but enough that I can kiss goodbye to peace and quiet and writing time. With the best will in the world, it's just not going to happen. Then I got to thinking. Here I was, pushing you away, and I *really* didn't want to…"

Seb wriggled, snuggling against Marcus's firm body. "I'm glad. My hole feels like it just went ten rounds with a baseball bat, but…"

"Are you sore?"

Seb couldn't miss the note of concern in his voice. He covered Marcus's hand with his own. "It's my own fault. We kissed some more, you got hard again, I got ideas… I could have said no, but it felt so fucking good I didn't want to." A reminder of why he preferred older men—they knew how to use what God gave them to its fullest advantage. And Marcus certainly knew what he was doing. His appreciative noises, grunts and groans painted a picture of a man who enjoyed sex, and a lot of it.

Three months without... Jesus, I'd have been climbing the walls if it were me.

"You want me to make it feel better?" Marcus whispered, his breath tickling Seb's ear.

Seb's breathing caught. *Fuck yeah.* "As long as you're not gonna use your dick to do it."

"Lie face down."

Seb did as he was told, and Marcus disappeared beneath the sheets. A moment later, Seb's cheeks were pulled apart by gentle fingers, and a warm tongue lapped over his hole. "Oh fuck." He shivered. "You can eat my ass all fucking day."

Marcus paused. "Now you know what *I* majored in."

"Feels like you did a masters in it too." He grabbed a pillow and shoved it under his hips, elevating his ass. "Fuck, don't stop." Seb buried his face in his pillow, fisting the sheet beneath him as Marcus loosened him up, his tongue warm, wet and insistent.

Another pause. "I'll stop when you come, how about that?"

Seb raised his head from the pillow long enough to reply. "Deal." Then he had a thought. He turned his head to the side. "Marcus... seeing that your family is going to be around for a while... and I'm here..."

Marcus chuckled. "I think July might turn out to be my favorite month." Then he went right back to blowing Seb's mind again.

Seb woke to sunlight pouring through the window and the smell of freshly brewed coffee. A glance at Gary's old alarm clock on the nightstand revealed it to be eight-thirty, and he smiled to himself. *I must've fallen asleep minutes after I came.* Then Marcus walked into the bedroom naked, carrying two cups. Seb sat up with a grin. "I could get used to this." Then he became aware of the state of the sheet beneath him, and grimaced. "I need to change the bedding." There was not one, but two wet spots, and that was down to both of them.

Marcus arched his eyebrows. "Do you feel the need to change them right now?" He placed the cups on the nightstand, then got into bed next to Seb, stuffing pillows behind him.

"No. They can wait till I've drunk my coffee."

Marcus's eyes gleamed. "Because I think we might get a little more use out of them."

Warmth spread through him in a slow tide. "What did you have in mind?"

"Well, that depends. How does your hole feel?"

Seb flashed him his widest grin. "Empty."

Marcus laughed. "A slow morning fuck it is then."

"Sounds like my kind of morning." Seb reached over Marcus for his cup, Marcus's warm, musky scent permeating his senses. Waking up with the smell of Marcus enveloping him was *all* kinds of sexy. He gave Marcus a speculative glance. "Ready for me to get in that ass of yours?"

Marcus's hesitation was telling. "Can we hold off on that for a day or two?"

Seb blinked. "Something you need to tell me?"

He sipped his coffee. "It's been a while, okay? Most of the guys I hook up with prefer to bottom. I kind of got stuck in the role."

"So when I said I wanted to fuck you…"

Marcus's eyes twinkled. "Yeah, best Fourth of July ever. I've got a butt plug back at the house. I just need a bit of stretching, that's all." He slid his hand down Seb's stomach and wrapped it around Seb's hard shaft. "I can't wait to feel this inside me." Then he stiffened. "Oh God." He released Seb's cock and sagged against the pillows.

"What's wrong?"

His brow furrowed. "I hope the kids don't venture into the summerhouse and start going through my stuff. I have visions of them running into the house, waving my shiny black double dildo and yelling, 'Uncle Marcus has a snake!'"

Seb became very still. "Double dildo?"

Marcus tilted his head to one side. "Have you ever played with one?"

"No, but now that you mention it…" He put on the most serious expression he could muster. "I think you need to bring your toys here, for safekeeping."

Marcus's lips twitched. "Oh you do?" He glanced around the bedroom. "I don't think you've got room here for all my toys."

Seb gaped. "Just how many do you have?" Then he caught the glint in Marcus's eyes. "You're yanking my chain, aren't you?"

Marcus's smile was positively gleeful. "Yup. I brought three butt plugs of varying sizes, a prostate massager, the double dildo, and a more normal-sized one." He gave Seb's cock a gentle squeeze. "Except maybe I need to rethink that. Because I think it's small compared to you."

"Is that why you need a butt plug?"

Marcus nodded. "One glimpse of that… anaconda of yours, and I knew some preparation was in order." He drank his coffee. "What would you like to do with the rest of your Sunday? That's assuming you want to spend some time with me."

The thought of having Marcus around for the rest of the day sent heat radiating through Seb's chest. "That depends on how we will be spending it."

Marcus's phone buzzed on the nightstand. "We'll come back to that thought." He put down his cup, reached for it and peered at the screen. When he sighed heavily, Seb had a feeling whatever plans he'd been making had just gone out of the window.

"Something wrong?"

Marcus tossed the phone onto the bed between them. "Apparently, you are invited to Sunday lunch."

"I am?"

"Mom says I'm not to take no for an answer, and she expects us at twelve. Lunch will be at one." He paused, glancing at Seb. "What do I tell her?"

Seb would have preferred some more alone time with Marcus, but he wasn't greedy. "Look, it's a special weekend. All your family is there, and they want to see you. So it's only right that you spend as much time as you can with them. As for me joining you…" He hesitated.

Marcus stroked his sheet-covered thigh. "What is it you're not saying?"

"It… it feels a little weird, that's all."

"In what way?"

Seb put down his cup and turned toward Marcus, propping his head in his hand. "Okay, for one thing, everyone will know what you and I were doing last night."

"And that bothers you, them knowing we fucked?" Marcus let out a wry chuckle. "You don't strike me as the shy type."

"You're right, I'm not, but I didn't expect to be seeing them again." Seb cocked his head. "Are your parents used to you bringing guys over for Sunday lunch? Or even bringing guys home, period?"

Marcus bit his lip. "You would be the first."

Seb nodded. "And Ashley seems to think we're already an item…"

He widened his eyes. "Ah. You don't want them to get the wrong idea."

Seb decided to go for broke. "I do a lot of hookups. I'm assuming you do too." Marcus nodded, and Seb breathed easier. "Okay. It's just sex, right? But parents don't understand the concept of hookups. Parents have this weird idea sex equates to something more."

"And you think they're going to assume there's more to us than meets the eye."

Seb nodded. "I like your family. I don't want to… mislead them."

"So if I promise to say 'He's just a friend' every time someone makes a comment like Ashley did?"

He gazed into Marcus's cool blue eyes. "You want me to do this, don't you?"

Marcus swallowed, and he ducked his chin. "I love my family too. But for reasons I don't want to go into, I was dreading this weekend. They're good people, but they're also the most inquisitive, persistent bunch. They know I've been at the house for a while, and I've lost count of how many times in the last couple of days they've asked why I'm not in New York."

"And you don't want to tell them," Seb surmised.

"No, I don't."

"And you think my being there will act as some kind of... buffer."

Marcus raised his chin. "It's a selfish reason, I know, but—"

The look on Marcus's face brought a lump to Seb's throat. "Hey, it's okay," he said softly. "I'll come to lunch. And about what you said earlier... If they're going to be around for most of July, then I've got a proposal."

"What kind of proposal?"

Seb smiled. "Remember the last time we met at the store? I told you to think of me as an escape route. So let's work on that. If there's a day when you want to write, or just get away from the family..." He pointed to the living room. "I'll give you the spare key. You'll have power, coffee, snacks, a comfy couch... I'll be gone every day from dawn till noon, so you'll have the place to yourself. If it gets too quiet, there's an ancient stereo system that plays CDs." He grinned. "You might wanna bring those from the house. I have no idea what kinda music Gary listens to, and frankly, I don't *wanna* know."

Marcus's face lit up. "I love this idea. If you're sure I won't be in your way…"

Seb laughed. "Are you kidding? I come home and dive in the shower, and there *you* are, waiting for me."

Marcus's sexy smile sent a trickle of arousal through him. "When you put it like that… And then of course there's your other wonderful idea."

"Which one?"

"Bringing my toys here."

That trickle swelled into a flood of pleasurable tingles and aches. "I'm obviously on a roll. But can we get back to *your* idea?"

Marcus frowned. "Which was what?"

Seb grabbed Marcus's hand and guided it to his dick that tented the sheet. "Getting the sheets real dirty before I wash 'em. I think you said something about a slow morning fuck? We've got a few hours to play with, right?" He shivered as Marcus molded his hand around it and squeezed it.

Marcus slowly pulled the sheet down and Seb's cock sprang up. He curled his hand around the base, his eyes glittering. "So how long do you think you can hold out before I make you come with just my mouth?"

Seb spread his legs wide. "How about we find out?"

Chapter Fifteen

Marcus stood by the window, watching Seb and his dad chatting animatedly while Dad flipped burgers on the grill. Judging by Seb's hand gestures, the topic was lobster hauling, and Dad appeared engrossed by the conversation. The kids were chasing one another in and out of the trees, with Ashley yelling now and then for them not to go too far, and the others sat around on patio chairs or on the low stone walls that surrounded Mom's raised flower beds. Music came from somewhere, and Marcus guessed that had something to do with either Mike or Jake. Mom and Lisa were in the kitchen, putting together the finishing touches to lunch.

It was a grab-what-you-want deal, and the patio table was covered with plates of lobster rolls, bowls of Mom's potato salad and coleslaw, a deep bowl of potato chips, and buns for the burgers and hot dogs. Bottles and jars of ketchup, mustard, mayo, and pickles sat beside the buns, along with yet more bowls containing lettuce, sliced red onions and tomatoes. Marcus had pulled out the canopy to shade everything from the sun. Dad had put out buckets filled with ice and soda bottles, and Jake had observed with a smile, 'What do we need ice for? This is Maine, not Florida.'

Then Dad had shot him down with a

comment about last year, when Jake had gotten sunstroke, and the temperature had climbed into the high nineties. Jake had the grace to flush. Of course, it could also have been the start of this year's sunburn.

It was a perfect summer's day with plenty of sunshine and a warm breeze, and the idyllic scene only heightened Marcus's ebullient mood.

What on earth was I panicking about?

The night—and subsequent morning—with Seb had surpassed his expectations. Marcus's fears had proved groundless, but maybe that was due more to the absence of anxiety. He'd let himself go, carried along on a tide of sensual pleasure that caught both of them in its swell. Seb's appetite mirrored his own, and maybe that too had played a part. Marcus knew what he'd feared most—that the sex would have left him unfulfilled—and when that fear wasn't realized, he'd finally relaxed.

"So he's just a friend, hmm?"

Marcus gave a start. Mom stood beside him, arms folded, peering through the window. "Mom, give a guy some warning, will you?" Then her words sank in. "And yes, he is."

"I like him." Mom stared at Dad and Seb.

"Mom…"

She turned her head toward him, her eyebrows arched. "Don't *Mom* me in that tone of voice. I'm just saying, I like him."

Marcus didn't respond. He had a feeling there was more to come.

"Of course," she continued barely a moment later, "I don't have anyone to compare him to, do I?"

That was a passive-aggressive poke if ever

he'd heard one. "Excuse me?"

"I knew you were seeing someone in New York, ages ago."

"How could you know that?" He hadn't said a word.

"The lines of communication dried up for a while. Your brother was the same whenever he met a new girl. When you didn't mention a name, or bring them to Boston, I figured it wasn't serious." She glanced at him. "It wasn't, was it?"

Apparently there was no getting out of this conversation.

"No, it wasn't. It was good while it lasted, but…" He shrugged. There was a reason Marcus never broached the topic of relationships with his mom—it felt awkward as hell.

"So…"

He steeled himself.

"Are we going to be seeing more of Seb, less of you, or a mixture of both?"

"Is this a comment on me staying out last night? Because if it is? For God's sake, Mom, I'm forty-four years old. So what if I stayed at Seb's?" He pointed to the family members sitting out in the garden. "They're not going to miss me. They didn't come here to see *me*. They came to get away from their regular lives and enjoy the sun and the ocean."

"Like you did," she commented.

Damn. He'd led her right into that one.

"Can't you tell me what happened?" she asked in her soft voice. "Because *something* drove you out of New York to this house. I thought at first you'd had a break-up, but now I'm not so certain." She laid her hand on his shoulder. "Marcus, I may be seventy, but I'm not clueless. I don't think there's anything you could tell me that would shock me."

Marcus wasn't so sure of that.

"What about your job?"

"What about it?"

"Is the company okay with you taking all this time off?"

"I told them I needed to step away from the job for a while, take a few months out, and they were fine with that." Except by now, his boss was probably beginning to wonder if he was coming back. 'A few months' had grown into four, and he knew he needed to think about what happened next.

I'm not ready to go back there.

"And what about your apartment?"

"I sublet it, initially for two months, and now we're playing it month by month." The guys renting it were there until the end of August, but soon it would be crunch time.

"But where's all your stuff?"

"In storage." The important stuff was in boxes in the summerhouse. He'd brought as much as he could squeeze into the car.

"You… you're not in any trouble, are you?"

Marcus couldn't bear to hear the worry in her voice. He enfolded her in a hug. "No, I'm not, I swear," he assured her in a whisper. "I'm just… taking a break, working stuff out, re-evaluating my life…" He released her. "Now, if we don't get out there soon, my nephews, niece, and little monsters will eat all the burgers and hot dogs." It was a lame-ass move, but if it got her away from the subject…

She hit his arm. "They are *not* little monsters. They're sweet little children."

He bit his lip. "That's not what you said a few days ago when they put a frog in your shoe."

Her eyes twinkled. "Which is no worse than what *you* got up to when you were their age."

"Me?" Marcus gave her his most innocent stare.

Mom burst out laughing. "Don't give me that look. It *was* you who taped a plastic cockroach inside my lamp? And it was you who snuck your dad's favorite cookies out of the cabinet, opened them, and replaced the creamy middle part with toothpaste?"

He grinned. "Wow. I was good."

She laughed. "You were incorrigible. I thought the worst was over when you hit your late teens, but then you pranked your dad with that fake audit letter. Sent his blood pressure through the roof." Mom leaned over and kissed his cheek. "But you're right. We should go outside." Her eyes twinkled. "Do I set a place for you at the dinner table this evening?"

He returned the kiss. "We'll play that by ear." Then he opened the French doors and they stepped out into the sunshine. Seb gave him a look that said *Help me*, and Marcus took pity on him.

"Hey, I've got something that might interest you in the summerhouse," he called out.

Ashley coughed violently, and Jake snickered. Chris blinked. "That's an improvement on 'Come up and look at my etchings', I suppose."

Seb smothered his mouth with his hand, and Marcus rolled his eyes. Seb followed him toward the summer house.

"If you pull down the blinds, we'll know what you're up to," Jess said in a stage whisper as they passed her.

"Playing hide and seek?" Sophia's clear voice was loud.

There was a moment of silence before the yard was filled with laughter.

"Out of the mouths of babes," Jess muttered. "Because I'll bet you're just *dying* to play Hide the—"

"Mom!" Jake gaped at her.

Seb erupted into a peal of laughter, and it wasn't long before everyone had joined in, with Sophia gazing at her older relatives in utter confusion.

Marcus opened the door to the compact building with its gable roof and cedar shakes, and windows on all four sides. "My granddad built this in the forties, when my Aunt Carol was a little girl, and Dad wasn't even born." It contained a bed, a table, and a recliner.

"It's cute." Seb glanced at the single bed and smiled. "That's tiny compared to the one in the master bedroom."

"And there's no shower either."

Seb's eyes twinkled. "Have to say, that shower gave me ideas." He took a step toward Marcus. "That bench was just crying out to be—"

"Down boy." Marcus gestured to the windows. "We have an audience, remember?"

"Well, if we're not here so you can—" Seb lowered his voice to a whisper. "Suck me off, what *did* you bring me in here for?"

Marcus pointed to a box at the foot of the bed. "Can you take that back to your place?"

Seb walked over to it, lifting one corner of the cardboard flaps. "Can I peek?"

"No. Save that for later."

He straightened. "Then there's going to be a 'later'?"

Marcus grinned. "Oh Lord, I hope so. I won't stay, though. That's not fair on you. I know you have to get up awful early in the morning."

Seb's eyes shone. "That's sweet." He reached into the back pocket of his jeans. "This is for you, before I forget." He placed a key in Marcus's palm.

"Thank you." Marcus added it to his key ring. "I promise I won't overstay my welcome."

"No, you come whenever you want." Seb gave a wistful glance toward the house.

"What's the matter?"

Seb bit his lip. "There aren't any blinds. Well shit."

Marcus laughed. "Are you perpetually horny? Wait—don't bother answering. I know, you're twenty-six. Stupid question." He inclined his head toward the patio. "How about we go have lunch, we stay a while, then we go back to your place."

"I can feed you tonight."

Marcus laughed. "Trust me, there'll be leftovers from lunch that we can take with us."

"*And* we're back to feeding the five thousand again." Seb's face glowed. "I really like your family."

"That's because so far, you've only had small doses."

Marcus had a feeling he was going to be using Seb's place as sanctuary sooner than he might think.

Seb dug his fingers into the edge of the mattress, his eyes locked on the mirror. Marcus covered Seb's back, powering into him, his gaze focused on Seb's reflection.

"You like my dick in your ass?"

"God, yes." Seb couldn't thrust up with his hips: Marcus had him pinned face down, his knees spreading Seb's thighs, his arm around Seb's chest as he fucked him.

"Jesus, I'm all the way inside you, and it feels amazing."

Seb stared at him. "Feels so fucking good." Then Marcus covered Seb's mouth with his hand, and just like that, they slipped into a higher gear. *Fuck, look at us…* Seb's eyes were huge and dark, his pupils blown.

Marcus drove his shaft into Seb with long strokes, sawing in and out, the bed rocking with each impact. Seb moaned into Marcus's palm as Marcus propelled him relentlessly toward orgasm. Then Marcus bared his teeth, driving into him with powerful thrusts, and Seb exulted to feel the throb inside him. He cried out, Marcus's hand muffling the sound, and Marcus bowed his head to kiss Seb's shoulder as he shuddered.

Then Marcus pulled out, and flipped Seb onto his back. "Your turn. Knees to your shoulders, baby."

Seb drew his knees up, and Marcus hooked his arms under them. He slid his shaft back inside Seb and moved slowly in and out of him. Seb grabbed his cock and tugged on it, his climax within reach. "Kiss me?"

Marcus's lips fused with his, and Seb tugged harder, faster, Marcus's thrusts quickening, his dick connecting with Seb's prostate again and again. And when he came, Seb let go of his cock and locked his arms around Marcus, clinging to him, shaking with each new jolt of electricity until at last Seb lay still beneath him.

He stroked Marcus's cheek. "All I said was, 'Come inside.' I didn't think you'd take it so literally." Not that he was complaining. Lightning fucks that took him by surprise were never a bad thing.

Marcus chuckled. "I thought it was an invitation. It's your own fault. You're impossible to resist."

"I know." Seb preened. "It's my superpower." He kissed Marcus's damp forehead. "And I think we both know what yours is."

Marcus eased out of him and rolled onto his back, his half-hard dick lying against his thigh. "Fuck, I needed that."

Seb stroked his sweat-slick chest. "Oh, *I* see. I'm your stress relief toy."

Marcus raised his head from the bed. "Do you mind?"

He smiled and leaned in to kiss Marcus on the lips. "Not for one second. How do you think I relax after a week of teaching?" Sunday lunch had been fun, but he'd been glad when Marcus had offered to take him home, seeing as he had a box to carry.

Yeah, no one in Marcus's family was fooled by that for a second.

Marcus tugged Seb onto him, parting his legs to give Seb room. "Maybe this is why we get along so well."

"Because we're alike?" Seb had had the same thought.

"Mm-hmm." Marcus pushed Seb's hair back from his eyes. "Although I have to say, when I'm around you, the rest of the world tends to disappear."

"Is that a good thing?"

Marcus's smile was answer enough.

"You know what else I'm good at?" Seb grinned. "Washing backs."

"Is that an invitation to take a shower with you? I accept."

Seb clambered off him and held out his hand. "Wait till you see what I use to clean your cock."

He led Marcus into Gary's small bathroom and even tinier tub, feeling more energized than ever.

July was shaping up to be an awesome month.

Chapter Sixteen

July 9

Marcus sat in the dining room, staring at his laptop screen, and trying to ignore the music pouring out of the living room. Jake and Mike were in there, on their phones, talking, and the TV was on too.

Whoever said men can't multitask was obviously not referring to the younger generation. They're a new breed of men.

After putting up with the cacophony for a further fifteen minutes or so, Marcus admitted defeat. He got up from the table and went into the kitchen.

His mom was sitting at the breakfast bar with Lisa, discussing crocheting and checking out yarn shops on the tablet. Mom gave him a half smile as he passed them, but it was clear her mind was on the conversation.

He went through the back door and out into the yard, heading for the summerhouse. At least there he was guaranteed some solitude. As he strolled toward the far end of the yard where the structure sat in the shade of tall trees, he caught the sound of children's voices, bringing with them the prospect of imminent invasion.

Do I need a No Entry sign?

Once inside, he sat at the table, opened his laptop, and started to read again. It had been several days since he'd even peeked at the manuscript, but a break from it was no bad thing. It made it easier to spot mistakes, paragraphs he wanted to switch around or delete altogether.

Ten minutes later, his peace was shattered as shrieks filled the air. He glanced through the window to where Sophia and Alex were playing a game. He had no idea what the game was, only that it was damn noisy.

Pity Granddad didn't think about soundproofing when he built this place. Marcus stared harder at the laptop screen, as if that would blot out the yells. *They won't be out here all morning, will they? It's nine-thirty, for Christ's sake.*

Then he stiffened. Chris was peering in through the window.

Marcus closed the laptop with a sigh as Chris stuck his head around the door. "Can I come in?"

Marcus regarded him with a straight face. "If I say no, will it stop you?"

Chris laughed and stepped inside, pushing the door to behind him. "Can we talk?" He went to the armchair and sat, extending the foot pad to raise his legs. "God. That's better. Getting old sucks."

Marcus huffed. "You're only forty-eight. Not exactly ancient. And I'm guessing 'Can we talk' was a rhetorical question." He turned his chair to face Chris. "What can I do for you?"

"I was just concerned, that's all. You don't seem your usual self. You've disappeared into here a couple of times over the last few days. Anyone would think you're avoiding us."

Apparently, Chris was more observant that Marcus gave him credit for.

He fixed Chris with a hard stare. "Isn't there some techie website you can go drool over?"

Chris gazed at him in mild surprise. "We used to be able to talk."

"And that was a long time ago. I think the older we got, the more we realized we are nothing alike." At least that had been Marcus's view.

Chris frowned. "Are we that different?"

"Mom used to say I was always in trouble because I took risks when I shouldn't have. You, on the other hand, never got in trouble because you never took risks. Yeah, I'd say we're different. And no, I haven't been avoiding you."

Pants on fire.

Chris laced his fingers. "Maybe that's partly my fault. I haven't been that talkative since we got here."

Marcus had noticed. "Jess said you've had some problems." He held up his hands. "She didn't elaborate, and I figured they couldn't have been all *that* huge because you hadn't said a word. If it was serious, I was sure you'd have gotten in touch." Their lives might have diverged, but they were still brothers, and Marcus would do anything in his power for his family.

"Oh, it's just Rachel, that's all. She got the house, but it doesn't seem to be enough." Chris snorted. "*You've* got the right idea."

"Hmm?"

"Staying single."

Marcus raised his eyebrows. "It's not a deliberate choice. Just haven't met anyone yet who's swept me off my feet." Not to mention he hadn't been looking either.

"And what about Seb?"

He stilled. "What about him?" Christ, his family couldn't resist, could they?

"Seems like an all right guy." Chris's eyes sparkled. "If he can cope with you, he's a keeper."

Marcus bristled. "Excuse me?"

That got him another derisive snort. "You're not exactly easy to live with. I mean, just look at the past week since we've been here. You've been stressed, moody, agitated…"

Marcus gaped at him. "That surprises you? I came here for peace and quiet, then chaos ensued."

"Don't give me that. You knew we were all coming. And you don't *have* to stick around. You can always go find your peace and quiet someplace else."

"You know what? That's the first sensible thing you've said since you came in here. So I'll do just that." He picked up his laptop bag from the floor beside the bed and shoved the laptop into it, along with his notepad. Then he grabbed his jacket that hung on the back of his chair.

"Hey, Marcus—"

He waved his hand. "I think you've caught me on a bad day. I'll be back when my mood is better." He strode through the yard, avoiding the kids who were running around whooping and hollering, and went back into the house. Mom glanced at his bag, and he paused long enough to kiss her cheek. "I'm going to Seb's. I won't be staying the night. But I don't know if I'll be back for dinner."

She nodded. "It's beef casserole. I'll save you some, just in case. Say hi to Seb for me."

"Sure." He walked out of the kitchen, stopped in the hall to grab his car keys from the table, and headed out of the door. As he reached the car, an idea struck him. Maybe a detour was required.

Seb stretched. *Hell, is it only Thursday?* After the week they'd had so far, he was more than ready to kick back when Sunday arrived.

"You heard from Gary?" Tim asked as he shoved the receipt for the lobsters into his pocket.

Seb snorted. "Not a peep. Have you?"

"I send him a text every day, tellin' him about the catch. Figure we're doin' okay 'cause he hasn't called me up to swear at me."

That made him laugh. "Maybe he's got enough on his plate, coping with his sister."

Tim gave him a speculative glance. "You've made it through four weeks—well, almost—and you ain't fucked up yet. You sure you wanna go back to teachin'?"

That made Seb laugh even harder. "Fuck yeah, I'm sure. At least with teaching, I don't go home every night smelling so bad that it can peel paint." He grinned. "'Ain't fucked up yet'? Hey, that sounded like a compliment. Watch yourself there, Tim. You're slipping."

Tim waved his hand. "See ya'n the mornin'."

Seb returned the wave and began the trek up Pier Road. He was bone tired, but that was nothing new. The sun beat down, and he was glad he had his baseball hat. It was a beautiful day, too fine to be spending what was left of it indoors. And just like that, his mind went to Marcus.

He'd been doing that a lot lately. He hadn't seen Marcus since Sunday, and although that had to be good, Seb couldn't help but feel disappointed.

What did I expect? For him to turn up every day so we could fuck like bunnies? Except it wasn't just the sex. Seb liked being around him. There was something about Marcus that put Seb at his ease. Yes, he was sexy as fuck, but Marcus was more than his looks. There was a keen mind behind those stunning eyes, and a sense of humor. He didn't make demands or assumptions, and most of all he didn't judge.

That counted for a great deal in Seb's book.

When he turned into the driveway, he spotted a familiar car, and his heartbeat sped up. *He's here.* Despite his fatigue, he quickened his pace. As he opened the front door, he caught a smell that made his mouth water. "Is that chicken soup?"

Marcus stood in the kitchen, stirring a saucepan. "And hello to you too. I brought you lunch. I'll have it ready for you by the time you've showered."

Seb laughed. "You're saying I stink, right?"

He grinned. "Put it this way. I could smell you when you reached the end of the driveway."

Seb gave him the finger and headed for the bathroom. He squirmed out of his jeans and layers and dropped them onto the floor, ready for the washer. As he stepped into the tub, he called out, "Wanna scrub my back?"

Marcus laughed. "Getting déjà vu here. You concentrate on the task in hand, and I'll concentrate on mine."

"Spoilsport." Seb flipped the shower on and let the hot water and soap remove all traces of the last seven hours. He gave special attention to his nooks and crevices, because *fuck*, it had been *four days*. Marcus surely hadn't come over just to make Seb lunch—he hoped. Judging by the boner he was sporting, part of his anatomy hoped so too.

As he dried himself, he debated strolling into the living room in just a towel, but then dismissed it. *Stop thinking with your dick.* Seb put on a clean pair of jeans, but paused at the choice of tee. He spread four or five on the bed, before finally choosing one. By the time he walked out of the bedroom, two bowls of steaming soup sat on the coffee table, along with two plates containing hunks of fresh bread.

Marcus took one look at his shirt and laughed. "You don't think maybe it's a little too subtle?"

He'd gone with a black tee emblazoned with the words *Queer as Fuck* in sparkly rainbow letters. Seb rolled his eyes. "And there you go again, using words that aren't in my vocabulary." He glanced at the lunch and smiled. "This looks great."

"I thought it would be a nice surprise for when you got home."

"It is." Seb sat back against the seat cushions, the bowl in one hand, his spoon in the other. Marcus joined him. "How long have you been here?"

"Only two hours."

Seb laughed. "Your morning was that bad, huh?"

"Let's just say I couldn't see it improving anytime soon."

The soup was delicious. "Damn, this is good." He glanced at Marcus. "Did you get anything done?"

"Today was mostly reading."

Seb enjoyed the comfortable silence while they ate. Some guys felt the need to talk all the time, but not Marcus. When he'd finished, he put down his empty bowl and spoon with a happy sigh. "That was just what I needed."

"Now that you're home and fed, I'll go."

He frowned. "Do you have to?"

"You must have things to do, and I don't want to be in your way." Marcus made no move to get up from the couch, however.

Seb folded his hands behind his head. "I gotta say, I expected you to turn up before this. When it got to Thursday and I hadn't seen you, I figured things were going well back at the house." He cocked his head to one side. "Unless you stayed away on purpose because you didn't want to be a nuisance." When Marcus blinked, Seb knew he had nailed it. "I meant what I said. You're not in the way. Don't put up with whatever is driving you crazy because you don't wanna put me out. You're welcome here, anytime. And just because we've finished lunch doesn't mean you have to go." Besides, he didn't want Marcus to leave.

"I'm not in the mood to write anymore."

Seb sat up straight. "Then let's do something."

"Such as?"

Seb glanced toward the window. "As I was walking back from the wharf, I was thinking what a lovely day it was. So why don't we go somewhere and enjoy what's left of the day—together. It's not something I get the chance to do often. We could take the skiff and head out to one of the islands. We wouldn't be going all that far, but at least we'd be out of the house and in the sunshine."

Marcus smiled. "I like the sound of that. I *am* surprised, however."

"What surprises you?"

His eyes twinkled. "I felt sure sex was going to be on the itinerary at some point."

Seb grinned. "Day ain't over yet." He had seven or eight hours before he'd have to think about sleeping, and he wanted to spend as many of them as he could with Marcus. And if a couple of those hours were spent in bed, even better.

Chapter Seventeen

The engine chugged as the boat headed away from the dock and out into the harbor. Marcus was feeling like a summer visitor in shorts borrowed from Seb, his sunglasses, and a pair of bright yellow flip-flops. "Not sure these are me," he murmured, gazing at his feet.

Seb laughed. "Anyone can carry off flip-flops in the summertime." He glanced down. "And Gary's shorts fit you better than mine would."

"These are Gary's?"

Seb snickered. "Relax. I did all his laundry the day I got here. Trust me, I wouldn't have loaned them to you before that."

"Where exactly are you taking me?" Ahead of them were several small islands, a sight he remembered from childhood when Dad had brought them out in the boat.

"Goat Island." Seb pointed to the left. "That one over there."

Marcus blinked. "Sounds… picturesque." He peered at the island, glimpsing a white shape. "Is that the lighthouse?"

"Yup. That's basically all there is. The island is a rock in the mouth of the harbor."

"Is it still working? I thought my dad said something about it being wrecked by a storm."

"That was the walkway between the lighthouse keeper's place and the tower. They rebuilt it in 2011. Apparently it looks like it did in the fifties. And yes, it still works. There's even a ghost."

"Seriously? There's no such thing."

Seb waggled his eyebrows. "I'm not so sure. Gary used to tell me stories when I was a kid." He pointed to an island on the right. "That's Bass Island. And we're not stopping there because that really is just a rock. Nothing on it."

Marcus peered ahead of them. "I don't think there's a lot more on Goat Island, from what I can see."

"We're not going there for sightseeing. We're going there to chill. I thought I'd take you somewhere peaceful."

That was fine in Marcus's book.

The boat cut through the water and stopped several feet away from the shingle-covered beach. "We'll drop anchor here, and wade in." Seb glanced at Marcus's feet. "Just take off your flip-flops. I don't want them floating away on the tide. Lost too many pairs that way."

Marcus frowned. "We *are* allowed to go ashore, right?"

Seb grinned. "Put it this way. If you see a Coast Guard boat, head back here pretty damn quick."

They jumped over the side and waded through the thigh-deep water to the shore. The lighthouse was visible to the right, a cylindrical white building. Farther off was a white house with a red roof, and Marcus guessed this was where the lighthouse keeper had lived. A covered walkway

connected it to the tower. Closer to the shore stood a pyramid-shaped tower covered in cedar shakes.
"What's that?" he asked, pointing to it.

"That's the new bell tower. They re-installed the original bell in 2011 when they did the renovations."

They strolled closer to the lighthouse, and Marcus spotted a flagpole. Lush green grass covered the area around the house. He stared at the walkway. "Does anyone still live here?"

"Not anymore. At least, I don't think they do."

"So is there really a ghost?"

Seb sat on a nearby boulder. "Dick Curtis was the caretaker here in the late nineties, Gary said—until Dick apparently fell overboard and drowned while he was coming over here by boat. The guy who replaced him said things started to happen not long after that. Items went missing, but always turned up on the kitchen table. Then he told a story about one cold day when he sat in Dick's chair and said,' Dickie, give me some heat', and an old electric heater that hadn't worked for years turned itself on. Then there were problems with the foghorn. It would go off frequently, even when it was clear. The Coast Guard tried new sensors, even disconnected the power, but it still went off. When they replaced the entire unit? *Then* it stopped." Seb froze as a figure came out of the house, gesticulating at them. "Fuck. There *is* a caretaker here. Time to go."

"Unless it's the ghost," Marcus said with a grin.

They ran back to the boat, laughing as they

splashed through the waves, Marcus clutching his borrowed flip-flops. When they were safely on board, Seb drew anchor and started the engine, the boat following a graceful arc in the water as it headed away from the shore.

"Well, that was a short visit."

"We don't have to go in yet," Seb told him. "We've got water, snacks… we can just stay out here and enjoy the peace and the motion of the water."

That sounded perfect.

Seb steered the boat around another island. "Seeing the ocean like this is *way* better than when I'm working." He gazed at the shoreline. "I keep forgetting what a beautiful place this is."

"It's a far cry from New York, that's for sure."

"Do you live in Manhattan?"

"Yes." Marcus couldn't change the subject, not when he'd been the one to bring it up.

"Do you *like* living there? Never saw the attraction myself."

"What counts as a big city in Maine?" When Seb gave him a puzzled glance, Marcus sighed. "I've been coming to Cape Porpoise since I was a kid. We'd go on day trips to York Beach or Kennebunkport, but that was about it. We stayed away from the more populated areas." Then he snorted. "Except I remember York Beach being pretty damn populated in the summer."

"I guess Portland is the biggest city. I don't go much farther north than that. Although I *have* ventured as far as Acadia with my friends."

Acadia National Park was on Marcus's bucket list. "I've always wanted to go there. It looks beautiful."

"One of my friends, Aaron, is a Park Ranger. He lives in Bar Harbor." Marcus chuckled, and Seb gave him another puzzled glance. "Did I say something funny?"

"No, it was just the way you said it. You sound like you're from Maine."

Seb rolled his eyes. "Well duh. You should hear Grammy, Levi's grandmother. Some of the things she comes out with make me scratch my head. Stuff you don't hear so much now, except from old-timers." Then he snickered. "And maybe fishermen." He gestured to the cooler bag. "Could you pass me a bottle of water?"

Marcus reached into the bag and removed two cold plastic bottles. He handed one to Seb, who drank from it greedily.

"I'll tell you one thing I do envy you about living in New York—the gay bars. There aren't that many around here."

"I think you mentioned Ogunquit?"

Seb nodded. "My regular is Maine Street, although sometimes I go to the Front Porch. It's a piano bar-cum-restaurant, and all the staff are gay. Well, *mostly* gay. It's a fun place. There are a few more in Portland, but I don't think they're as good. Blackstones is tiny and pretty old-school, then there's Bubba's Sulky Lounge. The Flash Lounge *says* it's a gay bar, but in my opinion it needs to be more gay."

Marcus laughed. "Yeah, there are a few gay bars in New York." And he'd probably seen them all.

Seb cocked his head. "You didn't answer my question. Do you like living there?"

Marcus's stomach clenched. *I did once.* Now

he wasn't so sure. "I'm not sure if 'like' is the right word. I work there. And I've sort of got used to it. Most of the city is huge and noisy, with *way* too many people. But there *are* quiet spots. Having said that, you're never far from traffic."

"You work in Manhattan?"

"Yes." *Now can we change the subject?*

Seb chugged some more water, then wiped his lips. "So, basically your job is to come up with ways to part people from their cash by making them buy something they didn't want in the first place."

Marcus studied him. "You've never bought something *solely* on the strength of an ad?"

"Nope, never… Well… I *say* that, but…"

"Come on, confess."

"I suppose when I saw the ad for the Slap Chop, I had to have it." Seb grinned. "Especially when the guy demonstrating it said, 'You're gonna love my nuts.' I think I spat out whatever I was eating at the time. No way did a straight guy come up with *that* line."

Marcus grinned back at him. "And you'd be right."

Seb's eyes widened. "No. Fucking. Way."

He nodded. "That was one of mine."

"Seriously?"

Marcus's eyes gleamed. "No, but I had you going there, didn't I?"

Seb stared at him. "*I* see. Funny guy, huh?" His eyes twinkled.

Fuck, he's such a breath of fresh air.

Marcus had had his fill of guys with agendas, who said one thing to his face and another behind his back, guys who went with the herd, instead of swimming against the tide.

I think I'm mixing my metaphors here.

Maybe living in New York had jaded him, but his life had become a list of guys he regretted getting involved with.

There were other regrets too, ones that had potentially far-reaching consequences. It was stupid to blame what had happened on the location, he knew that, but he couldn't help but wonder if the same events would have played out elsewhere.

Probably. What had ensnared him knew no boundaries.

Seb was nothing like any of the men he'd known. He was the epitome of What-You-See-Is-What-You-Get, and Marcus loved that. There was no duplicity in him.

"Hey, where did you go?"

Marcus dropped back into the moment. "Sorry. Guess I zoned out there."

Seb locked gazes with him. "I get the feeling wherever you zoned out to wasn't a good place." He kept his hand on the wheel as he steered them toward the dock.

"You don't *do* regret, do you, Seb?" The words were out before he could stop them. When Seb's brow furrowed, Marcus elaborated. "Because *I* get the feeling regret is another of those words that's not in your vocabulary."

Seb bit his lip. "You'd be wrong. Not that I blame you—you don't know me, that's all. If I'm honest, I don't think most of my friends do either. Sure, they know the guy they went to school with, the kid with the attitude. I couldn't be me at home, so I sure as hell was gonna be me when I was away from it."

"What do you regret?"

"Choosing to live my life the way I do. Don't get me wrong. I work hard, and when the weekend comes, I play hard. And like I said a while back, up until recently I wasn't interested in a relationship, but…" He drew in a long breath. "This seems an odd conversation to be having in a boat out on the ocean."

"Maybe it's because there are no distractions out here. It's easier to focus." Marcus knew he'd been seeing life differently ever since he'd arrived. *But isn't that what I came here for?*

"Maybe I should use this time to rethink my life," Seb mused. "Because I've been lying to myself. I've told myself over and over that this is what I want—no strings, no entanglements—but you know what? I'm only now realizing that living this way hasn't made me happy, so what's the fucking point?" He swallowed.

Marcus caught his breath. In that one moment, he *saw* Seb, with all the fears and insecurities he hid so well. "Maybe I know you better than you think."

Seb exhaled. "Okay then. What am I thinking right this second?"

Marcus didn't break eye contact. "That you want to take us back to the dock, take me back to your place, and shut out the world for a few hours. If you want us to fuck, that's fine. If you don't, that's fine too. You just want to be with someone who *gets* you, who won't make demands of you—who accepts you as you are, balls to bones."

Seb shivered, his eyes widening. "Fuck," he

whispered.

The skin prickled on Marcus's arms, and it had nothing to do with the breeze off the ocean. "So? What do you say?"

The boat picked up speed, and the dock loomed ahead of them.

Marcus had his answer.

They were barely through the door when Seb launched himself into Marcus's arms, their lips colliding in a long, unhurried kiss that sent warmth spreading through him. Marcus slid his hands under Seb's tee and moved them higher, grazing Seb's nipples with his thumbs, making Seb shiver.

"Too many clothes," Seb murmured between kisses.

Marcus could do something about that.

Standing beside the couch, he undressed Seb, taking his time, making sure to kiss each new bit of skin that came into view, until at last Seb was nude, his arms pebbled with goosebumps, his breathing shallow. His dick rose, stiff and long. Marcus removed his own clothing, dropping the shorts to the floor and stepping out of them. He cupped Seb's chin, ignoring the shaft that rubbed against his own erect cock.

"Well? What do you want?"

Seb curled his fingers around Marcus's dick.

"I want this inside me. No pounding, no bouncing on your dick, just a lazy, gentle fuck that lasts as long as we can make it."

Marcus pulled him closer, not letting go of Seb's chin, until their lips were almost touching. "Sounds perfect." Then he closed the gap and they kissed, a lingering kiss that sent tendrils of heat curling through him. Seb broke the kiss, grasped his hand, and led him toward the bedroom.

Marcus left his worries and regrets in the living room, along with his clothing.

None of them had any place in Seb's bed.

Chapter Eighteen

July 12

"Marcus."

"Hmm?"

"Dude, it's eight-thirty." Not that Seb wanted him to go.

Marcus's breath stirred his hair. "I fell asleep. You felt so warm, you sucked me right into a doze."

Seb chuckled. "You do realize your dick is still in my ass."

"It was happy there. I didn't want to disturb it." Seb laughed, and Marcus's breathing hitched. "Do that again. I can feel it all the way along my cock."

"And you say *I'm* a distraction?" With extreme reluctance, Seb shifted forward, freeing Marcus's shaft. He rolled over to find himself looking into Marcus's cool blue eyes. Seb ran a finger along Marcus's jawline. "This has gotten longer," he murmured, stroking the short gray beard. When they'd first met, it had been little more than scruff.

"Want me to shave it off?" Marcus's eyes twinkled.

"Don't you fucking dare." He sighed heavily. "Don't take this the wrong way, but I hope your family is a royal pain in the ass this week."

"Don't worry. I guarantee you'll come home

to find me on your couch a couple of times at least. I might even be making you lunch again."

Seb smiled. "That was really sweet, you know. I could *so* get used to that." He reached around to slide his hand down Marcus's back to the firm swell of his ass. "Still need to get in here."

"I said I'd work on that, didn't I?"

"Yeah, but that was a week ago."

Marcus laughed. "You impatient kid." He rolled onto his back, taking Seb with him. Marcus pushed Seb's hair back. "Let me see those pretty eyes."

"I have pretty eyes?" Seb batted his lashes. Then he did a slow grind of his dick against Marcus's hardening shaft. "Fuck," he breathed. "One more time for good luck?"

Marcus burst into more laughter. "The rate *we've* been going at it, we're the luckiest men in the whole state of Maine." He kissed the tip of Seb's nose, and the intimacy of the gesture made something flutter in Seb's belly. "Okay. If I *promise* to use the butt plug so you can have your wicked way with my ass, will you let me get out of here so you can get some sleep? I don't want you dozing off tomorrow and falling overboard."

"Deal." Seb clambered off him and knelt on the bed while Marcus got up and dressed himself.

Marcus glanced at the rumpled sheets. "Never mind working on the couch—I may work from here."

"Seriously? That couch is really comfortable."

Marcus pulled on his tee, then leaned toward him. "I wasn't thinking about comfort—I was imagining being surrounded by sheets that smell of you."

Aw fuck.

"You say things like that, when you're about to leave?" Seb grabbed Marcus and fell back onto the bed, taking Marcus with him. Marcus laughed, and suddenly Seb was at the mercy of Marcus's fingers that teased and tickled him until he was breathless with laughter. "S-stop that!"

Marcus relented, and got off the bed once more. "Now let me get dressed. Mom will already be complaining she's hardly seen me this weekend."

"Am I getting you into trouble?" Seb didn't want to be the cause of upset between Marcus and his family. He genuinely liked them.

Marcus let out a wry chuckle. "There are so many people in that house, she won't miss me."

"Any signs some of them will be leaving soon?"

Marcus nodded. "Chris is going home next weekend, and I think Jess and Lisa too. So if you want to say goodbye, you'd better come for dinner on Saturday." He smiled. "I'll let Mom know I've invited you. She won't mind one more mouth to feed."

Seb got to his feet. "If you're sure." He shifted closer. "How did you know I was ticklish?"

Marcus's eyes glittered. "I pay attention when we fuck." Then he drew Seb close and kissed him, his hands on Seb's ass, squeezing gently. "*You*, Seb Williams, are fucking addictive."

Seb smiled. "There are worse things to be addicted to, right? At least *this* addiction can't kill you."

Marcus stilled for a moment. "Not unless I

die from exhaustion." Another kiss, this time to Seb's forehead, then Marcus walked out of the room.

Seb squirmed into his shorts and followed him, watching as Marcus searched for his car keys. "They're in that bowl on the coffee table." Marcus grabbed them, then headed for the door.

"Get some sleep. I'll see you soon." Then he was gone.

Seb frowned. Marcus's departure seemed a little abrupt. Then all such thoughts were pushed from his mind when his phone vibrated against the coffee table. He picked it up and smiled when he saw it was a text from Levi.

It's been two weeks. Just checking you're still among the living.

Seb laughed and hit Call. "Dude. Really? Time sure flies when you're working your ass off."

"Were your ears burning today?"

"Why—was I a topic of conversation?"

"I met up with Ben, Dylan, Finn, and Joel, and we went for a hike up in Camden."

"Shit, that was today?" He'd gotten Levi's text a week ago about the meetup, but there'd been no way. "How did it go?"

"Great hike, and then we all went back to Ben's place and played Monopoly."

Seb cackled. "Was it as cutthroat as it used to be?"

"More. I think Dylan's gotten worse." They both laughed.

"Finn and Joel still loved up?" Levi's happy sigh said more than words. *Good for Finn.* "I'm glad it's working out."

"They asked how you were. Ben sends his

best."

"Aw. How is he? I got his text about getting the job—and who his boss is. Bummer."

Levi sighed. "He's… struggling. I think he's going to have it out with Wade. He needs to. He can't go on like this." He paused. "He was concerned about you, because he hasn't heard from you. None of them have."

Seb's chest tightened. "Yeah, I know. I've been pretty crap lately at keeping in touch."

"I made excuses for you. Told them you were having a rough ride, working hard… I didn't mention you'd met someone. I figured they didn't need to know you had the hots for someone who wasn't interested."

"Yeah… about that part…"

There was a moment of silence. "I swear, every time I call, the finish line has moved. Come on, hit me with the latest development. No, wait—I already know, don't I?"

"He says I'm addictive."

Levi laughed. "I take it you're happier than when we last spoke?"

"Yeah, but listen—don't tell the guys, all right?"

"Why not? They'd be happy to know you're not languishing on a lobster boat, that you're getting *something* out of being over there." Another pause. "Seb? What's wrong with telling them you're getting your itch scratched?"

Because it feels like more than that.

"Maybe I've decided my sex life isn't for public consumption. *Maybe* I've decided to keep my exploits to myself." He loved them like brothers, but… It was a feeling Seb struggled to articulate, even to Levi.

"I think I've hit a nerve." Levi's voice was quiet. "Something you're not telling me? I mean, it's not serious, is it?"

Seb had thought it wasn't, but the intimacy of the last moments he'd shared with Marcus had felt… special.

"It's a summer fling, okay?" Seb kept his voice light. "Come August, I'll be back in Ogunquit, and he'll be here or in New York or wherever." *Then why does it feel as if it could be so much more than that?*

"Okay. I guess I'd better let you sleep. It's probably already past your bedtime." A pause. "Seb, you know I'm here, if you ever need to talk, right?"

"Yeah, I know. Love you, man. Give my love to Grammy." They said goodnight, and Seb disconnected. He locked the front door, made sure everything was turned off that needed to be, and headed back to bed.

As he got beneath the sheets and laid his head on the pillow, what hit him was Marcus's smell, as strong as if he were still in bed with Seb. It was a comforting scent, and Seb pulled the sheets up to his chin, breathing him in.

He imagined Marcus's arms around him, the warmth of his body at Seb's back, his breath stirring Seb's hair.

I wish he was here.

Marcus let himself into the house and headed for the kitchen to pour himself a glass of water. Laughter and raised voices came from the living room. *Sounds like it's movie night.* He wasn't in the mood. The door opened and he swore inwardly, then sighed with relief when Jake walked into the kitchen.

"I thought I heard you come in." Jake leaned against the countertop.

"Hey. What's going on in there?"

"Oh, they're all watching some old movie Granddad was raving about."

Marcus raised his eyebrows. "What's your definition of 'old'?"

Jake grinned. "It was made before I was born." Marcus laughed. Jake bit his lip. "If you're not coming in… can we go someplace and talk?"

"Sure. Let's go to my space." He led the way, Jake following. Dad had turned on the lights and they lit up the yard, illuminating the path to the summerhouse. Once inside, Marcus waited till Jake was seated in the recliner, then pulled his chair across and sat facing him, leaning forward, his elbows on his knees, hands clasped. "Okay. What's up?"

"I have a… dilemma."

"That doesn't sound good.

"But it *should* be good," Jake remonstrated. "I've gotten invitations to two job interviews in the past two days."

"That's awesome. So what's the dilemma?"

"One is with a company in Boston, and the other is in… San Diego."

Marcus gaped at him. "This is your idea of a dilemma? If I had that choice, I wouldn't hesitate. California, here I come."

Jake nodded. "That was why I applied for the job in the first place. But I sent the application in months ago. When the closing date passed and I'd heard nothing, I assumed I'd been unsuccessful. Then… then stuff happened, and…" He sucked in a deep breath. "The San Diego job is perfect—so is the Boston one—but…" He looked Marcus in the eye. "*He's* not in San Diego—he's in Boston."

Marcus swallowed. "Thanks for trusting me with that. I won't say it's a total surprise, not after our last conversation." He cocked his head to one side. "And he still has no idea how you feel about him?" Jake shook his head. "So either you go to San Diego and forget about him, or you stay in Boston in the hope that something *might* happen between you?"

"It *can't* happen," Jake protested. "I know that makes no sense, but I really can't say any more than that. At least if I take the Boston job—assuming I get it—I'll be a damn sight nearer to him than I would be if I were way over on the West Coast." He leaned forward, his head in his hands. "Tell me it gets better."

Marcus sighed. "I *could* tell you that, but I'd be lying. Dealing with disappointment gets easier, I suppose, but only after you've coped with a shit ton of it." He paused. "I can make an assumption or two as to *why* nothing can happen between you, the number one reason being, he's married."

"No, he's not married, he's just… unattainable." Jake raised his chin and locked gazes with him. "Please, don't ask me why."

"Because you think it will make me think differently about you?" Marcus got off his chair and crouched in front of Jake, taking Jake's hands in his. "Listen to me. When I say I know exactly how you feel, it isn't just a line. If I told everyone in that house over there *why* I had to come to Cape Porpoise, I guarantee they would *all* look at me differently. Including you. And the same thing applies—don't ask me either. Just understand that I'm here for you, okay?"

"You're all right, aren't you?" Jake's brow wrinkled and his gaze grew pained.

"I'm fine. Actually, I'm in a better place than I've been for a long time."

Jake's eyes held a soft gleam. "Anything to do with a certain schoolteacher who doubles as a lobsterman?"

He laughed. "He might have something to do with it. But let's get back to you. Maybe you should tell this guy how you feel about him."

Jake gaped at him. "Why?"

"Because once you've told him, it's out in the open, and you can move on. You need to decide which is better to live with—the regret of doing something, or *not* doing something. You tell him, and that's it, done. You interview for the job you want most. What's your worst-case scenario? Him admitting he feels nothing for you?"

Jake shook his head. "No—him admitting he does. That would make things infinitely worse."

Marcus frowned. "I can't pretend to

understand that, but I accept you can't tell me more." He cupped Jake's cheek. "I just want you to be happy, kiddo."

Jake smiled. "You're the only person I'll let call me that. Thanks for listening, and for trying to help."

"You're welcome. Ready to go back to the really old movie?"

"I'd rather stay out here."

Marcus had an idea. "The WiFi is decent enough in here. Why don't I open Netflix on my laptop, and let you choose a movie? You can keep the recliner, and I'll sprawl on the bed."

Jake's eyes lit up. "There's popcorn left from last week."

"No way. They'll have eaten it all tonight."

"Not the box I stashed in my bag, they won't. Emergency supplies, I call it."

Marcus laughed. "Sneak into the kitchen and pop that corn. I'll see what Netflix has to offer."

Jake lurched out of the chair and was through the door in an instant.

Marcus shook his head. *What is going on, Jake?*

Chapter Nineteen

July 15

Marcus shoved his laptop into its bag, then added the power cord and his notebook. There was nothing else he'd need. Then he remembered his phone charger, and added that too.

"Going somewhere?"

Marcus almost jumped out of his skin at Jess's voice. "Christ, a knock on the door first would have saved me from my imminent heart attack." He glanced at her. "What are you doing up at this hour?"

"Thought I'd go out for the day and see some more of Maine before I leave Sunday." Her eyes glinted. "Going to Seb's again? Why? Surely he's out doing his thing in the middle of the ocean by now."

Marcus chuckled. "He's probably been out there four hours already."

"So I repeat—why?"

"I'm going there to work." He patted his laptop bag. "See? Work."

"You could work here."

He snorted. "Sure—until everyone else wakes up, the kids start running around, Jake or Mike plays music... There, I'll have peace for a few hours, then I'll make Seb's lunch so it's ready when he gets home."

Jess bit her lip. "Lunch? My, how… domesticated." He narrowed his gaze, but apparently that had no effect whatsoever. "How long have you been doing this?"

Marcus shrugged. "A couple of times." Okay, so this would be the third time this week. The look on Seb's face when he walked through the door and found Marcus there, slicing sandwiches or heating soup, made it worth the effort. And how much effort did it take to heat up some soup, or stop by the store to pick up something to make Seb smile?

Jess folded her arms and leaned against the door frame. "We haven't seen much of Seb since the Fourth weekend." Her lips twitched. "I'll bet all he sees is the boat and his bedroom walls."

Marcus couldn't resist. "We do it on the couch too."

Her eyebrows went sky high. "TMI, brother dearest."

He gave a hearty laugh. "Is there such a thing where you're concerned?"

"Hey!" Then Jess's expression grew serious. "You've talked to Jake, haven't you?" Marcus nodded, and she sighed. "He seems… I don't know… different. He's got interviews coming up, and whatever is on his mind, I don't want it to distract him."

"He's got my number. He knows he's free to call me anytime."

Jess's face glowed. "Thank you."

"And as for not seeing a lot of Seb, he'll be having dinner here Saturday."

Her eyes gleamed. "Great."

Marcus glared at her. "Jess…"

Those sparkling eyes widened. "What?"

"Don't make him feel awkward."

Jess snickered. "I may not have spent as much time around him as you have, but even *I* know there's not much that would make Seb feel awkward."

She had a point.

"Now go write more words, and feed your man." When he blinked, Jess smiled. "Hey, right now, he's the only man you've got, so I can say that with impunity."

Marcus walked out of the summerhouse, and Jess accompanied him as far as the side gate. When he paused there, she surprised him with a hug.

"What was that for?"

She stroked his cheek. "Just me loving on my big brother, who looks a damn sight happier than he did a few weeks ago." Jess grinned. "I think we both know why that is, without going into detail. And for the record, I'm green with envy." She kissed his cheek, opened the gate, and gave him a rough push through it, closing it after him.

Marcus was still smiling by the time he pulled up outside Seb's.

July 17

The boat chugged toward the wharf, and Seb was glad to see it. It had been a dismal morning, and the catch had been disappointing. *It's either famine or feast out here.* There had been similar days, but there had also been days which had put a smile on their faces.

"Who's that?" Tim demanded. "Anyone you know?"

"Huh?" Seb peeled off his oil pants.

"There's a fella on the wharf, starin' at us."

Seb looked up, and grinned to see a familiar figure. "Oh. That's Marcus."

"He the one you took fishin'?"

He nodded. "He's also made lunch for me every day so far this week." *And he's here, waiting for me.* Warmth trickled through him.

Tim's shaggy eyebrows shot up. "Has he now?"

Seb gave Tim an inquiring glance. "Something wrong with that?"

"Nothin' at all. Can he cook, or is he a 'open a can an' heat it up' kinda guy?"

Seb laughed. "He makes a great grilled cheese sandwich."

Tim grinned. "Ooh. A keeper then." He guided the boat closer to the wharf, then gave Marcus a nod. Tim patted Seb on the shoulder. "You go. I'll deal with the catch."

"You sure?"

Tim nodded. "Yuh. Ol' Donald will give me a hand. He works at Langsford's." His eyes were bright. "See you tomorrow, and don't be late. Your weekend doesn't start till noon Saturday, remember."

Seb climbed out of the boat, and Marcus drew nearer. Seb grinned. "You didn't need to meet me."

Marcus gave a shrug. "I wanted to. Lunch is done." They strolled back along Langsford Road, to the sound of creaking ropes, the shrieks of gulls, and the sound of water slapping against hulls.

"Oh? What are we eating?"

"Well… I tried something new. Mom bought a load of clams yesterday, so I asked her to show me how she made clam chowder." He snorted. "She didn't show me—she stood there giving instructions while I did the whole thing."

Seb came to a dead stop. "You *made* it? From scratch?"

"Hey, it wasn't that difficult. And I learned some things. I now know how to make a roux."

Seb laughed as they resumed walking. "I wouldn't know what a roux was if it bit me in the ass. I'm impressed."

"Like I said, it wasn't that difficult."

Seb gave him a warm smile. "It's not the difficulty that impresses me—it's more the fact that you took time out to do it. The grilled cheese sandwich had already set the bar pretty high."

"You'd better like the chowder. That's what we're eating tomorrow night." Marcus chuckled. "Let's just say, I made a lot."

"Ah, *I* get it. Send the family home with food poisoning. Nice." Marcus whacked him on the arm. "Hey!" Then they both laughed.

Seb was still blown away by Marcus's decision to meet him at the wharf. *Never had anyone wait for me anywhere.* It was sweet. Then again, who'd ever made him lunch before? Maybe Tim was right— Marcus was a keeper.

Except I can't keep him, can I? When summer

came to an end, so too would whatever it was they had going on. It wasn't dating, but it was more than just sex. Seb had gone from dying to get the hell out of Cape Porpoise, to wishing time would slow the fuck down.

And this is after knowing him for almost five weeks, and fucking him for less than two. By the time Seb had to pack up and go, he'd be a mess.

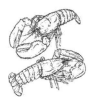

Seb scraped his bowl for the last little smidge of chowder, and dropped the spoon into it with a clatter. He set the bowl on the coffee table and let out a happy sigh. "Man, that was good. Wow. You can cook." He batted his lashes. "Marry me?"

Marcus guffawed. "You're easy to please. It's Mom's recipe. All I did was follow instructions."

Seb let out a derisive snort. "My mom couldn't follow a recipe to save her life. Which was why we lived on Hungry Man frozen dinners. So don't be so modest."

"Do you cook a lot?"

He bit back a smile. "There's a whole lotta Ramen in my cabinet, but yeah, I can do basic shit. I make a mean omelet, and I can grill anything you put in front of me. Generally, once school is out in June, I fire up the grill and that's me happy for the summer."

"Plus, you make great salads and baked

mackerel," Marcus added. "And that bass was awesome." Seb buffed his fingernails on his tee, and Marcus laughed. "Tomorrow night is Mom's meatloaf by popular request, after the chowder. If we're lucky, she won't ask Jess to mash the potatoes."

Seb blinked. "Something I should know?"

Marcus's eyes twinkled. "She's really good at leaving lumps the size of golf balls." They laughed. Marcus glanced at his phone and Seb's chest tightened.

"Can you stay a while?" The instant the words popped out, he regretted them. *Way to go to sound real needy, dickhead.*

Marcus's smile eased the constriction. "I wasn't planning on going just yet. Why, do you have something in mind?" There was that familiar twinkle again.

"How would you feel about going for a walk?"

"Before the family turned up, I did a lot of walking around Cape Porpoise. Since then, not so much. At the end of Land's End Road, there's Porpoise Cove. We could walk along the shore and see how far we can get."

Seb liked the sound of that. What he liked even more was that Marcus hadn't balked at the idea of *not* staying in and screwing each other's brains out.

Yeah. This was way more than just sex.

"I've missed this," Marcus commented as they stood on the rocky bluff, a warm breeze in his face, and the sunlight sparkling on the water before them.

"I get to see it every day, but from a different angle." He pointed to a boulder nearby. "Wanna sit a while and contemplate the view?"

Marcus had no problem with that.

He leaned against the warm rock, staring out at the boats dotted here and there, some with white sails, others that looked sleek, fast and expensive. He pointed to the biggest one out there. "There you go. The lifestyle of the rich and shameless."

Seb cackled. "Looks great. I'll take two." He closed his eyes and drew in a deep breath. "That air… On days like these, school seems so far away," he murmured. "I remember when I was a kid, the summer vacation seemed to last forever. Now? It feels as if it's over before I have time to really enjoy it."

"I know you said kids these days are getting more entitled, but surely there are good moments too, that reaffirm why you got into this career in the first place."

Seb smiled. "There are some *awesome* moments." Then his face fell. "Unfortunately, there's a lot of crap too. Sometimes I get the feeling they want us to entertain the students, not teach 'em, but we're competing for their attention that's already claimed by a whole lot of distractions. Too many distractions."

"Such as?"

"Sex, for one thing." Seb sighed. "Whatever happened to childhood? They know *way* more about sex than we ever did at their age. But is that such a surprise? They can get their hands on porn so easily these days. I mean, once or twice a year, I find boys jerking off in my classroom."

Marcus stared at him. "Are you telling me you never did that?"

"Okay, I *might* have done it once, on a dare." Marcus chuckled. "But earlier this year, I overheard a conversation between two fifteen-year-old girls, who were sitting at the back of my classroom. They didn't bother lowering their voices: they didn't care who heard them."

"What were they talking about?"

"One was telling the other about how she'd been spit-roasted the night before." Seb stared out at the ocean. "Kinda makes me want to rethink my whole attitude."

"What do you mean?"

"I'm not out at school, but you know what? Maybe I should be. Maybe it's not such a big deal. Because part of me says these kids wouldn't even care. They've grown up in a different world to the one I did. Hell, when I was their age—and we're only talking as far back as 2009—same-sex marriage was still a rarity. Look at the world now. Rainbows and unicorns wherever you look."

Marcus laughed. "I wouldn't go that far."

"Yeah, okay, maybe I exaggerate. But it's not

just the sex that's occupying their little minds day and night. There are other distractions out there. Vaping, for one thing. We catch three or four kids every week, vaping in the bathrooms. And then of course, there's the issue of drugs." He shook his head. "Only a few weeks ago, some of my students were caught using pot at a party. And we all know what a slippery slope *that* can be. What starts out as experimentation…"

Marcus was quiet for a moment. "Didn't *you* ever experiment?"

"With drugs? Hell no."

"Well, that was pretty emphatic."

Seb let loose another sigh. "There's a reason none of us experimented. When one of your best friends was left on his grandmother's doorstep by his druggie mom, it's not something you wanna touch. Drugs wreck lives."

Marcus's heart raced, and the hair lifted on his nape. His throat seized, and he couldn't have forced a word out even if he'd wanted to. Seb didn't seem to notice his lapse into silence. Neither of them spoke for several minutes, and then Seb got to his feet.

"Want to continue walking, *or* shall we go back to my place?" Seb's eyes sparkled.

Marcus hated himself for thinking it, but right then, fucking was way safer than talking. He didn't trust himself to speak, for fear he'd blurt out something he knew he would regret.

He cleared his throat. "Or. Let's go with or."

Seb's sexy smile reached his eyes. "And afterward, let me cook for you? I promise it won't be Ramen."

Marcus's breathing became a little easier. "Sure. Whatever you want to cook."

Seb cocked his head to one side. "Are you okay?"

"Why do you ask?"

"Not sure, just a feeling." Seb glanced around, then took a step closer. "Kiss me?"

The request caught Marcus off guard. "Now?" This was shakier ground.

Seb nodded. "Don't ask me why. I just got this urge to kiss you."

Marcus swallowed. "Then who am I to tell you to fight that urge?" He held his arms wide in invitation, and Seb stepped into them, looping his around Marcus's neck, pulling him in, until their bodies were connected from chest to crotch. Seb tilted his head, and Marcus took his lips in a gentle, unhurried kiss.

Seb broke away first. "Let's go home," he said softly.

Marcus nodded and followed him back along the path they'd taken.

It's not home, for either of us. But the prospect of stripping Seb naked and the two of them spending an hour or two lost in each other was so much better than the alternative.

'Drugs wreck lives.' Spoken with all the certainty and assurance that comes with youth. Marcus was *not* about to contradict him.

On that road lay disaster.

Chapter Twenty

July 18

"You didn't have to bring me home again," Seb commented as they got out of Marcus's car.

"Maybe I wanted to?"

"And it was a sweet thought, but you're gonna get a load of ribbing when you get back tonight." He snorted. "You think your family doesn't know why you were so eager to give me a ride?" Seb opened the front door, and they stepped inside.

"I didn't hear *you* protesting, or telling me strenuously that you *wanted* to stay and play charades." Marcus walked up behind him, slid his arms around Seb's front, and one hand covered his already stiffening dick while the other went for his nipple, teasing it. "Three things to bear in mind," he whispered, giving Seb's shaft a squeeze. "One—I *am* hoping for a load, although two or three would be even better. Two—Who says I'm going back there tonight? And three—I was also hoping you'd give *me* a ride."

Seb's breath stuttered in his throat. "Have you been using the butt plug?"

"Wrong tense." Marcus's teeth grazed his ear lobe, and he shivered. "It's still in there. Been in there all through dinner. Why do you think I kept squirming? And I didn't drop my napkin into my lap by accident. It was serving a purpose." He grabbed Seb's hips and ground his dick against Seb's ass. "You feel that?"

"Fuck yeah." Marcus wasn't the only one who wanted a ride.

"Well, this is me hard as a fucking rock at the idea of you inside me. So how about we stop talking and you fuck me?"

Seb's heart pounded at the thought of sliding between Marcus's downy ass cheeks. He turned around and looped his arms around Marcus's neck. "You got a cock ring in that box of tricks you had me bring here?"

Marcus frowned. "Possibly. Why? Do you think you're going to need it?"

Seb bit his lip. "I wasn't thinking about *me*. Seeing as you always come first, I thought it might help delay the inevitable." He waited for the explosion.

Marcus blinked. "Excuse me?"

"Well, you do," Seb retorted. "You're always the first past the finish line." He grinned. "Is it an age thing, or does my ass just feel that good?"

Marcus's eyes glittered. "Bet I can last longer than you do."

Seb was definitely up for a challenge. "Bring it on, honey. As long as you know?" He leaned in and kissed Marcus on the lips, slow and easy. "You're gonna lose that bet."

"Where's the box?"

"In the bedroom."

Marcus reached back and smacked his ass. "Then you stay out here while I go find what I need. Grab us some water from the fridge."

Seb tugged on his hair. "Yes, sir."

That earned him another smack, then Marcus disappeared behind the bedroom door. Seb went to the fridge, grinning. His night was looking better all the time.

He went over to the door and knocked. "Ready?"

"No, impatient brat. Wait."

"Who you calling a brat?" Seb cackled. "Not that you're wrong. That's what Grammy called me when I was a teenager. I think she pretty much nailed it." Then the door opened, and Marcus stood there, his eyes gleaming.

"*Now* I'm ready."

Seb peered beyond him to the bed, noting the lube was already there. Then he spotted the dildos, and he caught his breath. "Oh wow. Yes please." One was pink, thick and veiny, with a set of balls that also acted as a suction cup. The other made him grin. "Snake time." The double-ended dildo was shiny and black as Marcus had described, with veins that created a ridged surface, except for the smooth band that marked the center. "Christ, that's long." His hole contracted at the thought of them writhing on each end of it. "That is also seriously hot." Seb scanned the nightstand. "No cock ring, I see." He couldn't stop grinning. "Feeling confident, are we?" He dropped the bottles of water onto the bed.

"Oh yeah." Marcus curved his hand around Seb's cheek. "I have to tell you something."

"Is it gonna shock me?"

Marcus smiled. "Let's find out." He kissed Seb's neck, then whispered, "When we were having dinner tonight, all I wanted to do the whole time was kiss you."

Seb stifled a moan, loving the feel of Marcus's lips on his throat. Marcus's hand was on his back, stroking him with a languid up-and-down motion. "You might've shocked everyone else at the table," he murmured, "but not me. *Ashley* would've pitched a fit. Not in front of the children, remember?"

"Which is fair enough. They're nine and eleven."

"We're talking a *kiss*, not fucking on the dining room table." Seb shivered as Marcus slid his hands under Seb's tee. "Take it off," he whispered, holding his arms high. Marcus pulled it up and off, then tossed it to the floor. "My turn." Seb's fingers fumbled as he freed the buttons on Marcus's shirt. "You know what's good on shirts these days? Velcro."

Marcus laughed. "Good things come to those who wait." Except it seemed neither of them wanted to wait much longer. By the time they were both down to their briefs, Seb was vibrating with need.

He couldn't miss the damp spot on Marcus's white briefs, and rubbed his thumb over it. "You're already leaking. You're not gonna be able to hold it once I slide my dick over that sweet spot again and again."

Marcus smiled. "You know what comes with age? Stamina." Then he pushed Seb backward, and he landed on the bed with a bounce.

"Hey, don't break the bed. I don't wanna be the one to explain to Gary how it got broken." Before he could get another word out, Marcus was on him, and Seb instantly brought his legs up to hold

Marcus to him, shuddering as Marcus buried his face in Seb's neck and kissed him there. "That's cheating. It's a hot spot and you know it." He slid his hand down the back of Marcus's briefs, his fingertips encountering smooth plastic. Seb tapped it, and Marcus groaned.

"*Now* who's fighting dirty?"

Marcus shivered as Seb grabbed the plug's base and jiggled it in his ass. Seb's eyes sparkled. "It'll be me in there soon."

Marcus had thought of nothing else ever since he'd lubed up the butt plug and carefully slid it home. Every shift on his chair at dinner caused a reaction inside him, and he wasn't surprised he was leaking pre-cum. The way it had felt, he'd expected to see more of it.

"On your back, baby." Seb gave him a shove, and Marcus complied, his skin tingling as Seb leaned over him, stooping to kiss his neck, his nipples, and all the way down from his collarbones to just above the waistband of his briefs. Seb pressed his nose into the damp cotton and inhaled deeply.

"Like what you smell?"

Seb raised his head and grinned. "Fuck, yeah." He peeled Marcus's briefs back to reveal his hard cock, diving in to lick the pre-cum. Marcus ached to feel Seb's hot mouth enclose the head, but instead, Seb removed his briefs with almost prissy care before licking a path up Marcus's shaft. He rubbed his nose in the cleft between thigh and body, nuzzling him there. Then he shifted lower on the bed, and Marcus knew what was coming. He grabbed one leg, pulling it up toward his chest, revealing his hole to Seb's view.

Seb's grin widened. "This hole is mine." He grasped the base of the plug and gently eased it free, tossing it to the floor. A soft gasp fell from his lips. "Fuck, look at you. All stretched, ready for me." Seb circled Marcus's hole with his tongue, sending Marcus into a paroxysm of shudders. He rubbed his bearded chin from side to side over the pucker, and the sensation was exquisite.

"Aw, fuck." Marcus grabbed Seb's head, keeping him there. Seb chuckled against his hole, then penetrated Marcus with his tongue. "Jesus, baby." Marcus's shivers multiplied as Seb rubbed his face over Marcus's hole, taint and balls, before going back to tongue-fucking him. "Keep doing that and you'll make me come." Marcus craned his head from up the bed. "Except that's the point, isn't it?"

Seb grinned. He slid his own briefs down over his hips, balancing as he removed them, then crawled up Marcus's body to kiss him, rolling his hips, their shafts sliding over each other. His face was scant inches from Marcus's, his eyes bright. "Eat my ass?"

Marcus caught his breath. "Turn around."

Seb turned and crouched over him, affording Marcus the perfect view of Seb's tight little hole. Then Seb drew Marcus's legs up, and dove down to rim him again, forcing a groan from Marcus's lips.

He spread Seb's cheeks and gave as good as he got—until he caught sight of them in the mirror, and it almost stopped his heart.

Fuck, look at us. Marcus's legs were wrapped around Seb, crossed at the ankles, Seb curved around him, forming them into a circle of flesh, one form without end, while they both teased each other with their tongues and fingers.

"Marcus." It was a plea. Marcus licked over Seb's hole again and again, probing the tight muscle, noting the stony shaft that jutted out from Seb's body. Wet noises filled the air, heightening Marcus's arousal, until he couldn't take any more.

"I want you inside me. Now."

Seb scrambled off him. "Kneel on the bed."

Marcus did as instructed, and Seb knelt behind him, his cock hot and stiff against Marcus's back. He pointed to the mirror. "Look at you. So fucking hard." Marcus's dick pointed straight up, and Seb reached around him to give it a slow tug. "Ready for me?"

Marcus snorted. "I was ready hours ago."

Seb grabbed the lube, then eased him down onto all fours with a gentle push. He held out his hand. "Give me your phone. I need to show you how awesome you look." Marcus passed it to him and waited, shivering. Then he felt heat at his hole, and Seb moaned. "Reach back and spread yourself for me." Marcus pressed his head into the mattress and pried his cheeks apart. "Here I come."

Marcus had a feeling *he'd* be the one coming, and he breathed deeply, awaiting that initial penetration. When Seb drove all the way into him in one slick motion, he groaned. "Oh fuck. That feels amazing."

"It looks amazing too. Watching my cock slide into you." Seb moved in and out of him, and Marcus couldn't stay still. He shoved back, wanting more.

"Want me to take it slow?"

Marcus twisted to glare at him. "Fuck me, goddammit."

Seb smiled. "I'll take that as a no." He dropped the phone to the bed, gripped Marcus's shoulders, and proceeded to pound his ass, his body slamming into Marcus again and again. "Ass higher," he demanded. Marcus tilted his hips, and Seb filled him to the hilt.

"Oh, yeah, like that." It was fucking *perfect*. "Don't stop."

"I'll stop when you come first," Seb panted.

Marcus let out a joyful laugh. "You wish." He bowed his head and submitted to the sexual onslaught, jolted over and over by the impact as Seb fucked him with abandon. All he could hear were their harsh breaths and the erotic wet sound of Seb's cock sliding into him. It was almost too perfect, and he danced perilously close to the edge.

Seb paused to pull free of him, and kissed down Marcus's back, a soft brush of lips as he laid a trail to Marcus's crease. He spread Marcus's cheeks and teased his hole with his tongue. Marcus reached back to press Seb's head deeper, and Seb laughed quietly before easing his tongue into Marcus's body. Then the heavenly contact was gone, and Marcus bit back a groan of frustration.

"On your back." The breathless note in Seb's voice told Marcus he wasn't the only one on the edge.

Marcus dropped to the mattress and rolled over. Seb knelt at his ass, lifting Marcus's leg onto his shoulder. Seb aimed his dick and drove it home, his arms taking his weight as he thrust into Marcus, their gazes locked on each other. "Sexy fucking man," Seb murmured. He withdrew almost all the way, then thrust until he was balls-deep inside him. "Like that?"

"Yes," Marcus whispered, hooking his arm under his knee, one hand on Seb's nape as Seb rocked into him at a steady pace. Then Seb picked up the pace, slamming into him, accompanied by the slap of flesh against flesh. "God, yes, just like that."

Seb grabbed Marcus's knees and pinned them to his chest, folding Marcus in half as he plunged his dick into Marcus's ass with quick, short thrusts. Then he slowed as their lips met in unhurried drugging kisses while he stroked in and out of Marcus's body. Marcus held him close, one hand on the back of Seb's head, the other on his spine, their tongues meeting as Seb explored him.

Seb broke the kiss and gazed into Marcus's eyes. "Getting close?"

"You wish. In fact, let's turn up the heat." Marcus stretched across the bed and grabbed the double-ended dildo. "Let's see how much you can take of *this*."

Seb was out of him in a heartbeat. He flopped onto his back, grabbing his legs and yanking them up to his chest.

Marcus laughed. "Eager?" He slicked up one end and guided the slippery, shiny dildo into position. Seb's hole sucked it right in, about a quarter of its length. "Come on, you can take more than that." He held it steady around the center band and inched it into Seb, watching as more and more disappeared from view.

Seb shivered. "Fuck. That's deep."

"Hold it a sec." Seb grabbed it and held it steady while Marcus lay on his back. "Bring your legs over mine." When their asses were almost touching, Marcus brought the other end of the dildo to his hole and eased it inside. "Now ride it."

Seb rolled his hips, and Marcus mimicked the motion, bucking as the dildo slid deeper. They lay close enough to jerk each other off, tugging each other's shafts.

"Why have I never done this before?" Seb groaned. "Feels fucking good." He shuddered. "Fuck, right there."

"Want to try something different?"

Seb laughed. "I thought that's what we were doing."

"Take hold of it again." When Seb had it in his grasp, Marcus pulled free. "Knees to your chest." Seb did as instructed, rolling his ass up off the bed. Marcus slid the dildo a little deeper into him, then crouched over him as if to mount him. He guided the other end into his hole, then took control of the dildo, holding it firmly around its center band while he rode it, sliding it in and out of him. Seb rocked his body, taking it deeper and groaning when Marcus jiggled it in his ass. Seb's eyes widened, and Marcus grinned. "Revenge, baby, for the butt plug." He glanced at the mirror, catching his breath at the sight of them joined by the shiny black dildo, with maybe a hand's length visible.

Then they moved again, this time onto all

fours. Seb held onto it while Marcus backed up to him. Their ass cheeks brushed as they rode it, both of them in constant motion, their hips rolling.

"Marcus." Seb twisted to look at him. "Fuck me, please."

The entreaty in his voice couldn't be ignored. Marcus removed the dildo and tossed it aside. "Stay like that." He slicked up his dick and slid it deep into Seb's body, fucking him as Seb's moans multiplied. Marcus grabbed his phone and held it steady as he videoed Seb's hole swallowing his glistening shaft. Then he remembered the other dildo. He pulled free of Seb, dropped the phone, and reached for the pink silicone dick. One swipe of lube over its veiny surface, and he slid it deep into Seb's ass.

"Jesus, that feels huge." Seb impaled himself on it, hips bucking as he rode it.

Then Marcus added a finger, and Seb's moan rebounded off the bedroom walls. Marcus reached for his phone again. "Spread yourself for me."

Seb jammed his head into a pillow, his fingers digging into the firm flesh of his ass cheeks. Marcus started filming again, but now this time he added two fingers along with the dildo. A shudder ran the length of Seb's body. "Holy fuck."

"Want to try for three?"

"Christ. You're gonna fucking kill me." Then Marcus eased a third finger into him, alongside the dildo, and Seb turned his head to the side, his eyes wide.

Marcus removed his fingers and leaned over Seb's back. "Ever been DP'd?"

Seb's shudders intensified. "Couple of times, yeah." Another shiver. "Do it."

Marcus put down the phone, gave the dildo a twist until the balls were at three o'clock, and then brought the head of his cock to Seb's hole, just under the dildo. "Now, baby."

Then he squeezed his dick into tight heaven.

"Jesus fucking Christ." Seb had never been so full.

"You like that?"

"Give me a moment to catch my breath and I'll tell you."

Marcus stilled, and Seb took the time to take in several deep breaths, forcing himself to relax. Marcus's hand was gentle on his back. "Fuck, I can just about get my hand around them both."

"I can believe it. You should feel it from *my* side." Seb shivered.

Marcus stroked down his back. "Too much?"

A couple of breaths, and Seb was ready for more. "*Now* you can move."

Marcus slid his cock deeper into Seb. "Oh fuck, you should see this."

Seb could *hear* it, the slick wet sounds that had to be Marcus's shaft rubbing over the veins in the dildo.

"The base is pushing into my pubes, as if I were wearing a strap on. So when I do *this*…" He thrust, driving both of them into Seb, and Seb cried out from the sheer sensual pleasure that washed over him.

"Again," he begged. Marcus fucked him, his pace measured, and Seb struggled to keep away from the edge of the precipice that was suddenly in view. Another thrust, this time pegging his prostate, and it was all over. "Oh God. I'm coming."

Marcus picked up speed, sliding deeper, and Seb shot harder than he'd ever done. His cum seemed without end, and he shivered through every pulse onto his chest and belly. Marcus came to a stop, both dildo and cock still inside him, and kissed him as he lay there trembling.

"Oh, Marcus." He ached, his chest was tight, and warmth flooded through him. At last he lay still, his arms around Marcus's neck.

"Now it's my turn." Marcus slowly and carefully removed the dildo, placing it on the bed. He covered Seb with his body, his arms hooked under Seb's pits, holding him close as he began to move in and out of Seb's hole with a gentle stroke. "Can't last much longer," he confessed before taking Seb's mouth in a kiss that seemed to stretch out forever. Seb clung to him, sliding his hands lower to cup Marcus's ass, feeling his cheeks hollow as he rocked into Seb.

"Then come," Seb pleaded. "Wanna feel it inside me."

Marcus nodded, his strokes picking up a little speed, his breath quickening. Seb sighed as Marcus's cock throbbed within him, caging Marcus's sweat-slicked body with his legs, letting Marcus rock them both as he came. Marcus's low cry filled his ears, and his heart soared. When Marcus lay still on top of him, Seb cupped his nape and drew him into a long, chaste kiss.

"I don't think I was ever happier to lose a bet."

Marcus didn't move, but kissed his neck and forehead. "That was…"

Seb covered Marcus's lips with a finger. "Don't even try. There are no words." He looked Marcus in the eye. "You're staying the night, right?" Marcus nodded, and Seb sighed happily. "Good. Not that you're getting anywhere near my hole again for the rest of the night, but…" He smiled. "I like sleeping with you."

"Me too." Marcus eased out of him, and his eyes widened when Seb winced. "Did I hurt you?"

Seb smiled. "In the best way. Now lie down here and hold me. I'm not ready to lose this blissful feeling just yet."

Marcus curled around him, his chest damp against Seb's back. They lay in silence, and that was just right. Marcus's hand was over his heart, and Seb covered it with his own.

I could get used to this.

When the thought came, he couldn't hold it in. "Do you think you'll ever grow tired of hookups?"

Marcus stilled. "Where did that come from?"

"Just something that happened recently. A friend got into a relationship, and it looks like it's the real thing." He pictured the photo of Finn and Joel in bed, the happiness shining out of Finn, unmissable and heartachingly beautiful.

"And what's that?"

"You know… love. As opposed to lust. I saw

them together, and it made me think."

"Made you think what, exactly?"

Don't. Don't say it. But there was no holding it back. "That I could be missing out on something. That maybe there's more to life than a lot of sex." He twisted to look at Marcus, then both grinned as they said in unison, "Nah."

Marcus stroked down his arm. "I don't think I've ever really let anyone in."

Seb held himself so still. It felt like such a fragile moment, as if one false move would shatter it. "Why do you think that is?" It could have been *him* talking.

"Maybe I'm too scared they wouldn't like what they find."

Seb's breathing caught. "It's safer, isn't it? Keeping them at a distance, not letting them see what makes you tick… what makes you vulnerable. Because that gives them power over you."

Marcus kissed his shoulder. "Maybe that's what love is—finding someone you feel safe enough with to hand them that power." His breathing evened out, becoming deeper, and Seb knew he was drifting into sleep.

He lay there in Marcus's arms, surrounded by—and filled with—his warmth.

I think I could hand you that power.

Chapter Twenty-One

July 19

Marcus had no idea what time it was, but he was wide awake. Seb was still sleeping, and Marcus wasn't about to disturb him: with his schedule, Seb needed all the sleep he could get. Their last conversation flitted through his mind.

'Maybe that's what love is—finding someone you feel safe enough with to hand them that power.'

He felt safe with Seb—to a degree. Some of their conversations, however, made him wary. Nick's words came to mind, and although Marcus hadn't known Seb all that long, he didn't think Seb would be in the Who-gives-a-fuck? or the Good-for-him camp. Marcus's gut was already telling him to keep his past far, far away from Seb's ears.

Because it is *in the past. It's over.* And Marcus never intended revisiting it.

Seb stirred in his arms. "Wha' time is it?" He wriggled, emitting a yawn.

God, he was so fucking cute when he first woke up.

Marcus peered at the ancient alarm clock. "It's seven."

Seb rolled over and snuggled against Marcus's chest. "God, you smell good," he murmured, his arm slipping around Marcus's back.

"If I could bottle that smell, I'd make a fortune. *L'air de Marcus*. Got a nice ring to it."

Marcus couldn't resist the impulse to kiss the top of Seb's shaggy head. "Good morning."

Seb craned his neck, his eyes more alert. "How good a morning it is depends on what we do with it."

Marcus's chest tightened. "Well, I don't know what you're doing with *your* Sunday, but *I* have to go say goodbye to some of my family." Three of them were departing, and Marcus knew his mom and dad expected him to be there to see them off.

Seb let out a heavy sigh. "Do you have to go right this second?"

Marcus rolled him onto his back, his arms bracketing Seb's head. "Not right away, no." He leaned in to kiss Seb's forehead. "I guess we've got an hour before I need to get out of here." He couldn't see anyone leaving before Mom had put a huge breakfast in front of them.

Seb drew his legs up around Marcus's waist, and just like that, Marcus was a prisoner. "Is that a hint?"

Seb smiled. "Maybe?" He stretched out an arm toward the nightstand, and grabbed the lube.

"And who's doing what—or hadn't you gotten that far yet?"

Seb's eyes glittered. "How about we keep things versatile?"

"Sounds perfect." And it *was* perfect. Seb had remarked a couple of times that he could get used to whatever they had going on, and it was only now that his words hit home.

So could Marcus, in a heartbeat.

The cars were packed, and all that was left were the goodbyes. Mom and Dad hugged Lisa, Chris, and Jess, issuing invitations to come over for Sunday lunch when they were back in Boston. Jake, Sarah, and Mike were staying on another week, and Ashley and the kids would probably stay until mid-August.

Chris gave Marcus a firm hug. "Take care. Stay in touch."

Marcus blinked as Chris released him. "Seriously? We're doing the brother thing?"

"Maybe it's about time," Chris muttered. "Fifty is creeping up on me, and I don't want to get there and discover that somewhere along the way, we grew apart." He locked gazes with Marcus. "Okay, so I'm crap at keeping in contact. I can admit that. But so are you."

Marcus's throat seized. "It'll be better from now on, I promise." He just needed to get his shit together and work out what he was doing with his life. Because New York was looking less and less likely.

I don't want to go back. He'd left a part of himself there, one he didn't want to see again, and it felt as if returning there would be a retrograde step.

Chris gave him another hug. "I hope so," he whispered. Then it was time for one final hug to

Mom and Dad, and he got into his car.

Lisa hugged him. "Take care, cousin. It was good seeing you. And that nice young man too." Her eyes sparkled. "Got yourself a boy toy, huh?" When Marcus gasped, she shook her head. "I think I'm spending too much time around the younger generation."

"How does the saying go?" Jess said with a grin. "You're only as old as the man you feel? Then you're onto a winner, bro."

He rolled his eyes. "Go, before I smack you."

She opened her eyes in an innocent expression. "What? I think he's awesome. Go for it." She kissed his cheek before going over to hug Jake tightly.

When the cars had pulled out, everyone headed back indoors. Jake and Mike declared they were going to get changed and go for a run, and Sarah volunteered to strip the beds and do laundry. Dad retreated into his den, and the smell of his cigar wafted through the open door. It was a smell that took Marcus back to his childhood.

This was always my happy place.

Ashley announced she was taking the kids to the Nubble, and went into the kitchen to sort out water and snacks, while Sophia and Alex ran excitedly through the house, shrieking about going to see a lighthouse.

Marcus headed for the yard, a cup of coffee in his hand. He sat on the patio, enjoying the sun's warmth on his bare arms and legs. It was too warm for anything but shorts and a tee.

The French doors opened behind him, and he tensed for the onslaught of exuberant children, but it was only Mom. She sat at the table, staring out at the garden.

"It looks great," Marcus told her.

"It should. I've done enough work on it these past two weeks." She glanced at him. "Is there something you want to tell me?"

"About what?"

"Seb."

Marcus was getting to the point where he couldn't deny his feelings any longer, not to her at any rate. "I like him. More than I've liked anyone in a long while."

"That's good, isn't it?"

Marcus sighed. "Remember how Lisa used to rave about that movie, *Grease*?"

Mom chuckled. "I remember the endless gushing about how dishy John Travolta was."

He nodded. "And how does that movie start? It's a summer thing, right? Then it's over. Then they just *happen* to end up at the same high school." He sipped his coffee. "Seb has his life here, and in Ogunquit. I have mine."

Mom leveled a steady gaze at him. "You're saying when summer ends, so does whatever you two have going on?"

He nodded. "This isn't a Hallmark movie, Mom. Seb isn't going to change schools and move to New York to be with me. Life doesn't work like that, much as you might wish it to."

"It can if you want it to," she said quickly. "If it's something you want badly enough."

Just then his phone buzzed, and he frowned when he saw the text from Paul Douglas.

I know it's a Sunday, but can we talk?

His boss hadn't been in touch since—

Since I met with him back in April and told him I needed to take a step back for a couple of months. It didn't take any great stretch of the imagination to know why Paul was contacting him.

He got up from his chair, taking his cup with him. "Excuse me, but I have to take a call." He walked over to the summerhouse and went inside. Marcus took a deep breath and hit *Call.* "Hello, Paul."

"Marcus. Good to hear you. How are you?"

"I'm… doing better." That much was true.

"Look, I'm sorry to call you on a weekend, but… Well, we haven't heard from you, and I'm starting to get a bad feeling about it."

"I said I'd be in touch, didn't I?"

"Yes, but I expected to hear from you before now. It's almost August, for God's sake." He paused. "So I started to wonder… maybe there was more to this than taking time out? Maybe… you've been approached by another firm, and you're tempted to see if the grass really is greener elsewhere, and you've been too afraid to tell me."

Aw fuck.

"You've been with us for ten years, and I'm not lying when I say you're my top guy. I think that's why I've held off getting in touch with you for so long. I don't want to lose you."

What the hell do I tell him? Hey, Paul, I love my job, but the pressure has gotten too much lately'? I have way too many deadlines to meet'? Trying to keep on top of everything took me in a direction I really didn't expect'? I keep thinking if I return to New York, within six months I'll be back at square one'?

That last one was what scared him the most, because he knew in his bones it could happen.

"Your silence is scaring the shit out of me, Marcus."

Marcus cleared his throat. "You're not going to lose me, but…"

"But? Spit it out."

He inhaled deeply. "Maybe we need to make some changes. Don't ask me *what* changes just yet, because I'm still going over the options in my head." He *had* considered the options, that was no lie, but he didn't think Paul was ready to think about him going part-time, or maybe working from home. Hell, he'd thought about going freelance, but not right away.

All he knew was at some point, he'd need to go back to the office and discuss the situation, and it was a conversation he was dreading.

There was silence at the other end of the line. "Do you want more money? Is that it?"

"No, it's not about money," Marcus assured him.

"Then what is it? You had me worried, Marcus, I have to be honest. You seemed… strung out. That was why I agreed to you taking time off. I only wish you could have told me what was wrong."

There was no way on Earth Marcus could have done that.

"How much more time do you think you'll need?"

Marcus didn't want to alienate Paul any more than he already had done, but he couldn't face him right then. "A few more weeks?"

Yet more silence. Finally, Paul sighed. "Okay.

But then we need to talk."

Marcus agreed. "I'll be in touch." They disconnected, and Marcus was disconcerted to discover he was shaking.

Definitely not ready to go back. He wasn't ready to lose what he had with Seb.

Marcus composed a text. *Want some company?*

Seb's reply was almost instantaneous. *Sure. Was gonna veg out on the couch. Not feeling like doing anything strenuous. Wanna join me?*

That sounded like it was exactly what Marcus needed. *On my way.* A dose of Seb was the perfect balm to soothe Marcus's troubled mind. In fact, if Marcus had his way, he'd wrap himself up in Seb and wear him always, his very own warm, sexy security blanket.

Except it's like I told Mom. Life doesn't work like that. He recalled her words, and ached for them to be true.

'It can if you want it to. If it's something you want badly enough.'

Right then, Marcus wanted it so badly, it hurt.

The credits rolled, and Marcus had to smile. Seb was asleep in his arms, Marcus lying behind him on the couch. Not that they'd started out that way. Seb had been at one end, Marcus at the other, but as the movie progressed, Seb had inched his way closer and closer, until Marcus had remarked dryly that any nearer and Seb would be in his lap. He'd held out his arm and fixed Seb with a forthright stare.

"If you want to snuggle, then snuggle. I'm not going to stop you."

Seb had hesitated for all of two seconds before closing the gap between them and laying his head on Marcus's shoulder. Half an hour later they were stretched out together, Marcus's arms around him, Seb's back warm and firm against his chest. Marcus wasn't sure how much of the movie Seb had seen, but he didn't have the heart to wake him.

Except it was eight-thirty, and Seb had to be up very early in the morning.

Marcus bent down and kissed him softly on the cheek. "Hey, Sleeping Beauty."

Seb opened his eyes. "Hmm?"

"Wake up, Sleeping Beauty. It's time to go to bed."

Seb rolled onto his back, staring up at Marcus. "I don't want you to go," he said in a low voice.

It took Marcus a heartbeat of time to come to a decision. "Then I'll stay." He leaned in closer to take Seb's mouth in a leisurely kiss. Seb's lips were warm and soft and the gentle scrape of his beard against Marcus's sent a frisson of pleasure through him.

"Bed," Seb announced as they parted. He got up from the couch and extended a hand to Marcus.

"We're not going to sleep right away, are we?" Marcus asked as he got to his feet.

Seb's eyes held a warm glow. "No, we're not.

I want to fall asleep with you inside me."

That was fine by Marcus.

July 26

Seb removed the laundry from the washer just as his phone rang. He hurried out of the bathroom to retrieve it from the kitchen. He smiled when he saw Gary's name. "Hey, you're still with us then."

Gary's snort filled his ears. "She ain't killed me with her cookin', an' I haven't buried her in the yard—yet."

He laughed. "So how are you doing?"

"Saw the doc yesterday. He said I'm mendin'. So I'm hopin' to be home in a couple o' weeks. Then you'll be off the hook."

Seb's chest constricted. "Oh. Right."

"You don't sound too happy 'bout it, yow'un. Don't you want your life back?"

"Yeah."

There was silence for a moment. "What's 'is name?"

Seb's first thought was that Tim had said something. "Excuse me?"

Gary gave a wry chuckle. "You don't sound all that keen to leave. I don't think for a second you've decided the life of a lobsterman is for you, so that leaves a guy. Who's been warmin' my bed for ya?

And is it still in one piece?"

"Yes, it's still in one piece, and I'll change the sheets before you get here."

"Good. Don't wanna catch no gay cooties." He cackled. There was another pause. "Thanks, kid. Tim says you've been friggin' awesome. I'll have to take things a bit easy at first, but me an' Tim'll cope. You've got school to think about."

"Will you get off that phone and eat your breakfast?" Annie shouted in the background.

"Where's that shovel?" Gary mumbled.

Seb laughed. "Don't kill her just yet. You're almost there. Let me know when you're coming back, and I'll make sure the house is ready for you. I'll get the groceries in too."

"Thanks, Seb. You're a good man." Gary disconnected.

Seb put the phone down on the countertop, his mind in a whirl. *It feels like the ground is slipping from under me.* Marcus had gone to the house to say goodbye to Jake, Sarah, and Mike. Marcus had informed him Jake had a job interview lined up in Boston. And *then* he'd added that he'd spoken with his boss in New York.

It's all coming to an end so fucking fast, and there's nothing I can do to stop it.

Only thing was, Seb didn't *want* it to end.

His phone buzzed again. This time it was a text from Marcus, and the sight of it made Seb's heart dance.

They've gone. On my way back.

Seb took a deep breath. *It's not over yet.* He intended to take what time was left, and spend as much of it with Marcus as they could both manage.

If anyone had told me before this summer that in six weeks I could lose my heart to a guy, I'd have laughed my ass off. Yet here he was, in exactly that situation.

When Marcus went back to New York, a piece of Seb's heart would go with him.

Chapter Twenty-Two

August 1

"Got anythin' planned for't weekend?" Tim asked Seb as they left Langsford's. Then he snorted. "Forget I asked. I prob'ly have a good idea."

"Marcus is coming over later." The offer was there if he wanted to join what remained of Marcus's family for dinner, but Seb was feeling greedy.

He wanted Marcus all to himself.

"Not long left, yow'un." Tim cackled. "I think it'll be a while before you set foot in a boat again." He patted Seb on the back. "See ya Monday."

Seb nodded. "Don't do anything I wouldn't do."

He caught Tim's raucous laughter as he walked away. "That don't leave me many options."

Seb strolled along Langsford Road, tired but happy. *Marcus is coming.* It had to have been at least eight or nine hours since Seb had last seen him. He had to wonder what Sandra and James made of Marcus's new routine—the past week, Marcus had slept in his own bed once.

His phone vibrated in his jeans pocket, and Seb removed it, expecting to see Marcus's name. When he saw it was Pete Michaud, he grinned.

"Hey, Pete. If you're calling to invite me to Dueling Divas this month, I'm gonna have to decline."

"Where have you been? I haven't seen you at Maine Street in weeks. You okay?"

"Yeah, I'm fine." Seb filled him in on the events that had brought him to Cape Porpoise.

"Bummer. Although I'm kinda relieved to hear you're all right."

"Aw, how sweet. You were worried." Seb cackled. "Do you make a habit of calling up clientele you haven't seen for a while?"

There was silence for a moment. "You haven't heard, have you?"

Seb's skin prickled. "Heard what?"

"About Justin."

Seb came to a halt in the middle of the sidewalk. "Christ, what's he done now?" When there was no response, cold trickled through him, despite the sun's warmth. "Pete? What is it?"

"He's dead, Seb."

The cold turned into an icy sludge around Seb's heart. "When? What happened?"

"Mark Pelletier called me this morning. He said there was a party last night, and Justin was there, along with six or seven friends. They were all enjoying some naked fun, and Justin went to a bedroom to put his head down. Three hours later, someone decided they should check on him. Mark said he'd looked in on Justin before, and he'd been snoring. Only, when they found him, they couldn't wake him up. Mark's pretty cut up about it. We've all told him it wasn't his fault."

Oh, Justin. Seb's heart sank. "What had he taken?" Knowing Justin's habits, it was the only logical question.

"They think he mixed G and booze."

"Aw, fuck. And no one noticed him *doing* that? No one said anything?"

"Hey, they were all busy taking care of themselves. And besides, what did I say, dude? They thought he was asleep!" Seb could hear the pain in Pete's voice. He got that: everyone had liked Justin, including Seb.

He sighed. "Thanks for letting me know. Although it's not exactly a surprise, is it? We know what he was like. It was only a matter of time." As far as Seb was concerned, anyone who did drugs was asking for trouble, not that some of the guys he'd hooked up with would have agreed with him.

"There isn't a date yet for the funeral. I'll let you know if I hear something."

"Thanks, Pete." He disconnected and pocketed his phone, his heart heavy. It felt wrong to be standing in the sunshine, hearing happy voices raised as tourists went about their lives, and somewhere Justin was lying beneath a sheet or sealed in a body bag. *How old was he? Thirty-five?* Christ, that was no age. Seb resumed his walk, his feet as heavy as his heart.

When he reached the house, Marcus's car was outside, and the sight lifted his spirits. Seb let himself into the house, to find Marcus making sandwiches in the kitchen.

He glanced across at Seb, and his face lit up. "Hey, nice timing. Lunch is ready. And before you ask, no, I haven't been here since you left. I got back half an hour ago." Marcus gestured to the plates. "Chicken salad sandwiches, and yes, I added garlic mayo, just for you—" He froze, his brow furrowed.

"Hey. Are you okay? You look awful."

Seb was suddenly bone-tired. "I *feel* awful. Just had a call from the bartender at my regular bar. A guy we know is dead."

"I'm so sorry." Marcus was at his side in an instant, his hands on Seb's upper arms. "Were you close?"

"He was always at Maine Street in Ogunquit. We hooked up, ages ago, and we stayed friends." Marcus's arms enfolded him, and Seb leaned on him, bereft of energy. He could still see Justin, his muscles, his handsome face, his smile…

"Sorry, baby," Marcus whispered, his cheek pressed to Seb's. He guided Seb to the couch, and sat, patting the seat cushion beside him. Seb joined him, feeling hollow and worn out.

"I don't think I've ever had anyone I know die before," he muttered.

"The feeling never improves, I can tell you that." Marcus stroked his hair. "How did he die?"

"A combination of G and booze, by the sound of it." Seb sagged against the seat cushion. "I'm assuming you know what G is. GHB, right? Although nowadays you'd have to live in a cave not to know what it is."

Oh shit. Another one.

Marcus stiffened. "Yeah, I know what it is. I

also know you should never mix the two."

Seb huffed. "Hey, if it hadn't been that particular combination, the meth would've killed him at some point. In fact, if he hadn't done meth, he'd probably have survived this. Because I'd be willing to bet he took enough of *that* to make himself vulnerable to G."

Say nothing. Say nothing.

Except Marcus had come too far along this path to be silent.

"How do you know he did meth?"

Seb's eyes were closed. "Because he offered some to me, when we hooked up. I told him I wasn't interested. End of conversation." A sigh fell from his lips. "There were others who *were* interested, however. They're welcome to it."

Marcus's mouth had dried up. "How much alcohol did he drink in addition to the G?"

"I don't know."

"How much G did he use?"

Seb opened his eyes. "I don't know that either. What is this, twenty questions? You planning on writing his obituary or something?" His face tightened. "I'm sorry. I shouldn't have said that. It's still kinda raw."

Marcus could have left it there, but his It's-irresponsible-not-to-educate gene kicked in. "So you've no idea of the amounts involved, but you're going to blame it on meth anyway." It wouldn't be the first time Marcus had heard that theory.

Seb gaped at him. "Oh, come *on*. We all know about meth, right? You go to the same kinda clubs that I do, so you know how it goes."

Marcus took a deep breath. "Let me guess

what *you* know. A guy has his first taste of meth, and that's it, he's an addict. He'll steal to fund his habit. He'll even sell himself. It'll ruin not only his life, but the lives of any family member or friends who don't shake him off ASAP. He doesn't sleep. He's obsessed with sex. He's paranoid…" He arched his eyebrows. "Does that pretty much cover it?"

"I think you just about nailed it, yeah. Why the hell do you think drugs are such a big deal? Because they *ruin lives*, that's why. *That's* why schools run programs to educate kids, so that they don't slide down that slippery slope and become addicts. And it's a losing battle."

Marcus nodded slowly. "Okay, Teacher, you want to talk about education? School is in session, and it's Meth 101. Whatever you *think* you know? It's all bullshit. Not some of its effects, I'll grant you, but *everyone* becoming an instant addict? Total crap. You *can* be a functional user too. I'll agree that, for some, that first taste *can* be their downfall. Unfortunately, the only way to find out which of those two you are is to try it." He held up his hands. "Don't misunderstand me. I'm not advocating that you rush out and try it. I'm merely pointing out that what you *think* you know? Might not be the whole story. And if you want to know more, then do some research. And I *don't* mean Dr. Google. Look up Carl Hart, for one thing. He makes more sense than most of what you'll find online." *Christ*. He was a mess.

Seb lifted his chin, his eyes narrowed in confusion.

Marcus sat back, his arms folded. "Ask me. There's a question right there on the tip of your tongue that you're dying to ask, so ask it." His heart hammered, and his breathing quickened.

Seb swallowed. "Have *you* ever used meth?"

Crunch time. "Yes."

Fuck, Seb was so still. "More than once?"

He sucked in a breath. "Yes."

"Have you used it since you came to Cape Porpoise?" The cautious way he asked tore at Marcus's heart.

"No." Marcus tilted his head to one side. "Except now you're not sure you can believe that. Am I right?"

Seb's Adam's apple bobbed. "You're asking me to go against something I'm sure is true. I… I don't know what to say to you."

"There's nothing *to* say, not if you've already formed your opinion. If you want to continue with the All-meth-users-are-addicts-who-would-sell-their-own-grandmothers-to-fund-their-habit argument, then we really do have nothing to talk about." He got to his feet. "So… to save us both from awkward silences, I'll go." He sighed. "I know why you think the way you do. If *my* best friend's mom had succumbed to drugs, I think I'd probably feel the same. But you're speaking from limited experience. *I*, on the other hand, know whereof I speak." He grabbed his car keys from the table. "If you want to ignore everything you've heard from people who've never used it, are never *likely* to use it, and yet somehow know all there is to know on the subject, then you know where to find me."

"You… you're going?"

Marcus managed a shrug. "I've said enough. How does the saying go? 'A man convinced against his will is of the same opinion still'? You've got my number. If I get a call, great. If I don't?" He swallowed. "I'll understand. I won't like it, but I'll understand. It's hard to swim against the tide of popular opinion." Marcus walked toward the door.

"Marcus…" He came to a halt and turned. Seb's face was uncharacteristically pale. "Jesus, Marcus, that's it? You're gonna leave it like this?"

He bit his lip. "The funny thing is? If we'd had this conversation weeks ago, I'd have just walked out without saying any of this. But not now."

Seb's brow furrowed. "Why? What's different?"

Marcus speared him with an intense stare. "Tell me you don't feel we have something."

Another swallow. "I… I can't tell you that."

He nodded. "So it's not just me. Which makes it doubly hard to walk away. Because there's always the chance that it could be for the last time, and God knows, I really don't want to lose you." Marcus looked him in the eye. "But if you can't trust me, can't believe what I tell you… then we don't have a future anyway." And with that, he was out of there, walking—no, *running*—to his car, his heartbeat racing, his stomach like a rock as he fought the urge to throw up on Gary's meager excuse for a front yard.

What the fuck have I done?

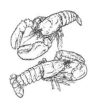

It felt as though time had slowed down.

Seb stared at the door, cold spreading out from his core, his head spinning.

What the fuck?

He sagged weakly against the cushions, replaying Marcus's words over and over in his head.

I can't deal with this. Not on my own.

He reached for his phone and speed-dialed Levi. The instant the call connected, Seb surged ahead. "Hey, you got a minute? I really need to talk."

"Give me a sec, I've just made Grammy some lunch. Let me take it to her, and then I'm all yours."

Seb forced himself to take deep breaths while he waited, his stomach churning.

"Okay. What's up?"

Where the fuck do I begin? "I just found out something about Marcus, and… I'm having a hard time getting my head around it." *Understatement of the fucking decade.*

"Can't be *that* bad."

"Oh yeah? Try this on for size. He's used meth. Past tense, because he says he isn't using now, but who the fuck knows?"

The sudden silence brought about a rash of goose bumps.

"Okay, I'm only going to say this once." Christ, Levi's voice was so quiet. "Don't walk away from that man—run. As fast as you can."

Therein lay the problem. Seb didn't *want* to walk away. "Look, I know why you say that, but—"

"But *nothing*. How many stories do you need to hear about another gay guy dying of a meth overdose? There was a case earlier this year, some guy on a gay cruise." There was a pause. "He didn't offer it to you, did he?"

"No, he didn't, and this is the first time he's mentioned it, okay? I thought I knew him but now? I don't know *what* to think."

Another pause. "Christ... You... you're in love with him."

"Yuh. And here's a newsflash for ya. He's in love with me—I think. Not that either of us has come right out and said it, but yeah..."

"So what are you going to do?"

"Right now I have no fucking clue, except for trying to survive this without getting my heart broken. And that's looking pretty fucking inevitable."

"Look, you know what I think. I'm here if you want to talk, okay? And yeah, I know my viewpoint is biased, but there are no gray areas where drugs are concerned. Do the research. You'll see I'm right." He paused. "But I *am* sorry, Seb."

"You and me both." Seb disconnected, then tossed his phone onto the couch beside him. He closed his eyes.

Were there any clues?

He racked his brain, bringing to mind any guys he knew for certain took meth. Sometimes they appeared not to have slept for three or four days, and sex became an obsession. Seb had been at one party where a few of the guys had slammed meth, and he'd watched them start their 'rush': there was a telltale flush, and he could almost see their hearts race, before they started pulling their clothes off and turning to anything sexual they could reach. There had been other parties too, where guys under the influence had sat around, everyone on their phones going through the hookup apps, searching for other men who might actually be able to get a boner going, and wanking their not-hard cocks for *hours*.

There was nothing hot about that *at all* in Seb's book, and he hadn't seen *any* of that with Marcus. Sure, he was horny as fuck most of the time, but then, so was Seb. That was why they were so fucking perfect for each other.

Maybe Levi hit on something. There had to be a whole lot of information out there on the subject, right? Something other than the 'Don't Do Drugs' message. Except he was pretty sure that was the message Levi intended for him to see.

Marcus said I don't know the whole story. So maybe I'd better go looking for answers. It was a better prospect than sitting there feeling sorry for himself. Then he thought about Marcus, and despite Seb's misgivings, his heart went out to him.

I hope he's okay.

Chapter Twenty-Three

Marcus stepped into the house's cool, quiet interior. Ashley had taken the kids out for the day, as it was Alex's birthday. He was grateful: the last thing he needed right then was noise.

What a clusterfuck. Yet he didn't think he could have handled it any other way.

"Marcus?" Mom came out of the kitchen, wiping her hands on a towel. "I thought we'd seen the last of you until tomorrow."

"Change of plan." He dropped his keys onto the hall table and headed for the living room. Dad sat in the big armchair, an open book in his lap. When he glanced up and saw Marcus, he frowned.

"What are you doing here?"

Marcus arched his eyebrows. "I was staying here, last time I looked." He was being obtuse, and he knew it, but he didn't want to talk about Seb. He went over to the liquor cabinet, removed Dad's bottle of Wild Turkey and a glass, then closed it. Dad cleared his throat, and Marcus realized that for someone who didn't want to talk, grabbing a bottle of whiskey was like putting a sign over his head that read, 'Give me the third degree because something is wrong.'

I should've waited till he wasn't around. Hindsight was a hell of a thing.

"Bit early for that, isn't it?" Dad commented dryly.

"No, not really." He didn't wait around for a response, but went out into the yard through the French doors. By the time he reached the safe haven of the summerhouse, he was shaking again. His fingers fumbled as he took off the cap.

"Son, what's happened?" Mom stood in the doorway, her brow furrowed.

Marcus poured himself a glass. "I can't answer that." When her frown deepened, he sighed. "What can I tell you? The jury's still out? Wait and see?" He sank into the recliner, the glass in his hand.

"You're not making any sense." She cocked her head to one side. "Did you and Seb have a fight? And don't tell me you're just friends, because I may have been born at night, but it wasn't *last* night."

He swirled the amber liquid, inhaling its pleasant fumes. "It wasn't a fight, exactly. We…" His throat seized. *I can't do this.*

"Do you need to go talk to him?"

Marcus took a sip for lubrication. "Nope. Ball's in his court now."

She walked over to where he sat, and tried to pry the glass gently from his hand, but he held on to it. "Sweetheart, that's never a good idea, especially when it isn't even one o'clock in the afternoon yet. Why don't I take the bottle, and put it back where it came from?"

He snorted. "You're using your teacher voice on me. That's not fair."

"I don't care if it's fair or not, as long as it works." She went over to the table and picked up the bottle. "I'm making a birthday cake for Alex. Why don't you come help me?"

"And lick the spoon, like I did when I was a kid?" Marcus sighed. "It might have cured all my ills back then, but trust me, it won't help this time."

"How do you know until you try it?"

God, he loved her so much. "I just do."

"Then what *will* help?"

He'd thought about that on the drive back from Seb's. "Maybe turn the clock back a couple of years?"

"Then you wouldn't have met him," she said simply.

"Yes, I would." He believed that. "I'd be here for the summer, so would he…" And with none of the baggage that was messing up any chance they had of being happy, being together.

I don't know that. He might actually do what I suggested and look for himself.

Yeah, right.

Mom cleared her throat. "Okay, I'm calling bullshit."

He blinked. "Excuse me?"

She gave him a frank gaze. "No, I don't think I will. Who's to say you'd have met him? If you're *that* good at fortune-telling, you'd have made your millions on the stock market by now, and retired before you were thirty." Her expression softened. "In case no one has ever told you, playing the what-if game is a losing proposition. You're sure speaking to him won't help?"

No, I'm not sure. It's just an assumption. Marcus gazed into the whiskey he no longer wanted to drink. "I have to let him work through this on his own. I've said all I can. It really is up to him now."

"It might help me understand better if I had some idea of what happened."

He shook his head. "You don't need to know." Marcus's stomach was in knots. He didn't want to think about Seb, because that only created more knots. He held out the glass. "Here. I don't want it."

She took it from him. "Then please, come into the house and talk to me while I make this cake." She glanced at the interior of the summerhouse. "And you don't have to sleep here anymore, not now most of them have left. I don't like the idea of you being out here, with only your thoughts for company."

"Mom, don't worry about me."

She gave him a sad smile. "That's like asking rain not to fall, or the wind not to blow. Moms worry. And it doesn't matter how old their children are."

He got up from his chair. "Then let's go see if licking the spoon really does help. Just as long as it's chocolate."

Mom chuckled. "As if I'd make any other kind."

He followed her out of the summerhouse and along the path to the kitchen door, focused not on cake but on Seb. The temptation to call or text was enormous, but he knew that was wrong. He had to give Seb space.

I said I'd understand if there were no call.

He'd meant it, too, but that didn't mean he wasn't hoping with every fiber, nerve, and cell in his body.

Seb had fallen down the rabbit hole.

He sat on the couch, his laptop balanced on his knee, and a bottle of water on the coffee table. His head was spinning.

Christ, there's so much here.

The first links he'd found were mostly articles sponsored by rehabs and addiction centers, which only made him more certain Marcus had it wrong—until he recalled something a professor had told them in college. Something about looking at the organization or individual funding whatever study or research, and seeing if they had a vested interest in the outcome—an agenda. All those rehabs and centers were paying huge sums of money to get their articles seen first, and they were in it for profit.

Find something else. There has to be something else.

Then he came across a post by a guy called Alexander Cheves, who maintained that queer culture was a drug-friendly culture. *That's for damn sure.* Some of what he said made a lot of sense, and one paragraph in particular caught Seb's attention.

Drugs, like sex, get glamorized and damned. To some, drugs are like forbidden fruit—they must *be wonderful. To others, they are the devil's work, the corrupter of youth, a commodity of society's lowlifes—they* must *be terrible. People have these same polarized views of sex, and like sex, drugs are both of these perspectives and neither of them—they are not as great or as terrible as anyone thinks.*

Seb's chest tightened as he read those lines. That second perspective could have been his own words to Marcus. And Marcus hadn't claimed drugs were wonderful. If anything, he'd tried to give a balanced view.

He wanted me to think for myself.

By the time he remembered the sandwiches Marcus had made, it was hours later and they were curling at the edges. He threw them into the trash, and heated some soup. Then he went back to the couch to continue his online search.

It was so easy to get mired in a site that got *way* too technical. He didn't want to know *how* the drugs did what they did—he was seeking confirmation. It was no longer a search to be told all drug users were a lost cause and irredeemable.

He wanted Marcus to be right, because the alternative didn't bear thinking about.

I want to believe him, to trust him again.

When eight o'clock arrived, Seb was exhausted. His research had branched off tangentially on several occasions, and it was only with a supreme effort that he'd forced himself back on track. It seemed as if everyone had their own opinion on the 'evils' of drugs. One site in particular had stopped him in his tracks. Marcus's mention of Carl Hart had intrigued him, but what he found on the man's website astounded him. Dr. Hart had written a book about drug use for grownups, but it wasn't that which gave Seb food for thought—it was a few lines from the book's introduction.

After reading this book, I hope you will be less likely to vilify individuals merely because they use drugs. That thinking has led to an incalculable number of deaths and an enormous amount of suffering.

Seb read those lines over and over. He couldn't deny his own perception of Justin had been colored by Justin's habitual drug use. *I claim to want to steer kids in the right direction and away from distractions, but when they succumb to those distractions, how do I react?*

He closed his eyes. *Fuck, I'm tired.* He decided to call it a night and rest his aching head, until a headline caught his eye.

The war on drugs is over—and drugs won.

What *kept* his attention on the article was the name of its author—Marcus Gilbert.

No way.

He read it through three times, and each time one particular part engrossed him.

The war on drugs as declared by Nixon and institutionalized by Reagan is over. And drugs won. By demonizing the chemical, we made it easy to castigate the user and the addict. It is likely that most who try a recreational drug initially do so out of curiosity or as a result of peer pressure, but research increasingly shows that sustained addiction is a symptom of a deeper problem, societally, socially, or emotionally. As we readily recognize as a cause of alcoholism, abusing a drug is far more often than not a means of self-medication; it has become for the addict a means of alleviating pain, grief, or anxiety. For a society to then add the shame of addiction to whatever the addict is already suffering does the addict far more harm than good, and more often than not drives him deeper into addiction. Hence if in our efforts to

*help those who would free themselves from drugs we only
address the drug use, we set all of us up for failure. If these
deeper problems are not identified and addressed, any addict
who might try to recover will find nothing in his life or
environment fixed, and will certainly be tempted to return to
self-medicating. We must stop taking the lazy way out,
suggesting that this is someone else's—i.e., the addict's—
problem. These difficulties they face are societal, too large for
the addict to change alone. Hence if we are to expect any turn
towards victory, we need to stop making this a "war on drugs",
or by frank extension a "war on addicts". We as a society are
causing this malaise; only we as a whole working together can
fix this.*

What struck him most was the *humane*
attitude toward addiction.

He knows what he's talking about. Seb shook his
head. *Of course he does. He's been through it, or at least
knows others who have.* The piece was insightful and
articulate, and he regretted the intolerance and
unwillingness to bend that he'd shown Marcus. And
the more he thought about it, the more Seb realized
his cookie-cutter image of guys who did meth was
seriously flawed. Not once had he seen Justin's habit
as anything other than a desire to get high. It had
never occurred to him to wonder what had started
Justin down that particular road in the first place.
And what about my students? Did I ever stop to think why
*they started using? I put it all down to experimentation, and
left it at that.*

Which led him to Marcus, and even more
questions that would go unanswered—unless…

Seb glanced at the laptop's screen. It was
already nine o'clock. Far too late to be calling
Marcus. Seb wanted to be wide awake and alert for

that conversation.

It can wait till tomorrow.

He climbed into bed, and it was as if someone flicked a switch, and all trace of fatigue fled, pushing his thoughts into overdrive. The conversation with Marcus replayed as though in a loop, to the point where Seb was seriously considering raiding Gary's bathroom cabinet in search of something to knock him out.

By the time sleep came, he sank into it, craving oblivion.

Chapter Twenty-Four

August 2

Marcus figured he'd had about two hours' sleep the whole night, which wasn't surprising given the circumstances. His inner turmoil only reaffirmed what he already knew. If Seb hadn't mattered, if he wasn't important, Marcus wouldn't have been such a mess. He would have simply walked away.

But I can't do that. Not now.

Sunlight poured through the windows, accompanied by birdsong. It was too early for the kids to be awake, so Marcus lay in his narrow bed, enjoying the peace—and wishing Seb was in his arms.

Ashley wouldn't be happy about that. The kids would have too many questions.

When his phone vibrated, Marcus snatched it up from the floor beside the bed and peered at the screen.

It was Seb. *Can we talk?*

Fuck. Those three words were enough to quicken both his heartbeat and his breathing. He clicked *Call.* "Hey. You're up early for a Sunday."

"Yeah, well… Sleep wasn't happening, so…"

Marcus could hear the fatigue in Seb's voice. "I hear ya. Same here." He paused. "I didn't expect to hear from you so soon."

Be honest. You weren't sure if you'd hear from him at all.

"I read your article," Seb blurted out.

Okay, he hadn't expected that, although maybe he should, if Seb had gone digging like he'd suggested.

"Marcus?"

"I'm still here. You took me by surprise." *So? What did you think?*

"I want to know more."

And there went Marcus's heart rate again. "Okay," he said in a cautious tone.

"In the article, you wrote about the reasons why people take drugs. Well… I want to know *your* reasons. How you started on this path. You say you're not on it now—I want to know why."

It wasn't the first time Marcus had been confronted with such a request, and he'd learned from the experience. "When I'm up and dressed, and I've had at least one cup of coffee, I'll be over there. I'm not going to stay," he added quickly. "But I *will* leave something with you that will hopefully answer all your questions."

"You can't do that in person?"

"You have to trust me on this. I've been down this road before, and it really is the best way." The last time he'd tried to have this conversation, there had been a barrage of interruptions, resulting in confusion and frustration. "If you still have questions after you've read it, then fine, I'll answer them." But hopefully he wouldn't need to.

Crickets.

"Seb? If… if that's not okay, I'll—"

"It's fine. I'll see you when you get here." Seb

fell silent, and Marcus's heart pounded. Then Seb sighed. "You gave me a lot to think about, stuff I hadn't considered. And you were right, by the way."

"About what?"

"I thought I knew the whole story. Turns out I didn't. Dr. Hart's site was an eye-opener."

The tightness around Marcus's chest eased a little, and he shuddered out a breath. "Thank you."

"For what?"

"Following my advice. You didn't have to go look."

"Yeah, I did. Because you were right about something else too." Another pause. "You and me… we could have a future. Not sure how that future would look, the logistics of it, but yeah, the possibility is there—and I don't wanna walk away from that."

Marcus sent up a silent prayer of thanks. "Me neither. Now let me get some coffee down my neck, so I can get my brain in gear."

Seb chuckled. "Go caffeinate. I'll be here." Then he disconnected.

Marcus lurched across the room to the table where his laptop and bag sat. He delved into it, searching for a USB drive. When he found one, he turned on the laptop and began downloading the document.

It didn't matter if the book wasn't polished or edited. It could tell Seb everything he'd need to know.

And then we can talk.

Seb opened the door as soon as he heard the car pull up outside. One look at Marcus's drawn face told him plenty.

Looks like we both had a rough night.

Marcus approached him with far more caution than Seb expected. "Hey."

Seb nodded. "Do you want to come in for coffee? I just made some."

"You know what? I'll pass." Marcus reached into his jeans pocket and removed a small object. He held it out to Seb. "Here. You can plug this into your laptop. There's only one file on it."

Seb had already surmised what Marcus was bringing. "This is your book, isn't it?"

Marcus nodded. "There's a lot of stuff that will bore the pants off you—stuff you've probably already found on Carl Hart's site. The parts *you* need to read are the autobiographical bits. I highlighted them in the index." He placed the USB drive into Seb's outstretched hand, his fingers brushing Seb's palm. "Read it all, read as much as you feel like—but when you think you've read enough, call me, and then we'll talk."

Seb nodded. "Sure." He cocked his head to one side. "Are you okay?"

Marcus's laughter had a bitter edge to it. "Not really. I've spent the past four months getting myself into a better place, both physically and mentally, and it feels like the last eighteen or so hours sent me back to square one again." He held up his hands. "I know that's an exaggeration, but it's how I feel right now." Marcus inclined his head toward the USB. "Happy reading."

"Thanks." Seb yearned to hug him, but the distance Marcus maintained between them quelled that impulse.

Marcus nodded and headed back to his car.

"Hey, Marcus," Seb called out as he opened the car door. He waited till Marcus was looking his way, and smiled. "Good to see you."

"You too." Marcus's weary smile made Seb's heart ache. "Hey. Remember how you asked me if I'd ever peeked into a guy's nightstand drawer, and I told you to be careful, because you might find something you don't expect?" Seb nodded, and Marcus smiled. "Well, that's how all this began—with a drawer." Then he got into the car and drove away from the house.

Seb went inside and closed the door. He poured himself a cup of coffee, got comfy on the couch, and fired up the laptop, his mouth dry, a tingling in his chest.

Let's see what we've got here.
The preface was direct.

You don't have to take everything I write in here as gospel.

You have the right to believe whatever you want.
But…

If you're going to engage me in conversation about some of the things I've written here, make sure you abide by the rules of evidence.

There were six or seven highlighted chapters, so Seb went to the first of these.

I know it sounds odd. How can a gay guy reach the age of forty-three and not have taken any drugs? And by drugs, I'm talking about the ones prevalent in gay culture—coke, Ketamine, E, GHB, and meth. (Those last three are MDMA, Gamma Hydroxybutyrate and methamphetamine, if you want to be really technical)

I know plenty of men who do partake, of course, but that wasn't me.

Until the night I met Drake.

I'd gone to a club in search of release. Work had been a bitch, and I was all kinds of tense. A hot hookup would cure my ills, and the moment I laid eyes on Drake, I knew we'd end up in the sack at some point. He was younger than me, with a body that would make any man drool. And when he casually dropped into conversation that his roommates were away for the weekend, it was a done deal.

Once we were in his room, we quickly established we were both on PrEP, and within weeks of our latest test. Then the clothes came off, and he directed me to his nightstand drawer to retrieve the lube. Except when I opened it, there was something else in there, and curiosity got the better of me.

"What is that?" There was a small blue plastic bottle containing a colorless liquid, and an equally small plastic bag filled with a whitish granular substance.

Drake smiled. "You don't do G or meth?"

"No. I've heard of them." Who hasn't? And peering at them was as far as I was willing to go. I was too skittish at that point to even consider touching them.

Drake cocked his head. "Would you mind if I did?"

"Why do you take them? What's the draw?" I'd

been curious for a while.

"G lowers your inhibitions." He grinned. "Makes you super horny. But then, so does meth. I take 'em together."

"Why, if they both produce the same effect?"

"One counteracts the less desirable side effects of the other. G is a depressor, and meth is a stimulant that works against it."

I picked up the bottle. "I have been curious about this." I glanced at him. "Can we?"

Drake held up both hands. "Hey, I don't wanna be the one to get you into this. We don't need it. We can just fuck."

Except now I was seriously contemplating trying it.

"Or we could fuck and do G," I suggested.

Drake sighed. "Look, I like you, okay? You're here, we're naked... I don't wanna overdo it, all right?"

"Are you afraid this will screw things up?"

Drake sat on the bed, pulling me down next to him. "Here's the thing you need to realize. Your attitude toward the drug is everything. You think it'll screw it up? Guess what? It'll screw things up. You think it'll give you a good time, and enhance shit? Then that's what it'll do."

I knew in that moment I was going to try it. What Drake was offering was the opportunity to try it in a controlled, safe environment.

"Let's do it."

Seb hadn't expected that first step to be so... simple. He liked that Drake hadn't done a hard sell on Marcus: if anything, he'd been reluctant to let him dip his toes.

He skimmed through the rest of the first chapter, until a line caught his eye, and he stopped to read more.

I have never bought G or meth. I have never consciously sought them out.

But...

If I hooked up with a guy who had them, I used them. Suddenly it felt as though more and more of the guys I hooked up with were users.

I never injected. I wasn't into slamming. I expected to crave the drugs, and when I didn't, I'll admit, I was confused.

Despite Drake's assurance that my attitude would color my experience, I'd gone into it with no small amount of trepidation. I knew meth's reputation for being addictive, after all. And as time went by, I learned a lot about both drugs.

In a nutshell...

As much as we hear over and over that someone died of a meth overdose, though, this is almost never the case; the amount that would have to be taken... well, the person would be vilely ill well before that stage is arrived at.

I'm going to repeat that.

Nobody dies of meth overdose.

GHB, however, which we gay men wink at all the time, is the real killer. Meth ruins lives, but it doesn't really kill. I've seen guys who had been functional occasional users for quite some while, for whatever reason suddenly get sucked down the slippery slope into full overuse. And yes, between the lack of sleep, the sexual obsession it can cause, the potential paranoia, the possible psychosis, the neglect of one's body and hygiene that can result... As you can imagine, yes, this drug can fuck up a person's life monstrously.

So what did I learn?

It's hard to categorize G, as it's a chemical that's in our bodies anyway, related to neurotransmitter and dopamine production. There's a sense of euphoria and a relaxing of inhibitions. It aggrandizes senses, makes music or bodily contact mean so much more, and the sense of sexual arousal is strong.

When you take it, your sense of time is altered, and you have to be very careful about not having too much in your system. Timing subsequent doses is vital. I saw house parties where cooking timers were set, and at ninety minutes when the bell dinged, *someone said, "G o'clock!" and the next dose was prepared. At such parties where someone was being particularly cognizant, everyone took their dose together so nobody got confused. However, under the influence and without a timer, it got beyond easy to believe that the high from the previous dose had run its course and you were ready for another far too soon.*

G is a deeply dangerous drug on a few levels. One, it's seriously mercurial: the same dose from the same batch on two different days can have wildly different effects. One day it gets you high, and the next, it misses the target.

DO NOT MIX G AND ALCOHOL.

Use of poppers while on G should also be discouraged. G by itself may lower blood pressure a bit; this is why a bit too much G in the system causes a "G out"; the person goes limp and essentially falls asleep. If this happens in a club, the guy needs to be made to move, needs to be made to keep his circulation up. He needs to be given fluid, and he must not be allowed to rest. Most often he'll be fine, but if security sees him, they will probably ask him and anyone with him to leave, and they may insist on calling medical attention for him. However, especially in combination with alcohol, this blood pressure drop may prove fatal.

Oh my God.

In one paragraph, Marcus had hit upon the circumstances of Justin's death. *Did his friends know what to do in case of a "G out"?* Because to Seb's new way of thinking, responsible drug use implied knowledge of how to deal with its consequences. Then he realized how far he'd come, because up till then, he hadn't known there *was* such a thing as responsible drug use.

He read a few lines down from that, and stilled.

G is highly addictive, and although you have to take fairly substantial quantities for quite some time to arrive at this point, it can have some vile, deeply unpleasant withdrawal symptoms.

And as for meth…

A lot of the guys who took it experienced euphoric highs, but there were others who simply became focused and clear-thinking while taking it. I was in the latter camp. Intrigued by this difference, I did some research.

It's instructive to think of methamphetamine as being a kissing cousin to amphetamine, which is the Adderall some of my friends take for ADHD. They are essentially the same substance.

However…

There is an aspect of meth which affects brain chemistry specifically related to how memories are formed and retained; by causing or facilitating a recurrence of the same memory over and over, and by loosening the constraints that keep memories from changing over time, meth allows a heavy user to rework memories and thoughts, detaching from reality. In the instances where this does happen, much of the time the person just gets confused when memory and reality fail to match later on. Frequently, the recurrence of the faulty memory amplifies itself; catching a glimpse from the corner of your eye of what looked like eyes peeking in a window can, a few days later, become an absolute certainty that the neighbors or the

CIA are spying on you. The fact that the window is four stories off the ground is immaterial...

I was never a heavy user, but I hooked up with a few guys who were, and time after time, I got to experience their paranoia at first hand.

What surprised the hell out of me was that meth really has no chemically addictive properties. Why, then, was it so hard for so many to set aside?

With a little research, I had my answer.

Meth allows the user to reprogram his own thinking so that he absolutely believes that he needs the drug—the psychological *addictiveness of meth is what screws up so many. Couple that with this drug having a huge sexual aspect for most—horniness can be almost unmanageable, although the degree of stimulant will prevent a hard-on from even having a chance of forming for most guys—and this drug has become associated with sex to the point that many guys believe they are unable to have sex without it.*

And that was the trap into which I plummeted.

Seb's heart hammered. *Oh, Marcus.*

I found myself caught up in an endless cycle. As my work-related stress levels increased, I sought relief in more and more sexual encounters, with more and more partners who took chemicals to enhance their experience—and who shared these chemicals with me.

Ultimately, that affected my work, which increased my stress, which made me seek relief through sex... On and on it went. Now and then, I'd hook up with a guy who didn't use, and while the sex brought relief, it didn't feel as... enhanced, which in turn sank me into depression. To combat this, I went back to hooking up with guys who used. It got to the point where I was having a hard time conceptualizing having sex without drugs.

I tried to stop, but telling myself I wouldn't partake while remaining in that same environment was a nonstarter. The cycle needed to be broken.

Seb set the laptop on the coffee table, then sagged against the cushions.

Well, now I know why Marcus left New York.

It left Seb with a few unanswered questions, however—and a lot of remorse.

He grabbed his phone and composed a short text.

Come on over. We need to talk. And I need to apologize.

Chapter Twenty-Five

Marcus got out of the car, aware of an empty feeling in the pit of his stomach. *We need to talk* hadn't given much away, but Seb's desire to apologize at least gave a hint at the way things might go. His pulse quickened as the door opened.

Seb stood there in his sweats and tee, his hair tousled and his feet bare. "Hey. Coffee's on."

"Music to my ears." Marcus drew closer. He'd never wanted to hold Seb as badly as he did in that moment, but he tamped down hard on the impulse: Seb would have to make the first move.

Seb stood aside to let him enter, then closed the door and went over to the coffee pot. "By the way, you were wrong. I didn't find any of it boring. In fact, I think I got quite an education."

Marcus sat on the couch. Seb's laptop was on the coffee table. "I know it got a bit technical. And I also know there will be people who read it who think it's TMI. Fuck them. Too many people have strange and potentially dangerous ideas about drugs. I thought it important to put it all in the right context."

Seb came over, carrying two cups, and handed one to Marcus before joining him. He propped his feet up on the table. "You left New York to break the cycle, didn't you?"

Marcus nodded. "And to get away from my so-called friends."

Seb frowned. "What do you mean?"

"Word got around. 'Marcus is a meth addict.'"

"But you're not. Anyone who talks to you for more than five minutes knows that."

Marcus locked gazes with him. "You say that *now*, but did you think it yesterday?"

Seb had the good grace to flush. "Please, don't remind me."

"But what has really *changed* since yesterday? I'm the same man I was then. All that's happened is you've had your preconceptions challenged, and you've been re-educated."

"I'm guessing you weren't so successful with your friends. Did you tell them you weren't an addict?"

Marcus nodded. "It didn't make any difference. I denied it, and got the reaction 'Well, of *course* you deny it, because that's what addicts do. So you *must* be an addict.' I could tell them I didn't have a problem till I was blue in the face. I was obviously lying because addicts lie about their habits, right?" He scowled. "What really got me was the hypocrisy of it all."

"Hypocrisy?"

"Sure. They're happy to take E when they go clubbing. I bet you know lots of guys who take E, right?" Seb nodded. "Well, E is MDMA. What do they think that MA stands for? Methamphetamine. And I know one guy whose boyfriend is on Adderall. *He* doesn't have ADHD, but that doesn't stop him taking his boyfriend's meds and popping it like candy before he goes out dancing, because it helps him stay awake. But it's not meth, right?" He sagged against the cushions. "There is such a stigma attached to meth. It's like I said to you yesterday. People hear 'meth' and…" He locked gazes with Seb. "You believed what people told you, didn't you?"

Seb nodded. "Because I didn't know any better." He tilted his head. "Were you really scared you couldn't have sex without it?"

"Yeah, I was. I have to say, that fear went out the window after one night with you."

Seb grinned and preened. "Damn, I'm good."

Marcus's heart soared to see a glimmer of the Seb he'd known up till then. He leaned over and whacked him on the arm. "Your hole did *not* cure me, okay? It might feel amazing on my dick, but magic it is *not*."

Seb arched his eyebrows. "Hey, it could be. Maybe we should try it again, just to make sure."

Marcus narrowed his gaze. "Subtle, Seb. Very subtle." He sighed. "I was in a different place. No work, no stress… Maybe that helped. Maybe these few months acted as a… reboot of sorts." He smiled. "I've been set back to my factory settings. But while *that* fear proved groundless, there was another waiting to take its place."

"And what was that?"

Marcus looked him in the eye. "That you'd turn out to be like everyone else."

"And for a moment there, I was." Seb swallowed. "I'm not proud of how I reacted."

Marcus shifted closer. "You didn't know. You'd been fed the same diet as most of the gay men out there." He cupped Seb's chin. "You know what's listed as one of the most dangerous drugs out there? Alcohol. But saying you drink doesn't get the same reaction as saying you take meth." He stilled. "But you were different. *You* listened."

"Because you asked me to." Seb's voice was so quiet, his breathing harsh.

Marcus seized his courage. "And if I asked you to kiss me?"

Seb rolled his eyes. "Thought you'd never get there." Then his arms were around Marcus's neck, their lips met, and Marcus sighed into a kiss he'd believed he'd never experience again. Seb pushed him onto his back, then lay on him, his body warm and firm in Marcus's arms.

He rested his head on Marcus's shoulder. "I'm sorry."

Marcus tilted Seb's head, his fingers under Seb's chin. "You've already apologized."

"Yeah, well, I'm doing it again. I should have trusted you."

Marcus traced the line of Seb's jaw with his fingertips. "In the grand scheme of things, you've known me for what, five minutes? Guys who've known me for more than a decade leaped onto the bandwagon in a heartbeat. And not *one* of those guys has come to me and said, 'Hey, Marcus... I was wrong.'" He tightened his arm around Seb, holding him so close, he could feel Seb's heart beating.

Then Seb moved, shifting higher, and kissed him, a slow, tender kiss that was balm to Marcus's bruised soul.

"You feel good," Seb murmured against his lips.

"You feel better," Marcus countered. He ran

his fingers through Seb's unruly hair, pushing it back from his face so he could see those blue eyes he lov—

But it's not just his eyes, is it?

He lay still beneath Seb, his heart pounding. "Know what else makes you different?"

Seb raised his chin. "What?"

"All those friends? I could never see them again, and I wouldn't lose any sleep over it. Well, most of them." *Maybe not Nick.* He stroked Seb's cheek. "But I couldn't bear the thought of losing you. And leaving you is going to be a wrench, but I have to."

Seb was off him in a heartbeat. "You're leaving?"

"Not right this second, but yes. *You'll* be leaving too. And I have no clue where we go from there." He sat upright.

"But you're not going back to New York, are you?" Seb's eyes widened and his face paled. "You can't. You said it yourself. You can't go back into that environment."

"But I have to," Marcus said in a gentle voice. "I need to see my boss, and work out what happens next." He squeezed Seb's thigh. "When does Gary get back?"

"He says a couple of weeks."

Marcus nodded. "And I've got another week, two at the most, before I need to go. I've kept him hanging long enough."

Seb's face tightened. "Then we'll make the most of what time we have left."

It didn't take a genius to work out what was going through Seb's mind.

"You think I'll leave, and that will be it. Back to our own lives."

Seb gave a shrug. "You have your career, I have mine."

His forced nonchalance didn't fool Marcus for a second. "There are weekends. Ever heard of those? Vacations? Holidays?" He grinned. "You think you're getting rid of me *that* easily?"

"You say that *now*," Seb remonstrated, "but you don't know for certain." His chest heaved. "You know, whoever said it's better to have loved and lost was full of shit."

Marcus's heartbeat stuttered at his words. Then he told himself it was just a saying. *It doesn't mean anything.*

But *dear Lord*, he wanted Seb to mean it.

Seb stroked Marcus's cheek. "You look as tired as I feel."

"Not surprising, really. I doubt either of us slept much last night."

Seb got up off the couch. "Come on. A nap will do us both good."

He arched his eyebrows. "A nap? Really?"

"Well, we *could* take a nap…" Seb's eyes sparkled. "After."

Marcus didn't need to ask after what. "How about we get as far as the bed, and take it from there?"

After all the anxiety and turmoil of the past day or so, Seb's smile was beautiful to behold. He took Marcus by the hand and led him to the bedroom. When they reached the bed, Seb locked his arms around Marcus's neck. "I couldn't bear the thought of losing you either," he murmured. He stroked Marcus's nape with gentle fingers. "You and me? We fit. And I'm not just talking about the sex, although that's a huge part, for both of us, I think."

Marcus kissed him softly on the lips. "And that's changed too, for me at least."

Seb's eyes gleamed. "So I'm not just a way to relieve tension?"

His stomach clenched. "I'll be honest. Remember when we went for a walk, and we ended up talking about your students? We got onto the topic of drugs, and…"

"And you got panicky." Seb's eyes widened. "That was also the day we came back here and you fucked my brains out."

Marcus nodded. "It was an escape. If we were fucking, we weren't having conversations that turned me inside-out. But that was the only time."

"Wanna know why we're such a good fit in bed?" Seb's breathing hitched. "Because our appetites match. It could be an hour after we've both come, and I want you all over again. And then I realize you want me too."

Marcus slid his hands down the back of Seb's sweats, grabbing both bare ass cheeks and squeezing. "How could anyone not want this ass?" He insinuated a finger in Seb's crack and brushed it over the tight pucker. "This hole?" Then he eased Seb's sweats over his hips. Seb moved as if to help him, but Marcus stopped him. He lowered Seb onto his back on the bed, then lifted his legs into the air and shoved them toward Seb's chest, rolling his bare ass up off the mattress.

"Okay, this is kinda kinky. You're not letting me take them off?"

"Not yet." Marcus leaned over, Seb's calves coming to rest on his shoulders as they kissed, while he rocked his now hard cock against Seb's ass. Then he grabbed the lube from the nightstand, slicked up a couple of fingers, and slid them into Seb's hole, seeking his prostate while he reached under the soft fabric of Seb's sweats to work his erect dick.

"Oh, that feels good," Seb said with a sigh, wrapping his arms around his knees and hugging them to his chest. Marcus stroked in and out of him, Seb's body tight around his fingers. "One more," he begged.

Marcus dribbled more lube over his fingers, then added a third, loving the low moan that fell from Seb's lips as his hole stretched to accommodate them, clinging to them as he gently fucked Seb with them. When he paused in his task to free his own cock, Seb rolled his eyes. "Finally."

Marcus stripped off his tee, and shoved his jeans past his hips. Then he lubed up, and smacked the head of his dick against Seb's hole. "Ready for me?"

Seb gave him a mock glare. "If you don't get that cock in my ass real soon, I may have to kill you." He expelled a drawn-out "Oh" of pleasure as Marcus guided his dick into position and slid into him. He grabbed Seb's feet, high in the air, and held onto them as he rocked in and out, keeping a leisurely pace.

"Your ass feels great," he said with a moan. Marcus pulled free of him and shoved his jeans roughly to the floor before kicking them off impatiently. "Flip over." When Seb complied, Marcus was confronted with the sight of Seb's back, his tee clinging to it, his sweats around his thighs, and Seb's bare ass, tilted up.

Lord, he wanted in there.

Marcus got onto the bed and straddled Seb, aiming his dick between Seb's cheeks. He sank into Seb's warmth with a sigh.

"Fuck, yeah." Seb rocked up to meet his thrusts, and the bed shook as their bodies slammed together, the pace quickening in a heartbeat.

Somewhere along the way, Seb rid himself of his clothing, and Marcus let go, plunging his cock into Seb's body, Seb's groans punctuating his thrusts. Then he tugged at Seb's hips, forcing him onto his hands and knees, before yanking him back onto Marcus's shaft again and again.

"Fuck, right there," Seb moaned, and Marcus made sure to aim for that spot. "Marcus… not gonna last long…"

Marcus was out of him in a heartbeat. He flipped Seb onto his back, and with Seb's ankles on his shoulders, he sank once more into Seb's heat. He cradled Seb's shoulders and head in his arms, holding Seb to him as they kissed, his dick sawing in and out, driving both of them closer to their goal.

"Let me know when you're close," Marcus ground out, hips bucking.

Seb panted as they rocked together, his hands tight around his knees. "Babe… I'm there." He shuddered, and Marcus's cock was sheathed in tightness.

"Oh God," he gasped as he shot deep in Seb's ass, warmth on his belly as Seb came, his dick untouched. Marcus let loose a single cry, their bodies locked together as Seb threw his arms around

Marcus's neck and held onto him. Marcus claimed Seb's mouth in a heated kiss, his cock wedged in Seb's ass.

"Holy f-fuck." Seb shivered in his arms, jolted now and then, their kisses becoming the soft brushing of lips as they held each other.

Marcus pushed Seb's hair back from his damp forehead. "I guess we crossed the finish line together that time."

Seb expelled a breath. "Tell me that wasn't a one-off. Tell me you can repeat that. Because you just rocked my world."

Marcus kissed his forehead. "That's good. Because you rocked mine."

Chapter Twenty-Six

August 7

Seb stood with the mourners, Marcus beside him, their hands joined. As the coffin was lowered into the ground, he gripped Marcus's hand tighter still, feeling cold despite the afternoon sun's warmth. Virtually all the people standing around the grave were gay men, and he recognized many of them. Justin's mom couldn't get to her feet, but sat on a chair, weeping, her husband's arm around her.

One by one, the mourners dropped single roses onto the coffin, and when it was Seb's turn, Marcus came with him. Seb tossed the red rose into the grave. "Goodbye, sweetheart." His throat seized, and Marcus put his arm around Seb's shoulders. Seb turned to him, unable to prevent the tears that welled in his eyes. "He's in a better place."

"You believe that, don't you?" Marcus murmured. When Seb nodded, Marcus kissed his cheek. "Do you want to go to Maine Street with the others, or do you want to go back to Cape Porpoise?"

"I want to go home with you."

Marcus stroked his face. "Then that's what we'll do. You must be tired. Tim did say you could have the day off."

Seb shook his head. "I needed to keep busy.

But you're right. Now I feel wiped out."

"Then when we get back to the house, we'll curl up in bed and take a nap."

He smiled. "I'd like that."

Together they walked away from the grave, their fingers laced.

"I was thinking about what you wrote," Seb murmured as they strolled.

"Hmm?"

"That GHB is the real killer. Maybe if Justin had known the risks, he'd still be alive."

"We'll never know for sure."

Seb squeezed his hand. "Finish that book, Marcus. Get it out there. So there are no more Justins."

"I don't think my book could accomplish that feat."

"But if it saves even one life?" Seb shivered.

Marcus kissed his cheek. "I'll finish it."

Seb shuddered out a breath. "Thank you. Even if it's only one starfish at a time, it's something. Because it will matter to the ones we save."

Marcus frowned. "Starfish?"

"You never read that? About the old guy walking along a beach covered with thousands of starfish that had been washed ashore? He comes across a boy who's throwing them back into the ocean, one by one. He tells the old guy he's doing it because when the sun comes up, it'll fry 'em. The old guy tells him that with there being so many, the kid won't make that much of a difference." Seb smiled. "The kid picks up another starfish and hurls it as far as he can into the ocean. Then he tells the guy, 'It made a difference to that one.'"

Marcus's eyes glistened. "Then yes. We'll save as many as we can."

August 15

Someone somewhere had flicked a switch, and time had sped up. At least, that was Seb's explanation why the past week seemed more like a couple of days. His mornings dragged, but he made sure to keep his mind on the job: Tim needed him to be on the ball. But as soon as the wharf came into view, his thoughts went to Marcus, who he knew would be waiting for him.

His afternoons were filled with walks, day trips, and a lot of bed time. Couch time. The kitchen and bathroom saw some action too. His evenings were spent mostly with Marcus, but two or three times, they'd had dinner with Sandra and James.

His nights were spent in Marcus's arms.

Gary called to say he'd be home on the sixteenth, so that meant Seb's last Saturday was spent cleaning the place until it sparkled. Marcus volunteered to help, which was sweet, and they divided the chores between them.

It was almost lunchtime, and the house was spotless. The drier rumbled in the bathroom, every surface was free from clutter, and the place smelled a damn sight more pleasant than it had the day Seb arrived.

And how long will that last? Knowing Gary, about five minutes.

Marcus's phone buzzed, and he picked it up to peer at the screen. "It's Mom. She probably wants to invite us to lunch." He lay on the couch and answered it. "Hey, Mom. Yeah, it's going well."

The little devil on Seb's right shoulder chose that moment to whisper into his ear. He got onto the couch, and spread Marcus's legs. Marcus gave him a puzzled frown—until Seb slowly lowered the zipper on Marcus's jeans.

No. No, he mouthed, his eyes wide.

Seb merely grinned as he fished out Marcus's dick that stiffened as Seb's fingers touched it.

"What was that? Oh, sure. Lunch. We'd love to." Marcus's gaze was locked on Seb, his mouth open as Seb worked the shaft with one hand. Marcus's breathing quickened. "What? Oh. We're… still cleaning. Yeah. Still a load to do."

Seb grinned. "You said load," he whispered. Then he bent over Marcus's crotch and took the head of his cock into his mouth.

"God!" Marcus shuddered. "Sorry, Mom. A… a huge spider just ran over my foot." Seb raised his head, and Marcus glared at him. As if Seb paid him any mind. He went back to his erotic task, enjoying the slip and slide of Marcus's dick filling his mouth over and over.

"What was that? I don't know, I'll ask. Seb, Mom wants to know if you like tuna casserole."

Seb released Marcus's cock. "Tell her I love it." Then he went right back to sucking him off, only now with more vigor, his head bobbing. Marcus rocked his hips up off the couch, one hand on Seb's head, forcing him to swallow more of his shaft.

"You heard that? Great." Marcus's voice sounded strained. "Okay, we'll see you at one o'clock. Yeah, we'll have it all done by then. Bye."

Seb chuckled around Marcus's dick, then pulled free. "I'll have *you* done any second now." Then it was back to blowing him. He knew the signs: Marcus was about to nut.

Marcus tossed the phone aside and applied both hands to Seb's head. "*You* are going to swallow every... single... drop." He groaned as he arched off the couch, and Seb tugged on Marcus's balls, holding his dick steady as Marcus shot hard. Seb took it all, and when Marcus was done, he licked the shaft clean, loving the shivers that coursed through Marcus when Seb flicked the little knot of nerves under the head with his tongue.

Marcus grabbed Seb and hauled him, until Seb lay on top of him. "You are evil, do you know that?"

Seb grinned. "I couldn't resist. Don't tell me you didn't enjoy it."

"Oh, I won't deny that. But my mom was laughing her ass off at the end. She probably knows exactly what we were doing."

"That should make lunch interesting." When Marcus's face fell, Seb had a fair idea what had gone through his mind. "I know, babe. The last lunch." The following day, Seb would be back in Ogunquit, and Marcus would be driving to New York.

"When do you think Gary will get here tomorrow?"

"Probably around noon. It's a four-hour trip from Annie's place." Seb cocked his head. "Why?"

"Because I want one more night with you, and I want to avoid the situation of Gary walking in on us."

Seb let out a sigh. "I was gonna ask you to stay, but I didn't want to push."

Marcus wound his fingers through Seb's hair and drew him close. His lips brushed against Seb's cheek before he took Seb's mouth in a leisurely kiss.

"How long do we have before we need to be out of here?" Seb murmured against his lips.

"Maybe an hour?"

Seb sat up and stripped off his tee, then unbuttoned his jeans. "Perfect."

They weren't about to waste time moving things to the bed.

Marcus gave the summerhouse a final glance. "I think that's everything." He'd packed up all his belongings, and the boxes and suitcases stood by the door.

"If I find anything, I'll let you know," Mom said from the recliner.

Marcus gave her a quizzical glance. "Where's Seb?"

"In the den with your dad. They're talking trains this time. Apparently Seb has a friend who's built an entire town above his parents' garage."

He laughed. "Watch out, Mom. Dad'll get

ideas about the attic."

"*Ideas*, I can cope with. If he wants to put any of them into practice, I'll put my foot down." Her eyes twinkled. "He's already got far too much stuff hoarded up there. He's *not* adding a model railway." Mom tilted her head to one side. "If I *do* come across something you've missed, I could always ask Seb to drive over here and collect it. Ogunquit's not that far from here, and he'd probably see you before we did."

Marcus shook his head. "And I thought *Seb* was the king of not being subtle."

"It's a Mom thing. I want you to be happy. I want *all* my children to be happy." She met his gaze. "And I think Seb makes you happy."

Marcus sighed. "I *know* he does."

"So what are you going to do about it? Have the two of you made plans? Have you—"

He held up his hand, and she fell silent. "No plans. There's still too much that needs to be worked out before I can think about the future."

Mom's eyes were kind. "I don't know what circumstances brought you here, and it's obvious after all this time that you're not going to tell me. But I hope being here helped."

"More than you'll ever know."

"Your dad and I have been talking." She gestured to the house. "Once we've left, this place will be empty until Labor Day, and then after that until God knows when. So... if you need a breather... a time-out... whatever you want to call it... come here. Don't waste time asking us first. Just turn up. We'll make sure you have a key before you leave. And... if you want to bring Seb here? That's okay."

Marcus bit his lip. "This feels as if you're giving us your blessing."

"I think the two of you are a good fit," she said with a shrug. "And like I said… I want you to be happy."

"I suppose I should be relieved."

Mom blinked. "What do you mean?"

"Well, I remember vividly your reactions on meeting some of Chris's girlfriends. They didn't get such glowing commendations."

She flushed. "Oh dear. Was I that obvious?"

Marcus laughed. "Only to us." He walked over to the recliner, bent down, and kissed her cheek. "If anything changes between me and Seb, I'll let you know. And I really do appreciate the offer to use the house. This is my happy place."

"I'm glad." She got to her feet and hugged him. "Am I feeding you this evening, or will you be at Seb's?" Her lips twitched. "Stupid question."

"I'll put everything in the car. That way, I can set off tomorrow morning from his place." Marcus grinned. "I'll get Seb to help. He probably needs rescuing by now anyway." It pleased him that his parents had taken to Seb. He wanted to tell his mom he and Seb would stay together, but he wasn't about to make promises he couldn't keep.

Let's see what New York has in store for me first.

Seb knew from the sound of Marcus's breathing that he wasn't asleep. "What's on your mind?"

"How did you know?"

He laughed softly. "*How* many nights have you spent in this bed?"

Marcus's arm tightened around him. "I loved coming to Cape Porpoise as a kid."

Seb snickered. "I wish I could say the same, but my summers here were very different. Child labor. I *might* have mentioned that once or twice."

Marcus laughed. "Yeah, I picked up on it. What I'm *trying* to say is… This has always been a happy place for me, but I think this summer has been the happiest—and that's due entirely to you. In fact, I'll go further." He nuzzled Seb's neck, his breath warm on his skin. "*You* are my happy place, Seb Williams."

Warmth flooded him. "And you've changed the way I feel about Cape Porpoise, which is no mean feat." He brought Marcus's hand to his lips and kissed his fingers. "From now on, it's always going to be 'the place where I…'" Seb swallowed. He couldn't bring himself to say the words 'where I fell in love for the first time.' That would be too much like tempting fate.

"Where you what?" Marcus kissed his neck, and Seb shivered.

"You're fighting dirty again." Seb reached down to where Marcus's leg lay hooked over his, and stroked his thigh. "And I was *going* to say, 'the place where I met the most incredible guy.'" The lie tripped smoothly off his tongue.

"I'm going to miss you."

Seb's throat tightened, and he turned in Marcus's arms. "Me too." He couldn't push aside the overwhelming fear that what they'd shared was about to end. Their lives were going to diverge, and neither of them had any way of knowing if their paths would cross again.

I know what I want to happen, but wanting won't make it so.

As if he'd read Seb's thoughts, Marcus brought his lips to Seb's ear and said quietly, "This is not a summer fling. I think we both know that. And it doesn't have to end, not if neither of us want it to." He kissed Seb on the lips. "So tomorrow we'll say goodbye. I'll go back to New York, and you'll go back to Ogunquit. Just don't think you're getting rid of me, okay?"

Seb wrapped his arms around Marcus. "I love your positivity." It was the nearest he could get to saying the words that lay on his heart.

"I have to be positive." Marcus pulled Seb closer still. "It's the only thing keeping me going right now." He paused. "Are you sleepy?"

"Not remotely."

Marcus gently rolled Seb onto his back. "Then let's make love until we fall asleep."

Seb couldn't think of a more perfect way to spend their last night together.

Please, God, don't let it be our last night.

August 16

Marcus glanced at his phone and knew he couldn't put the moment off any longer. "Time to go," he murmured into Seb's hair. Seb's body was warm against his as they snuggled on the couch. Marcus chuckled.

"What's so funny?"

He kissed Seb's head. "You turned me into a snuggler. How did you manage that?"

"Maybe you always were. You just needed to meet me to bring it out." Seb straightened with a sigh. "You're right though. Gary should be here soon."

"Have you changed the bedding?"

Seb laughed. "I did that while you were taking a shower. The sheets are in the washer."

Marcus got to his feet and held a hand out to Seb. "Walk me to the car?"

"Why? Do you think you'll get lost on the way?"

He grasped Seb's hand. "No, but at least I get a little more time with you."

Seb led him out of the house and over to the car. "You sure you've got everything?"

"There's one thing missing, but I can't fit you in my suitcase." Marcus opened his arms wide, and Seb walked into them. Marcus drank in his smell, the feel of him, burning them into his senses.

"You've got my number," Seb whispered.

"Your number, your email, your mailing address…" Marcus kissed him. "And you've got mine." He held him close for one final kiss, then pulled away with a heavy heart. "Take care. I'll call, okay?"

As he opened the car door, Seb hurried over to him. "Marcus!" He stilled, and Seb grabbed his hand. "Listen… if you feel stressed, under pressure, anxious… call me?"

Marcus heard the words Seb didn't utter. "Don't worry. I won't let things get that bad. But if they do, you'll be the first to know."

Seb released his hand. "Take it easy. Don't let that boss bully you into taking on more than you feel comfortable with." He took a step back. "*Now* you can go."

Marcus got behind the wheel and turned on the engine. He wound the window down, and gave Seb a wave. As he backed away from the house, a car pulled onto the gravel driveway, and Marcus caught a glimpse of a grizzled face in the passenger seat.

That has to be Gary.

He drove to the end of Pier Road, then turned right.

New York was over three hundred miles away, and every one of those miles would take him farther from where he longed to be.

Chapter Twenty-Seven

August 22

Seb's books were on the table, along with his notes, but preparing for the new semester was the last thing on his mind. His heart wasn't in it. Aaron had texted a week ago to invite him and all the others to a barbecue the following weekend, and then he'd texted *again* that morning to find out if Seb had got the text.

Seb hadn't replied because he didn't know what to say.

Never thought it would come to this, that I don't feel like spending a weekend with the guys.

He'd been home a week, and contact with Marcus had been sporadic at best. There had been texts, sure, and one voice call, and even then Marcus had sounded distracted.

Maybe I was right not to get my hopes up. All the signs pointed to the two of them going nowhere, but despite his fears, Seb couldn't help but feel concerned for Marcus. *I hope he's okay.*

When his phone buzzed, he grabbed it, but his heart sank when he saw it wasn't Marcus, but Levi. Seb grimaced. *I really have been a shit friend lately.* He clicked on *Accept*, and Levi's cheerful voice filled his ears.

"Hey. Since Mohammed won't come to the

mountain… We haven't spoken for *three weeks*, dude. I was starting to worry."

"I know. I'm sorry. I've only been back here a week."

There was a pause. "You're in Ogunquit? And you haven't come over?" Seb couldn't miss the hurt in Levi's voice, and that only twisted the knife in a little more.

"I wouldn't be much company." He hesitated, but the thought lay so heavy on his heart, he had to share it. "I miss him."

"Oh, Seb." Levi's voice was soft. "I know. But this was always going to be a shit deal. You did the right thing, walking away."

Fuck.

Seb's mouth was suddenly devoid of spit, and there was a tightness in his throat. "Levi, it… That wasn't the way it happened."

"What do you mean? Did *he* dump *you*?"

This is getting worse. "Look, there was no dumping, okay? After you and I spoke, I did exactly what you suggested—I did some research— and… I got some surprising results."

"If you were surprised, you were looking in the wrong place." A hard edge crept into Levi's tone.

There was no way around this. "Levi, you know I love you, right?" Seb said in as gentle a voice as he could muster. "We think alike on so many issues. But… on this one, I'm gonna have to differ. This… This isn't as black-and-white as you think it is. I understand how you feel, and believe me, if I were in your shoes, I'd probably feel the same way. But—"

"There *is* no but, not about this." Levi's voice

hardened even further.

"Yes, there is," Seb insisted. "I don't want us to fall out over this, but… I thought the same way you did, okay?"

There was a pause. "That implies you don't now."

"No, I don't. And about Marcus… He's not an addict, okay? Yes, he did meth, but he doesn't now, and I don't know if he'll ever do it again. Even if he does, he can do it responsibly. And before you blow up at me, I'm gonna send you a link. Once you've looked at it—and I *mean* look at it, read it, digest it—if you still feel I'm deluded, then okay. I'm just gonna have to live with that." Jesus, this was hard. "I'm hoping we can come through this though." Seb didn't want to lose his brother.

"But… you said you missed him."

"Yeah, dude, 'cause he's in New York. Before he left, he said there was still an *us*. I'm finding it a little more difficult to hold onto that, but…"

"You're going to send me a link? Let me guess, it's a site full of opinions from people who've deluded themselves into thinking they can handle it."

Seb had known it wouldn't be easy. "This is a reputable source, not just something I found on Dr. Google, okay? You'll realize that as soon as you see it." When the thought came to him, he debated ignoring it, but then relented. "Levi… you said a while ago that we all know how society treats addicts. You don't even know Marcus is an addict, but you've already judged him. So how are you any different from the rest of 'society'?"

Crickets.

"I know that sounds harsh, but I had to say it."

Seb caught the sound of a car engine outside, and got up from the couch to peek through the window. His heart pounded. "Levi? Marcus's car is in my driveway."

Levi sighed. "Then I guess this conversation is ended. Stop talking to me, and go see your man. I don't pretend to understand any of this, but you're not stupid. I have to assume you know what you're doing. So send me your link. I promise I'll read it. I'm not promising I'll come over to your way of thinking, but I'll read it."

Seb expelled a breath, his heart a little lighter. "Thank you. That's all I ask." He disconnected, and hurried to the front door. When he opened it, Marcus stood there in his faded jeans and dark blue tee, his face drawn.

"I could really use some coffee if there's any going."

Seb swallowed. "You didn't drive three hundred miles for a cup of coffee. And I'm sure it wasn't to apologize for not calling me either." He peered past Marcus to the car, and stilled. It was full of boxes. Seb arched his eyebrows. "Something you wanna tell me?"

Marcus laughed. "Don't I even get a kiss?"

"What, and give all my neighbors a free show?" Seb grabbed his hand and yanked him through the doorway, kicking it shut behind them. Then he was in Marcus's arms, and they were kissing, the past week fading from memory with every second.

Seb pressed his cheek against Marcus's, breathing him in. "God, I missed you."

Marcus pulled back. "I didn't have *time* to

miss you. I hit the ground running and I didn't stop."

Seb led him to the couch, and they sat. "So? What's going on? Why are you here? And why does your car look as if you couldn't even fit a cigarette paper in there?" He kept hold of Marcus's hand, as though releasing it would somehow make him vanish, and prove to be a dream.

"I'm on my way back to Cape Porpoise. My parents are home in Boston, and I'll be living in the house until I can find a place of my own." He met Seb's gaze. "In Maine."

Holy shit. "But… your job…"

Marcus sagged against the cushions. "Yeah, about that. I met up with my boss, and we did a lot of talking. It soon became obvious that no matter how often he said things would change, things would get better… I saw the truth. Sure, things *would* get better—for a while—and then it would be like it was back in April. Deadlines, pressure, more deadlines, more pressure… Hell, the backlog that awaited me was proof of that. So… I made a decision." Marcus held his head high. "You are looking at an independent copywriter. I'll be working from home from now on—all I need now is the home part."

Seb had to rein in the impulse to yell 'Move in here.' *He's just got here.* "You sure you wanna do this?" It seemed like an awful huge step.

"I'm good at what I do, and enough people know my work if I need endorsements. It might be slow to take off but I'm prepared for that." He drew in a breath. "And… I meant what I said at Justin's funeral. I'm going to finish the book."

Seb's heart was getting lighter by the second. "I'm glad about that. What you have to say is important." His throat tightened. "I still can't believe you're really here. I thought we were done. When I hardly heard from you…"

Marcus hauled Seb into his lap, holding him close. "I'm sorry, baby. I was working so hard to pull all this together in a week. There was my apartment to see to. I went through everything I had in storage. I threw so much into the trash, keeping only what was necessary. *Then* I realized something was missing." His eyes twinkled. "My box of toys. *You've* got that."

"Did I forget to put it in your car?" Seb asked innocently. "Gee, that was remiss of me."

Marcus laughed. "Well, it can either come back with me to the house, or stay here."

"We could share them," Seb suggested. "Joint custody? Swap on the weekends?" He swallowed. "That is, if we're going to keep seeing each other."

Marcus's hand was warm on his nape. "I didn't drive three hundred miles just to start a new career. I came back here for *you*." He pulled Seb in, and kissed him, a soft brushing of lips. Then Marcus drew back. "And I think it's time I was honest."

Seb's heart felt as if it was about to explode.

Marcus cupped his cheek. "I think you already know what I'm about to say."

His pulse raced and his breathing quickened. "Yeah, but you don't *say* it."

Marcus laughed. "You want your love scene, is that it? Okay." He looked Seb in the eye. "I love you. I don't want to be without you. I know things are kind of up in the air right—"

Seb silenced him with a kiss, pouring his heart and soul into it. "Love you too," he murmured against Marcus's lips. Marcus's hands were so goddamn gentle on his neck and cheek.

"It won't be easy, balancing our careers."

"We'll work it out," Seb uttered with confidence. "My biggest problem right now? Learning to be patient." He still had the urge to tell Marcus to move in, but he knew it was all too damn fast. "So, now what?" He leaned into Marcus, heat radiating through his chest.

I guess this is what happy feels like. It was so good, Seb could become an addict.

"Well, after I'd had my coffee, I was going to drive to Cape Porpoise and unpack all my stuff." Marcus kissed his head. "I was hoping you'd come with me."

"I've still got work to do for the next semester, but I can bring that with me. I'll stay for the week." Marcus's smile was all the response Seb needed. Then he remembered. "Oh. Next Saturday. You know you said you wanted to visit Acadia?"

"Yes," Marcus said, drawing out the syllable.

"Well, one of my friends, Aaron—the one who lives in Bar Harbor—is having a barbecue. Kind of a let's-celebrate-the-end-of-summer thing. All the guys will be there, I think. I wasn't sure if I was going to go or not."

Marcus frowned. "But I thought you loved getting together with them."

Seb bit his lip. "I was feeling kinda low."

"That was my fault, wasn't it?" Marcus's eyes widened. "You want to go—and you want to take *me* with you."

Seb grinned. "I knew you were a smart man." His gaze narrowed. "Do they even know about me?"

"Only one of them does." And if they did go, Seb was in two minds as to whether he'd tell Levi.

"And you're just gonna turn up?"

"Hey, Finn did it. We had no clue about Joel—well, the others didn't." Seb had been in the loop.

"So I'll be the entertainment." Marcus's voice was a little strained.

He looped his arms around Marcus's neck. "These are the people I love most in the world, and they need to meet you." Seb smiled. "Right now I feel so freaking happy, I wanna shout it from the rooftops, but telling the guys is a good start."

"When you put it like that…" Marcus cocked his head to one side. "Who knows about me?"

"Levi."

Marcus's face tightened. "Shit." His gaze met Seb's. "How *much* does he know? Because given his history, if he knows mine? This could get awkward."

"Trust me, it'll be fine." At least, Seb hoped it would. "And by the sound of it, something else has been arranged for the entertainment." Aaron's second text had said something about a surprise, but there'd been no clue as to what. He kissed Marcus on the mouth. "By the way, you won't be the only old dude at the party."

Marcus arched his eyebrows. "Excuse me?"

Seb grinned. "Hey, you're older than me. But Joel is in his early forties, I think."

"Thank God. I thought for a minute there I'd have seven more of you to cope with." His eyes gleamed.

"Hey, what does that mean?"

Marcus kissed him, a long, deep kiss that went all the way to Seb's dick. "One of you is more than enough."

"Then you'll come?"

He nodded. "I'm nervous as hell about this, but yes I'll come." Then he smiled. "But there's a catch. If I go to the barbecue with *you*, the following weekend *you* have to come stay at the house for Labor Day." He grinned. "I want my family to *officially* meet my boyfriend. Not that any of them will be surprised in the slightest."

Seb liked that idea. "Will there be as many of them as last time?"

"No idea. But we'll be in the summerhouse. I just need to go shopping before then."

"For what?"

Marcus's lips twitched. "Blinds."

Seb snorted. "Do they make soundproofed blinds?"

"Alas, no, but I do have a solution." Marcus kissed him lightly on the lips. "I'll just gag you."

He grinned. "I have only one word to say— Ditto."

Marcus laughed. "Okay, so I'm not quiet either. But back to now… How long do you need to pack a bag for the week?"

Seb widened his eyes. "Do we have to go right now?"

"Why? Do you have something else in mind?" Marcus's eyes glittered. "Stupid question. Forget I asked. Maybe this is the time when you give me the guided tour of your place—starting with the bedroom."

Seb let out a happy sigh. "I love it when you

read my mind." Then he frowned. "What about this coffee you keep mentioning?"

Marcus's eyes gleamed. "Sex beats coffee every time."

He got up off Marcus's lap, took his hand to hoist him to his feet, then led him toward the bedroom.

Practicalities could wait. Making love to his man was way more important.

They had some catching up to do.

Chapter Twenty-Eight

August 23

Marcus awoke to birdsong, the ticking of the clock in the hallway, and Seb's measured breathing beside him. Light seeped through the pale curtains, bathing Seb in a warm glow. Marcus leaned over and kissed his chest, and Seb stirred, stretching.

"Is it coffee time?"

Marcus chuckled. "Was that a hint?"

Seb reached for him, enfolding Marcus in his arms. "Put it this way," he murmured drowsily. "If you give me coffee, I'll reward you."

He smiled. "And what form would this reward take?"

Seb's eyes held a soft gleam. "I ride you, you ride me… it's all good."

Marcus kissed his forehead. "Then I'll be right back with coffee."

"See? I knew there was a reason why I love you." Seb's eyes were suddenly alert and bright. "And I do, you know."

"I know." Marcus kissed him again.

"But I'll love you even more if you bring me coffee," Seb added. He let out a contented sigh. "This bed feels awesome. I slept great." Then he peered at Marcus. "You're still here."

Marcus laughed. "That's *your* fault for being so

gorgeous when you wake up. I can't tear myself away from you." It wasn't entirely a joke.

He got out of bed and walked naked into the kitchen where he'd left his phone on charge. He set up the coffee pot, then glanced at the screen.

Apparently, Nick had called three times.

Marcus clicked on *Call*, and Nick answered on the third ring. "Hey. I thought I'd see how you were doing. It's been a while."

"At the risk of repeating myself, I've been meaning to call you."

"Where are you?"

"In Maine, where I've been since we last spoke, apart from one week in New York to wrap things up."

"Wrap—Okay, fill me in."

Marcus ambled over to the back door to stare out at the yard filled with sunshine. "Not much to tell. I quit my job and I'm working independently from home. I'm staying at my parents' place in Cape Porpoise until I find something more permanent. And… I've met someone."

Nick laughed. "And that counts as 'not much to tell' in your book? Christ, it all sounds life-changing. Who's the guy?"

"He's a teacher. He lives in Ogunquit, but he's staying with me for his last week of freedom before school starts. He's smart, beautiful, funny…"

"He's obviously good for you. You sound so… happy."

Seb was right there in his head, his hair in his eyes as usual, that cheeky smile… "I came back here for him."

There was a pause. "We didn't exactly finish on

a good note, did we, the last time we spoke?"

Marcus sighed. "Not really. But you know what? It's okay. Think whatever you want about my past. There's a guy in my bed who heard the same things you did. *He* believes me, and that's all that matters."

"You told him?"

"Everything."

"And he's okay with that?"

He let loose another sigh. "Nick, I said this to you back in June, and I'll say it again. You're talking about the past. What matters to me right now is the future." He paused. "If we ever make it to New York, I'll stop by and say hi, so you can meet him."

Nick gave a wry chuckle. "Believe me, I want to meet the guy who claimed *your* heart. Take care, Marcus. Call me, sometime?"

He laughed. "Okay. Give my best to Juan." They disconnected. It was then Marcus remembered Nick's thoughtful gift, and he smiled.

Maybe it was time to use it.

Such thoughts would have to wait. Right then, there was a gorgeous man in his bed, lube on the nightstand, and the whole of Sunday stretched out before them.

August 24

Seb made notes, aware of Marcus humming in

the kitchen as he made them lunch. He smiled.

Happy was a great look on Marcus.

"Hey, can you come in here a sec?"

Seb got up from his chair at the dining table, and entered the kitchen as Marcus put two plates into the fridge. "What's up?"

Marcus crooked his finger. "Come here."

Seb went over to him, smiling. "Bossy." Marcus took him in his arms, and Seb sighed into his kiss.

"You've been at it all morning. Time for a break." Marcus stroked his cheek. "What are you working on?"

Seb bit his lip. "Something I should've done when I first started teaching." When Marcus arched his eyebrows, Seb sighed. "I'm designing a display for my classroom. It's an LGBTQI+-friendly display, all about non-discrimination." He raised his chin and looked Marcus in the eye. "I think it's time I hoisted a virtual flag in there, and showed my true colors."

Marcus's face glowed. "I like that."

Warmth trickled through him. "I'm glad." Then he frowned. "Although I'm not sure I need a break. I can do another hour before lunch."

Marcus's only response was to kiss him, only now his hands were on Seb's ass, sliding into his shorts and spreading his cheeks.

Seb shivered, his cock filling. "*You* are a distraction, Mr. Gilbert."

Marcus had to laugh. "Oh, the irony." He moved his hands higher, stroking Seb's back, his touch light. Then he propelled Seb backward, until his butt smacked into the kitchen table. "I'm reminded of a conversation we once had in this very room." Marcus's voice grew a little husky.

"Which conversation would that be?" Seb's dick tented his shorts, straining against the soft fabric.

Marcus leaned in to kiss Seb's neck, and his shivers multiplied. Marcus brushed his lips against Seb's ear. "I said if we'd met a year or two ago, I wouldn't have been able to keep my hands off you."

Heat raced through him as he recalled the rest of Marcus's words, and the solid wood of the kitchen table at his back suddenly took on a whole new meaning. Before he could tell Marcus he really, *really* liked that idea, Marcus removed Seb's tee, unbuttoned his shorts, and shoved them to the ground, leaving him naked. He lifted Seb onto the smooth wooden surface, then squirmed out of his own shorts. Marcus yanked open a drawer in the table to take from it a bottle of lube.

Seb gave a mock gasp of surprise. "You planned this."

Marcus's eyes gleamed. "And your point is?"

Seb raised his legs to rest them on Marcus's broad shoulders. "Fuck me." He sighed as Marcus slowly inched his slick cock into him, stretching him, Marcus leaning over to grab the edge of the table behind him as an anchor.

School work would have to wait.

August 26

Marcus smiled when he saw Jess's name. "Hey, sis." Beside him on the couch, Seb glanced up, then went back to watching the movie, his head resting on Marcus's shoulder.

"I'm not interrupting anything, am I?" Her voice held amusement.

"We're watching TV. What can I do for you?"

"Actually, I want to pick your brains. It's about the end of September. You know what happens then, right?"

He snorted. "No, I'd completely forgotten it's their Golden Wedding anniversary."

She laughed. "Well, I had an idea, but seeing as you're living at the summer house, I need to run it by you first."

"Go for it." Marcus was in a blissed-out state. He'd agree to anything—within reason.

"I wanted to plan a surprise party for them. I'll arrange everything," she added quickly. "The caterers, the decorations… All *you* have to do is get them there. Invite them to stay for a weekend with you and Seb. Mom would love that. Then when they arrive, the house will be full."

Marcus could do that. "Sure. I think it's a great idea."

"Excellent. I'll get right on it." There was a pause. "Hey, Marcus? In case I forgot to mention it last time we spoke? I'm really stoked you and Seb are together."

"Thanks. We're pretty '*stoked*' about it too."

A pause. "You're laughing at my vocabulary again, aren't you? Jesus, you did that when I was a kid. Well, laugh it up. We both know you and Seb getting together is all because of me."

He blinked. "Excuse me?"

"Well, *I* was the one who invited him to have dinner with us, wasn't I? Would *you* have done that?"

He sighed. "Probably not." Then he glanced at Seb's tousled head. "Although... he *might* have worn me down eventually." Seb's eyes met his, and Marcus bent to kiss him on the lips, a lingering, sweet kiss that made him warm inside.

Jess coughed. "Hey, still here, you know. And before I forget... Jake got the job. He heard this morning. He'll be working with a company in Boston. We're looking for a place for him right now."

"That's great. Tell him congratulations. Will we be seeing him Labor Day?"

"He says yes." She coughed again. "And now I'll let you go back to whatever you're watching. Say hi to Seb for me."

"I will. See you on Labor Day." He disconnected, then stretched to place the phone on the side table. "Jess says hi."

"Hi, Jess." Seb reached up and popped the first button on Marcus's shirt.

"Can I help you with something?" Marcus asked with a chuckle.

Seb ignored him and popped another free. "Seems the Gilbert Curse missed Sandra and James." Another. "What do you think our chances are of escaping it?" Another.

Marcus cupped his chin and lifted it, looking Seb in the eye. "I don't believe in curses," he said in a quiet voice.

Seb slid his hand under the cotton, his

fingertips sending shivers through Marcus as they brushed over his nipple. "Neither do I." He stilled. "What *do* you believe in?"

Marcus pushed him onto his back, then covered Seb with his body, cradling Seb's head and neck in his hands. "You, baby. I believe in you."

Then Seb wrapped his arms and legs around him, and the TV was forgotten.

August 28

Seb was singing in the shower, and Marcus had to laugh. Despite Seb's earlier claims not to be able to carry a tune, he was doing a passable rendition of 'Wake Me Up Before You Go-Go," and Marcus imagined the lyrics were accompanied by bumps of the hips and using the nozzle shower head as a mic.

Marcus hadn't bought it for that express purpose, but hey…

He'd told Seb to take his time, and paying no attention to Seb's puppy dog eyes had been tough, but Marcus had a job to do. He was just about finished when his phone rang. Marcus was going to ignore it, until he saw it was Jake.

"Hey. I'll be seeing you next weekend."

"I know, but I probably won't get the chance to talk with you. You're living at the house, aren't you?"

"For the moment, yes."

"Well… would it be okay if I came up for a visit sometime? I'd call first."

There was something in Jake's voice that tugged at Marcus's heart. "You can come over whenever you like," he replied at once. "Has something happened? Apart from getting the job, I mean."

There was silence for a moment. "I've decided you were right. I'm going to tell him how I feel."

Marcus took a deep breath. "If you need me, you know where I am. This is a safe space, okay? No one's going to judge you here—*whatever* you tell us."

"Thanks, Marcus. You've no idea how much that means. I only hope you feel the same way when you know the truth."

Shit. Is it that bad?

"Anyway, I'll let you get back to whatever you're doing. Say hi to Seb for me. I'm really happy for you guys." And before Marcus could respond, he disconnected.

Damn. Marcus was about to hit *Redial* when he heard the water shut off in the bathroom. He hit it anyway.

Seb wasn't going anywhere, and this was important.

"Did I forget something?" Jake asked as the call connected.

"You're going to be all right, aren't you?" Marcus blurted out.

Jake sighed. "I'll be fine. And if I'm not, I'll come find you, and we'll talk. Okay?" He paused. "I know I made it sound pretty bad, but that's just me. Glass-half-empty guy, right? I'm not gonna do anything… stupid, I promise."

Marcus breathed a little easier. "Okay. Love you, kiddo."

"Love you too—*Guncle* Marcus." Jake was laughing as he hung up.

Marcus placed the phone on the nightstand, then removed his jeans and tee. He walked into the bathroom, just as Seb was toweling himself dry. His eyes lit up when he saw Marcus's naked state, then he narrowed his gaze. "Not sure I'm talking to you."

"What have I done?" As if he didn't know.

"Here I was, in this big, beautiful shower, with its own bench, and you were MIA."

"How was the new nozzle?"

Seb grinned. "Perfect. Now I want one for *my* place." He cocked his head to one side. "Were you on the phone just now?"

He nodded. "Jake called."

"Is he okay?"

Marcus wasn't sure how to answer that.

Seb sniffed. "What can I smell?"

"Do you like it? I've got my oil burner set up in the bedroom. There's chamomile and jasmine in it at the moment."

Seb smiled. "Smells heavenly." He lowered the towel, hanging it on his erect cock.

Marcus burst into laughter. "Now you're just showing off." He grabbed the towel and hung it on the warming rail. "Come with me." His heartbeat sped up.

This was virgin territory.

Seb caught his breath as they walked into the bedroom. "Oh wow."

Alongside the glorious scents that filled the air, there were flickering tea lights on every flat surface, their light dancing on the walls and ceiling.

He turned to Marcus, aware of a lightness in his chest. "This is beautiful."

Marcus took him by the hand and led him to the bed. "I wanted it to be perfect." He pulled the sheets back and got in, taking Seb with him.

"Oh, it is, but perfect for what?" He lay down beside Marcus, breathing in the relaxing scent.

Marcus leaned over him, his hand gentle on Seb's face. "Making love." Then their lips met, and Seb moaned into the kiss, exulting in the feel of Marcus's body against his. He shivered with each trace of Marcus's tongue over his skin, every brush of his fingers over his nipples, his belly, his cock…

His heart hammering, Seb cupped Marcus's face. "Love you."

Marcus didn't blink. "Love you too." He sighed. "I'm glad you like the candles. I've never done this before."

Seb gestured to the tea lights around them. "No one has ever done this for me."

"You know why that is?"

He stilled. "No."

Marcus's smile was enough to make Seb

thankful he was lying down—it was the kind of smile that would make any man weak at the knees. "Because no one has ever loved you the way I love you."

The only adequate response to that was to claim Marcus's mouth in a kiss.

Chapter Twenty-Nine

August 29

When Marcus apologized for the tenth time, Seb had had enough. "Look, it wasn't your fault that guy called you on the weekend." The traffic on 95 had worn his patience pretty fucking thin as it was: he didn't want to lose it with Marcus.

"Yes, but I could've said outright that it wasn't convenient. I mean, who makes business calls late on a Saturday afternoon?"

Seb reached across and gave Marcus's thigh a squeeze. "But it was a good call, wasn't it? He sounds like he's gonna send a lot of business your way." Judging by Marcus's smile when he'd disconnected, it had been a *great* call.

"That's true. But we should've been at Aaron's hours ago."

It was almost nine o'clock, but Seb wasn't overly concerned. "I guarantee, we'll walk into that yard, and there will still be enough beer to sink a battleship." His stomach grumbled, and he sighed. "Food, on the other hand, might be another matter." He was pretty sure Aaron wouldn't let them starve.

"Where are we?"

Seb pointed to the left. "That light out there? That's the Egg Rock Lighthouse. And next vacation, we'll go see it, I promise. This is just a short visit."

He headed down Main Street, hoping to find a place to park near Aaron's. He'd called Aaron a few hours before to warn him they'd be late.

Well, that I'd *be late.* Seb hadn't mentioned Marcus.

"Grab my phone, will you? And send a text to Aaron. He's on the Contacts page. Just say, 'ETA a couple of minutes.'" He fired off the code to unlock it, and Marcus's thumbs slid over the screen.

"You like to make an entrance, don't you?" Marcus said with a chuckle.

Seb knew his amusement was to hide his nerves. "It'll be fine, I promise. They're a good bunch. By the time we leave tomorrow afternoon, you'll know that too. And depending on where we end up sleeping, you'll also know who snores and who doesn't."

"What *are* the sleeping arrangements?"

Seb cackled. "If you see a space big enough to fit a camp bed, grab it." Marcus grabbed his own phone and scrolled. "What are you looking for?" Seb demanded.

"A hotel. I had no idea."

He laughed. "You never did sleepovers when you were a kid?"

"No, and I don't intend starting now. Besides, does Aaron's place have a hot tub? Heated outdoor pool? Because the Bar Harbor Grand Hotel does, and they've got a room. A deluxe King room. Think about it, Seb. A nice big bed." Marcus's voice became silky.

Seb groaned. "You had to mention the bed, didn't you?"

"Hey, I only fight as dirty as you do. So? Do

I go ahead and click *Book this Room*? We can always come back tomorrow morning for breakfast or brunch or whatever." Marcus stroked Seb's thigh. "And I get you all to myself for the night."

"Book it," Seb snapped. "Great. Now I get to walk into Aaron's place with a hard-on."

"I'd offer to help you take care of it first, but we're late enough as it is. Plus there's always the chance we'd be arrested."

Seb turned left into Wayman Lane and searched for a space. There was one, a few houses down from Aaron's, and he parked the car. As they got out, he heard laughter, and grinned. "What did I tell you? Party's still going strong."

Marcus drew in a deep breath. "Okay. Lead the way."

They approached the house, but as they drew closer, Marcus came to a halt. "I left my jacket in the car. I'll just go get it." Seb tossed him the keys, and he turned back.

Seb went up to the side gate, which was ajar. He walked through it, to find the guys sitting around the fire pit.

And here we go.

He grinned. "Tell me you guys haven't eaten all the food. I'm starving." Then he caught sight of the beer bottles in their hands, and rolled his eyes. "Fuck." He went back to the gate and called out, "Grab the beers, babe. They're in the trunk. Which means they'll probably go off like rockets when we open 'em." Then he returned his attention to the group—and came to a dead stop.

Everyone was so still, their gazes locked on him.

"Why are y'all staring at me like that?" Then he realized what had slipped out.

Ben was the first to react with a smirk. "'Babe'? And who is 'babe'?"

It wasn't exactly what he'd planned, but hey…

Seb feigned reluctance. "That… would be my boyfriend." Then he awaited the explosion, inwardly buzzing.

He didn't have to wait long.

For a moment there was silence, broken by a chorus of raised voices, as synchronized as if they'd rehearsed it.

"What the *fuck*?"

Seb gave a shrug. "Surprise?" He caught sight of the guy standing beside Ben, and for a moment his mind went blank. Because no *way* could that be Wade Pearson. *Why the fuck did Ben invite his boss?*

Then he realized there was a much more important issue to be addressed: Ben and Wade were holding hands.

"Holy fuck."

Ben gave an identical shrug. "Surprise!" Beside him, Wade stared at Seb in obvious trepidation. It was that rabbit-in-headlights look that stopped Seb cold.

Okay, what's going on?

Aaron strolled over. "I did warn you," he murmured. "Which is more than *you* did, you asshole. Boyfriend?" At that moment, Marcus came through the gate, carrying the box in which bottles clinked. Aaron gave him a broad smile, his hand extended. "Hi. I'm Aaron. And you are?"

"Marcus Gilbert. I'd shake your hand, but

mine are a little occupied right now."

Before Seb could step in and help, Ben hurried over and took the box from him. "Hi there. I'm Ben. Let me set this down somewhere, then we can do all the introductions." He glanced at Seb. "And explanations." He took the box into the house, and Wade accompanied him.

Seb stared after them. "I'm not around for eleven weeks, and the world drops into the *Twilight Zone*?"

Beside him, Marcus smiled. "Have I missed something already?"

"It's a long story," Finn assured him, before walking over and squeezing Seb's shoulder. "But what *you* need to know is… it's all good."

Seb blinked. "But… that *was* Wade, wasn't it?"

Aaron nodded. "And for the record, I think you're the one he's been dreading meeting. So go easy on him."

"Yeah." Shaun took a bottle from Dylan's hand, and thrust it at Seb. "I think you need this." He smiled warmly at Marcus. "I'm Shaun. And you look like you could use a drink too."

"Thank you." Marcus gave him a grateful glance, then nudged Seb's arm. "Baby? Close your mouth, you're catching flies." That had them all chuckling.

Dylan looked from Seb, to Marcus, and back to Seb again. "Okay, *I'll* say it, even if none of *you* is going to. When did the last trumpet sound? I think I missed it. Because Seb getting a boyfriend has to be one of the signs of the coming Rapture, right?"

There were a few seconds of silence, and

then the laughter erupted.

Seb turned to Marcus. "Welcome to my family."

Which was getting bigger all the time.

Noah inclined his head toward the firepit where Marcus and Aaron were sitting, drinking beer, and talking about Acadia, from what Seb could make out. "I can't really complain about you not keeping us informed, because Ben was just the same. Did anyone know? About Marcus, I mean."

"Just Levi." And speaking of Levi, Seb had a feeling they weren't out of the woods yet. He'd given Marcus a cool reception. When Marcus gave Seb a glance that was obviously I-told-you-so, Seb couldn't respond.

Levi'll come around. He hoped.

"So, have you gotten over the shock yet?"

Seb frowned. "What shock?"

Noah grinned. "The *other* surprise of the evening." He tilted his head to one side. "Have you spoken with Wade yet?"

Seb sighed. "Yeah. Hard to believe it's the same guy. I mean, he is *smitten*." Seb was happy for them. It was hard to be anything else when he saw how Ben just glowed every time he and Wade were together.

"He's not the only one." Noah bit his lip.

"*You've* got a good case of 'smitten' going on too. Never seen you look so happy."

Seb gazed at Marcus. "Can you blame me?" He still had to pinch himself sometimes.

"Guys?" Aaron stood up. "It's getting late. The party isn't over, but I'm going to move us indoors." He grinned. "I have great neighbors, and I want them to stay that way."

Amid laughter, everyone filed into the house, while Aaron doused the fire.

The living room was full of chairs of all shapes and sizes: two couches, dining chairs, and a rocking chair. There were also large floor cushions lying about the place. Seb pointed to the rocking chair and nudged Marcus. "You can have that one."

Marcus's lips twitched. "Just so you know? I'm taking notes. And when we get home, there will be retribution." Then he kissed Seb on the lips, and that made it perfect.

"Hey, Seb, you got a minute?" Levi called out from the other end of the living room.

Marcus gave Seb's hand a squeeze. "Go talk to him," he said in a low voice. "You've got some bridges to build." He smiled. "I'll be right here."

Seb drew in a deep breath and went to talk to Levi.

As if he didn't know what the topic of conversation would be.

Marcus sat in the rocking chair, trying not to watch Seb in conversation with Levi.

They need to talk.

The couch beside his chair was fully occupied. Joel sat at the end nearest Marcus, Finn on a cushion at Joel's feet, talking with Dylan. Next to Joel was a quiet guy—*Shaun? Is that his name?*—who'd said a couple of words since Marcus's arrival.

He looks like his mind is someplace else. Like, on whoever was texting him.

"It's confusing at first, isn't it?"

Marcus blinked and refocused. "Excuse me?"

Joel regarded him with a warm smile, then gestured to the group. "Remembering all their names. It does get easier. This is my second such meet-up." His eyes twinkled. "I was the surprise last time. And now with Ben pulling the same stunt, and then Seb, I'm starting to think this is what they do—it's a competition to see who can create the biggest stir."

Marcus laughed. "You may be closer than you know. I asked if I was to be the entertainment. I think I nailed it."

"Your *existence* might have come as a shock to us all, but not your age."

He grinned. "Seb likes older guys. Yeah, I *might* have picked up on that."

"I think it's great. It'll be good to have another guy at these shindigs who doesn't laugh when I suggest watching a DVD, or listening to a CD."

Finn craned his neck to gaze at Joel. "CDs? Aren't they those silvery coaster thingies? I found a bunch of them when I unpacked your stuff. They're great for putting cups on." Joel gaped at him, aghast, and Finn's eyes gleamed. "Gotcha."

Marcus burst out laughing. Seb was right about his friends—they were a great bunch. *Well, most of them*. He'd exchanged less than ten words with Levi all evening. For Seb's sake, Marcus hoped the situation would improve.

"So, Joel, Finn said you're writing a book?"

Joel flushed. "I'm *trying* to write. There doesn't seem to be a lot of time for that, what with my business taking off." He shrugged. "It can wait. Right now there are other more important things to occupy my mind." He stroked Finn's head. "Such as the possibility of *this* guy here building a home for us." His eyes shone.

Finn nodded. "We can talk about this tomorrow."

Ben came over, dragging a floor cushion, and flopped down onto it next to Finn and Dylan.

Joel chuckled. "Wow. We're honored."

"What does that mean?" Ben's brow furrowed.

"You managed to tear yourself away from Wade. I was beginning to think you two were surgically attached." Ben gave him the finger, and he laughed. Then Joel leaned forward and kissed the top of Finn's head. "And I totally understand why you wouldn't want to be apart," he said as he straightened.

Ben flushed. He addressed Marcus. "Did Seb warn you about all of us?"

"I'm not sure 'warn' is the word I'd use. He's talked about you, and I knew me meeting you was important to him."

"If it feels as if they're all watching you and weighing you up?" Joel grinned. "Don't worry. That's because they are. At least you weren't the only surprise of the night."

Ben gazed across the room at the other couch where Wade, Aaron, and Noah were talking. "Hey, *most* of you knew about Wade, right?"

"Knowing is one thing," Dylan observed. "Hearing the guy who made your life hell announce to everyone that he loves you? That was the shocker." He smirked. "At least, it *was*—until Seb strode in with a boyfriend."

Ben laughed. "Totally stole my thunder, dude." He leaned in conspiratorially. "I think you were such a shock because Seb hasn't been in touch all summer."

Marcus sighed. "I take it he doesn't usually keep things to himself?"

Ben snorted. "Seb? Hell no. But we knew he was finding it tough being stuck out there, with no one around to talk to." He bit back a smile. "Except he wasn't alone, was he? No wonder he didn't call. He was obviously *busy*," he air-quoted, and Dylan coughed. Ben continued. "But that's what's so awesome about this lot. There's always someone to turn to if you need a helping hand, or just someone to listen." He gazed warmly at Finn and Dylan. "I don't know what I'd have done if these guys hadn't had my back. They visited me, they took my calls, even when it was the early hours of the morning." His eyes twinkled. "Of course, Dylan *said* he was working the night shift at reception at the hotel at the time, but we know what he was *really* doing."

Finn blinked. "Speak for yourself. *I* don't know what he was doing."

"Watching porn on his phone," Ben said in a stage whisper.

Dylan's jaw dropped. "I never said that."

Ben guffawed. "You didn't have to. But what *I* want to know is… was it het porn or gay porn?"

"Ben can want all he likes," Finn said to Dylan in a firm voice. "You don't have to tell him anything. Because it's none of his business what you watch—isn't that right, Ben?" He gave Ben a hard stare.

Ben flushed. "You're right. Sorry, dude." He got up and went over to the other couch where Wade, Aaron, and Noah were still talking. Dylan's cheeks were red.

Marcus had the impression Ben had hit a nerve.

"Did you say we get a room to ourselves?" Joel asked Finn. When Finn nodded, Joel's eyes sparkled. "Want to show me where it is?"

Finn was on his feet in a heartbeat. He grabbed Joel's hand and tugged him up off the couch, then led him toward the door.

Dylan coughed again. "Well, *that* was subtle." He got up and took Joel's place on the couch. "Listen, about what Ben said—"

Marcus held up his hand. "Before you say another word, can I point something out? Finn was right. What you watch is no one's business but yours."

"Yeah, but he makes it sound like I was watching porn when I should've been working. I'd get fired for that."

Marcus arched his eyebrows. "The night shift at a hotel reception desk? That has to be one of the deadest shifts going, right?"

Dylan nodded. "It's not what I usually do, but a couple of times recently I've ended up working it as a favor. And it was just me manning the desk. A guy could get bored to death just sitting there." He nibbled on his lower lip. "And about that other thing he said…"

Marcus had a feeling he knew what was bothering Dylan. "Doesn't matter if you watch guys with girls, girls with girls, guys with guys… whatever helps." He leaned in. "I may be gay, but I've watched straight porn."

Dylan blinked. "Really?"

Marcus nodded. "Of course, I was pretty much focused on the guys' asses and dicks."

"Some of their cocks are *huge*," he whispered. "Sometimes I take one look and I swear, it hurts just *thinking* about taking it." His eyes widened. "Not that I have. Taken one, I mean. I'm not gay."

Marcus had been around long enough to spot a bi-curious guy with relative ease. And judging by Dylan's rapid blinking, the way he tugged on his lip, his knee that bounced as he sat beside Marcus, this was one very nervous, curious man.

"It's okay, you know," he said in a low voice. When Dylan froze, Marcus nodded. "It's okay to be curious. And if the opportunity should arise to be more than curious? Don't panic about it. I have a nephew, in his early twenties, and recently I gave him this advice. I told him he needed to decide which was better to live with—the regret of doing something, or *not* doing something."

Dylan's breathing quickened. "It's like that FOMO they all talk about. You know, fear of missing out? Well, sometimes I wonder if *I'm* not missing out on... something."

Marcus smiled. "Mark Twain once wrote some very wise words. Let me see if I can remember them correctly." He paused, then recited, "*Life is short, break the rules, forgive quickly, kiss slowly, love truly, laugh uncontrollably and never regret anything that made you smile.* Everyone always quotes that bit, but he goes on to say *Twenty years from now you will be more disappointed by the things you didn't do than the ones you did. So throw off the bowlines. Sail away from the safe harbor. Catch the trade winds in your sails.*" Marcus paused. "He ended with three words. *Explore. Dream. Discover.*"

Dylan swallowed. "Sounds like he was a very wise man."

Marcus realized he'd have to cut the conversation short. "Where's the bathroom?"

"Through that door," Dylan said, pointing, "and to the left."

Marcus thanked him and got up to go take a leak. When he walked out of the bathroom, someone called his name from the kitchen. Marcus went to investigate, and found Levi pouring himself a glass of water.

"I thought we should talk." Levi spoke quietly. He gestured to the door. "You might want to close that."

Marcus's heart raced, but he did as instructed. "Knowing a little of your history, I figured we'd be having a conversation at some point."

Levi leaned against the countertop. "I guess we both know things about each other." He inclined his head toward the door. "But I didn't think this was something you'd want to be common knowledge." He took a drink from his glass.

"Could I have one of those too?" Marcus's mouth had dried up.

Levi put down his glass and filled another. He handed it to Marcus. "You must be a pretty amazing guy. I've never seen Seb so happy."

"And yet we're in here, talking."

Levi swallowed. "I've known Seb most of my life. He's the closest thing I have to a brother, so… I look out for him."

"Of course you do. Which is why you told him to walk away from me." When Levi arched his eyebrows, Marcus nodded. "He told me. I don't blame you for that. And yet we're in here, talking," he repeated. "So you must have something on your mind."

"I read your article."

"I see." Fuck, his heart was hammering.

"I also went to a link Seb sent me."

"And now you don't know what to believe. I get that."

Levi nodded. "Seb is no fool. He clearly trusts you. Hell, he loves you."

"Which is good, seeing as I love him." Marcus was not going to hide a damn thing. "So where does that leave us?" Levi took a deep breath, but Marcus got in first. "I've just walked away from my life in New York to make a new one here in Maine—with Seb. I am *not* going to hurt him. Now, I fully understand why you don't trust me, but I'm asking you to put aside that distrust, for Seb's sake. You can watch me like a hawk if you want, but personally, I think there are better ways to spend your time. If you're waiting for me to slip up, to slide into my old ways, then you will have a long, long wait, my friend."

"I'm not your friend."

"No, you're not—but I'd like you to be. I *want* a friend who's not afraid to speak their mind. I want a friend who will be honest with me. If there's one thing Seb has that I envy, it's all of you."

Levi's breathing hitched, but he remained silent.

"I want you to trust me, and I know that'll take time. Well, I'm not going anywhere."

The door opened, and Seb came into the kitchen. He stilled when he saw them. "They say the best parties always end up in the kitchen. What have I missed?" His tone was light, but his face was taut, his back stiff.

Before Marcus could respond, Levi smiled. "Marcus and I were just getting to know one another, that's all."

Marcus got the message: a truce had been declared.

Seb's shoulders slumped with obvious relief. "I came to find you because I'm ready to leave."

"You're not staying?" Levi asked.

Seb put his arm around Marcus. "There's a King bed with our name on it at the Bar Harbor Grand Hotel. We'll be back tomorrow."

"Good, because Aaron has bought some great-looking steaks for lunch, and I know he's hoping you'll do the honors." Levi met Marcus's gaze. "I'm glad we finally got to meet."

"Me too." Then Seb took his hand and led

him from the kitchen. After a chorus of goodbyes, they left the house and went to the car to collect their overnight bags from the trunk. According to his phone, the hotel was a short walk from Aaron's place.

Seb laced their fingers as they strolled through the quiet streets. "So… wanna tell me what that was all about?"

Marcus sighed. "Levi was looking out for you, that's all."

"The jury's still out, I guess."

Marcus squeezed Seb's hand. "You didn't expect him to capitulate *that* easily, did you?"

"I suppose not."

He raised Seb's hand to his lips and kissed it. "Give him time. Let him see us together. Stay in touch with him. Make him a part of our lives. Share our successes."

"Give him a copy of your book when it comes out," Seb added.

"Maybe." He glanced at Seb. "Want to tell me about your conversation with him? Because from where I was sitting, it seemed pretty intense."

Seb heaved a sigh. "He asked me what I would do if you ever…"

"If I ever used again?" Marcus suggested. Seb nodded. "And what did you tell him?"

"I said you'd started because of a very specific set of circumstances, that you are fully *aware* of those circumstances, and that they won't be repeated, because you've removed what caused them in the first place." They came to a halt in front of the impressive-looking hotel, and Seb turned to face him. "I'm right, aren't I?"

Marcus nodded. "Yes, you are." He drew Seb to him. "Thank you."

"For what?"

"Defending me. Believing in me." He gestured to the hotel door. "No more talk of Levi tonight, okay? I want to enjoy our first night in a hotel bed, and although it's a King, there's only room in it for the two of us."

"I like the sound of that."

"And tomorrow we'll go back to Cape Porpoise, pick up the rest of your things, and then we'll drive to Ogunquit."

"'We'?"

Marcus smiled. "You bet. I'll be giving Teacher a ride to school on Tuesday. That's if he likes the idea of showing up with his boyfriend."

Seb caught his breath. "Yes, he does."

"And when school is over, I'll be waiting for you, with a foot rub, a head massage, a cuddle, whatever you need. And then you can bend my ear about the little brats." Seb's eyes glistened, and Marcus' heartbeat sped up. "Did I say something wrong?"

Seb wiped his eyes. "No, quite the opposite." He leaned in and kissed Marcus on the cheek, then brought his lips to Marcus's ear. "Now take me up to our room and make love to me."

Marcus kissed his forehead. "All night long."

The End

Coming next in the Maine Men series!

Dylan's Dilemma (Maine Men Book Four)

Dylan has been curious for a long time, but is he ready to confront his desires?

A difficult decision

Dylan Martin has worked in the same Ogunquit hotel since he was eighteen, and he knows the drill: anything that might damage the hotel's reputation has to be reported. So telling the uptight manager there's a gay porn shoot about to take place should be a no-brainer.

Except Dylan recognizes one of the performers. He's been watching Mark Roman's scenes for so long, he could describe every inch of Mark's ripped body, from the silver at his temples and in his beard, right down to the tattoo on his ass. Not to mention Mark's sexy smile that sends heat hurtling through Dylan every time he sees it.

But if Dylan says nothing, it's his job on the line. And then his hand is forced…

An eager student

Mark's shoot is a bust but there's a silver lining, in the shape of a cute, sexy guy in the local bar. Except the guy seems familiar—and nervous—and suddenly it's clear who let the cat out of the bag. When Mark jokes that Dylan owes him a scene to make up for it, Dylan refuses point blank, but the longing in his eyes is hard to ignore: Dylan obviously wants him, even if he can't bring himself to say it.

Mark wants to be the one to undress him, to show him how sensual a man's kiss can be. He wants to set Dylan on fire, to make him shudder with pleasure. Most of all, he longs to hear his name on Dylan's lips when Mark brings him to the edge.

It won't be any more than that. Mark's 'career' has proved a stumbling block in the past, and he doesn't expect Dylan to be any different.

Mark may know a lot about desire, but Dylan's about to give him a lesson in love.

THANK YOU

A huge Thank You as always, to my wonderful team of betas. You guys ROCK.

Special thanks to:
Jason Mitchell, for continuing to be the most wonderful alpha and the best sounding board ever.

Donal Mooney, for allowing me to use part of our conversation in a dialogue.

Alexander Cheves, for his words.

Kazy Reed, for her invaluable assistance. She's been there for the first three books of the series, but this one needed a lot more expert knowledge, and she provided it.

Jack Parton, for yet more invaluable Maine knowledge, but also for his advice. I couldn't have written this book without him, and I'd never have discovered Dr. Carl Hart. Thank you for breathing life into Marcus.

More Maine-isms

Yes, I added a few more...

Pull-haul: to argue, contend
Culch: any kind of trash or rubbish; occasionally used of a person held in low esteem
Barvel: A fisherman's apron made of leather or oilcloth
Yow'un: young person
Gaumy: awkward, inept, stupid
Number than a hake: More colorful way to say someone is stupid

Appendix

According to neuroscientist and drug abuse specialist Carl Hart, most of what we have been told about drugs and addiction is wrong. Growing up in an impoverished and predominantly African-American neighborhood of Miami, Carl witnessed and experienced the multitude of factors that lead to addiction. A "combination of choice and chance" led him to leave his community and attend college, starting Carl on a path that culminated in his appointment as the first African-American tenured professor of the sciences at Columbia University. His scientific research and personal experiences have informed the thrust of Carl's book **The High Price** — that addiction is less prevalent and problematic than we have been led to believe, and that drugs have been scapegoated for problems related to poverty and race.

High Price: A neuroscientist's journey of self-discovery that challenges everything you know about drugs and society.
Hart CL. (2013). Harper-Collins: New York.

https://drcarlhart.com/

Also by K.C. Wells

Learning to Love
Michael & Sean
Evan & Daniel
Josh & Chris
Final Exam

Sensual Bonds
A Bond of Three
A Bond of Truth

Merrychurch Mysteries
Truth Will Out
Roots of Evil
A Novel Murder

Love, Unexpected
Debt
Burden

Dreamspun Desires
The Senator's Secret
Out of the Shadows
My Fair Brady
Under The Covers

Lions & Tigers & Bears
A Growl, a Roar, and a Purr

Love Lessons Learned
First
Waiting for You

Step by Step
Bromantically Yours
BFF

Collars & Cuffs
An Unlocked Heart
Trusting Thomas
Someone to Keep Me (K.C. Wells & Parker Williams)
A Dance with Domination
Damian's Discipline (K.C. Wells & Parker Williams)
Make Me Soar
Dom of Ages (K.C. Wells & Parker Williams)
Endings and Beginnings (K.C. Wells & Parker Williams)

Secrets – with Parker Williams
Before You Break
An Unlocked Mind
Threepeat
On the Same Page

Personal
Making it Personal
Personal Changes
More than Personal
Personal Secrets
Strictly Personal
Personal Challenges

Personal – The Complete Series

Confetti, Cake & Confessions

Connections
Saving Jason
A Christmas Promise
The Law of Miracles
My Christmas Spirit
A Guy for Christmas

Island Tales
Waiting for a Prince
September's Tide
Submitting to the Darkness

Lightning Tales
Teach Me
Trust Me
See Me
Love Me

A Material World
Lace
Satin
Silk
Denim

Southern Boys
Truth & Betrayal
Pride & Protection
Desire & Denial

Maine Men
Finn's Fantasy
Ben's Boss

Kel's Keeper

Here For You
Sexting The Boss
Gay on a Train
Sunshine & Shadows
Watch and Learn
My Best Friend's Brother
Bears in the Woods
Double or Nothing
Back from the Edge
Lose to Win
Teasing Tim
Switching it up
Out for You
State of Mind

Anthologies

Fifty Gays of Shade
Winning Will's Heart

Come, Play
Watch and Learn

Writing as Tantalus
Damon & Pete: Playing with Fire

About the Author

K.C. Wells lives on an island off the south coast of the UK, surrounded by natural beauty. She writes about men who love men, and can't even contemplate a life that doesn't include writing.

The rainbow rose tattoo on her back with the words 'Love is Love' and 'Love Wins' is her way of hoisting a flag. She plans to be writing about men in love - be it sweet or slow, hot or kinky - for a long while to come.

Printed in Great Britain
by Amazon

65496298R00218